Place

Patrick Norhden's novel, *The Perfect Place*, is the second in his series following his debut of *The Crystal Monkey*. *The Prefect Place* is a compelling story revolving around the journey of Min Lee as she escapes the cultural revolution of Communist China and comes face to face with the corruption of a modernizing China, including organized crime and human trafficking. It is story of honor, duty, and triumphs and hardships of life. This page-turning novel is a great read and wonderfully written. Norhden is a wonderful story teller creating likable characters and a moving, powerful plot.

-- Debra Hellen, Author of *Chasing Evil's Shadow*:

There is a subtle yet captivating simplicity to Pat Nohrden's *The Perfect Place* that contrasts well with the complications of personal, familial, and cultural tragedy that weaves throughout the story of Min Li. The tragedies, misfortunes, and vagaries of life that surround Min Li are also threaded with her good fortune, a fortune born of Min Li's tenacity and strong character. The perfect place that Min Li discovers is not a physical space or even a circumstance, but a hope that rises above the often calamitous conditions of life.

--Joseph Bell, Director of Deaconate Formation and Chancellor, Diocese of Reno:

The Perfect Place is the excellent second part begun by the first book *The Crystal Monkey*. The first novel acquaints us with the horror of the Chinese Cultural Revolution and the chaos that spread to all of China. The second focuses on the struggle of a poor peasant farming family trying to survive and prosper in the chaos. The oldest daughter has completely rejected the path laid down by the Party. She is determined to survive and prosper and help her family do the same. Severely hampered by an abusive father who is a product of the new China, caring only for himself and blowing all of the family's money on himself, and constantly abusing is wife whose health is getting worse, Min Li becomes a successful business woman, but her mother, her dearest treasure, will not live to enjoy it. She wants a special place for her tomb where her husband will never go. The found a place that made her mother's heart happy. Then, in a final twist of irony, she meets the American she fell in love with a decade ago, and they are reunited. Finally, hope triumphs amid the chaos of modern China.

--Larry Hyslop, International Education Consultant

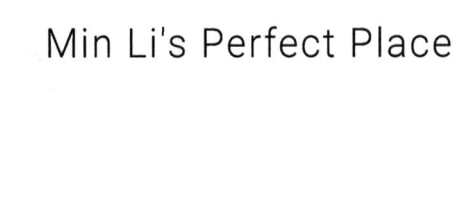

Min Li's Perfect Place

Min Li's Perfect Place

Patrick Nohrden

Dedicated to my wife and soulmate Mindy Nohrden (formerly Guo Limin), who taught me to see China in different ways.

One

The valley below shimmered in the early afternoon sun, the view distorted by the layer of suspended dust made humid by the sweat of men and women working the fields. Each field laid out in a haphazard patchwork of no particular geometric shape, Min Li pretended she could make out the field claimed by her family and imagined she saw her mother hoeing the rows of waist-high corn. From her childhood hiding place atop Pàotǎ Shān, a small hill outside her home village of Shangguang, Min Li easily surveyed what was once the extent of her known world, an alluvial plain near the Bohai Sea in Liaoning Province.

The landscape had changed little since Min Li lived in Shangguang, the summer sky constantly grey by the suffocating humid heat of Northeast China, the ever-present dust in the air, the sounds of summer insects eagerly eating crops before harvest, and the smells of what few livestock shared the village with the villagers, and the outhouses. Now, however, the smells were mixed with those of the factories from the nearby city of Huludao, and the skies seemed a different shade of grey. Min Li thought of the novel by the English writer Thomas Wolfe *You Can't Go Home Again*. She added to that title her own thought, *because there is a reason you left*. And so long as home never changes, the reason for leaving will always be there.

The last time Min Li returned to Shangguang was during the lunar New Year holiday four years earlier. Before that, she returned home every year, the filial obligation of every Chinese, the second day of the holiday being reserved for wives to visit their own parents. That last visit was also the last straw, and Min Li could no longer tolerate her father lording over the family household, ordering her mother about, being waited on hand and foot, and spending evenings with his friends, coming home drunk every night. Had he at least contributed in some way to the household, she might have felt differently. But her father lived in faraway Panzhihua in Sichuan Province, coming home every year only for the lunar New Year, the Spring Festival, to remind his family that he was in charge.

Throughout the year, Min Li's mother, Lian Min, and her sisters Hong Qi and Hai Tian, worked their small field growing corn. What corn they sold, and what meager earnings her older brother Xiong Yong brought in from doing odd jobs, was the only money the family had. Lian Min used this money to support the family and to pay for Min Li's school fees while she was in high school. There was not enough money to pay for her sisters' school fees, so they stayed home and learned to farm. Their father, who by now was a supervisor at an iron ore mine in Panzhihua, often bragged about the money he earned and the bribes he took to assign workers to less dangerous jobs. But none of that money ever made its way to Shangguang.

Min Li remembered that lunar New Year four years ago which found Lian Min disabled with pneumonia. She had purchased a small pig which she planned to butcher for the upcoming holiday, but Hai Tian had left the gate open one evening when she went out with her friends. The pig escaped, and Lian Min spent most of the evening looking for it in a freezing winter rain. She found the pig, but by the time came to butcher it, was so sick she could not leave her bed. Hong Qi, who was married by then, offered to do it, but it was the first time for her. When she had finished, the pork had been butchered poorly, and some of the meat had been wasted.

Min Li's father, Zhang Zhi Hao, arrived the next day and saw evidence of the carnage in the small front year. Lian Min, too sick to meet him at the door, remained in bed, but Zhang Zhi Hao would not tolerate a lazy wife and ordered her out of bed to make dumplings. He reasoned that if Hong Qi had no skills to kill a pig, she could not properly make dumplings.

Lian Min would not argue with her husband, and complied with his wishes, remaining out of bed to prepare the traditional food for the New Year celebrations. When Min Li arrived from Shenyang, she found her mother bent over a bench rolling dough for dumplings, pale as a ghost, drenched in sweat from the fever. Min Li ordered her mother to bed and finished preparing the dumplings.

Min Li was making the dumplings when her father entered the house following an afternoon of drinking with his friends.

"Where's that lazy wife of mine?" demanded Zhang Zhi Hao.

"In bed where she belongs."

"That's not where she belongs. She belongs in the kitchen cooking for her husband."

'she's sick," responded Min Li.

'she can't be that sick," retorted Zhang Zhi Hao. 'she's still breathing, and she's my wife."

"Leave her be," Min Li warned. "Give her a chance to get better. You're lucky she's still alive."

Her father merely grunted and entered the other room where he scolded Lian Min for being lazy and for allowing his ungrateful daughter to make his dumplings. Before he came back into the main room where Min Li was working, she had already grabbed her still-packed suitcase and left the house. As she walked to the bus station, she amused herself with her father's slight limp resulting from the time she stabbed him with a pen while he beat her for refusing to marry Cao Hong Bo.

By now, Hong Qi worked her own small field with her husband Liu Yuncun, and Xiong Yong worked in the local granite quarry as a stonecutter. Lian Min continued to work the family field with the help of Hai Tian, except at harvest time when all the neighbors, all former members of the same production team, helped each other bring in the ripened corn. During the Cultural Revolution, most of the villagers worked in production teams farming huge tracts of ancient farmland, nearly sterile from the centuries of farming, and benefitted from none of the harvest, but for ration coupons with which they could exchange for food and other essential items. When that era ended, the government disbanded the production teams and divided the land between the individual members, each receiving about an acre. Some families received two acres, because both husband and wife worked on the production team. Lian Min received only one acre, because her husband worked in another province. She had to make do with that.

Min Li refused ever to be a farmer and immersed herself in the urban world of Shenyang, the capital of Liaoning Province. It had been fifteen years since she ran away from Shangguang, and the memory of that night never left her. In an attempt to court favor with a local Communist Party official, Min Li's father sold her into a marriage with the official's son, Cao Hong Bo, who had twice before attempted to rape her. Min Li should have gone to study at a university and had won full scholarships at both Beijing University and Xinhua University. Her father smashed her hopes when he told her she was marrying Cao, so she ran away to Shenyang. College now out of the question for her, she could at least do what she could to avoid marrying the scum that wanted to rape her.

Now she sat on a stone atop Pàotǎ Shān and allowed more pleasant memories of her childhood to seep into her thoughts. She came here often with her brother to play. Then, the young trees were too small to climb and very few animals disturbed them. But now, the trees had grown tall enough to provide shade, giving Min Li a respite from the hot sun, and rabbits, squirrels, and many varieties of birds abounded. Min Li pondered the absence of animals before and could think of no reasonable explanation. Maybe her memory had changed. Over time, Pàotǎ Shān had become a more pleasant place. It gave Min Li a chance to relax and to review the problems she faced in her daily life. She came here to gather her thoughts. Climbing through the thicket that had overgrown the trail she and her brother had often used scrubbed the troubles from her mind. She needed to think, to gather her inner strength before she returned home to meet her father, and Pàotǎ Shān gave her what she needed. For that, it was the perfect place.

Min Li's mother asked her to come home this weekend. Her father had just retired and the family would celebrate his sixtieth birthday, a momentous occasion in China representing the culmination of two life cycles when the twelve animals of the Chinese zodiac coincided with the five elemental cycles for the first time since a person is born. Chinese custom obligates the adult children to plan a large celebration, the first major birth celebration after a child's first. Guests will bring red eggs, red envelopes with money, and steamed buns shaped to look like peaches. Her father would be the guest of honor, an honor that he expected, and he will look forward to spending his retirement with his family. As his eldest daughter, Min Li will cook him long noodles representing a longer life.

Min Li steeled herself from her hilltop hideaway and pushed through the bushes along the old trail. She had to go to her family's home to celebrate her father's retirement and his sixtieth birthday. Her mother expected her. Her brother and sisters expected her. The whole village expected her. Zhang Zhi Hao would lose face if his eldest daughter failed to return for his occasion. That would cause shame to her mother, and Min Li would not allow her mother anymore shame.

Two

Sweat formed small rivulets etching the dust caking Min Li's face by the time she reached Shangguang. The humidity prevented her perspiration from achieving any affect, and what sweat had not been absorbed by the dust dripped from her body. None of the small businesses in Shangguang had air conditioning, so she could find no relief from the midday sauna making movement so difficult. She continued toward her family's home with only the thought of what relief the well pump would provide her.

No longer used to life in the village, Min Li dwelled only on the life she led in Shenyang with indoor plumbing, air-conditioned restaurants, bathhouses, and taxis. She entered the broken gate that led to her former front yard and headed straight for the pump, pumping the handle six or seven times to half fill the bucket. Her sister Hai Tian watched Min Li from the open door of the small house as Min Li hoisted the bucket and poured the cold water over her head before filling it again.

"You're going to catch a cold, Jie Jie," Hai Tian yelled from the doorway.

Min Li ignored her little sister and continued rubbing the mud from her face with her wet hands, then pouring the bucket over her head again. "How are you doing, Mei Mei?" Min Li finally responded.

'same as I always am," Hai Tian responded.

"Well, you're just in time to help me make dumplings. You always made the best dumplings, Jie Jie."

"Give me a chance to rest up," protested Min Li. I have no strength from this oppressive heat and humidity."

"Don't you have heat and humidity in Shenyang?" Hai Tian queried.

"Yes, but there you can find relief, go shopping in an air-conditioned market, go to the neighborhood shower shop. Here, the only relief is this miserable pump."

"It'll be cooler this evening."

"Not cool enough. Then we'll have to fight off mosquitoes."

"I haven't seen you in more than four years, and all you do is complain," whined Hai Tian.

'sorry. I miss you and Hong Qi and Mama, but I don't miss this place."

"But at least you got away. I'll be here until I die."

"You don't have to stay. Marry a rich guy," Min Li answered with her usual advice for Hai Tian.

"Find me a rich guy. It's not like their dropping out of the trees here in Shangguang."

"What trees?"

"There you go. If they were falling out of trees, none would fall in Shangguang."

Shangguang had few trees, as most had been cut down many years ago before 1963. What few existed were apricots, apples, and jujube trees, all planted by local people hoping to supplement their corn crop income. Hong Qi and her husband had planted six apricot trees, although none had yet to bear fruit. Lian Min and Hai Tian had planted a jujube tree many years earlier, but it yielded only enough fruit for their small household.

"You can come back to Shenyang with me," Min Li offered. "I've told you that a hundred times."

"Then who will help Mama? Xiong Yong is working at the granite quarry. Papa will be home soon, but do you think he will be any help?"

'maybe he's changed."

"He's the same every year when he comes home for New Year," Hai Tian argued. "He spends his time out with his friends drinking, stealing our things to sell for more liquor, and sleeps half the day. Do you think he'll be any different now that he's retired? I'm not looking forward to it."

"Another good reason to come back to Shenyang with me."

'really, Min Li. You used to be more serious."

"Why do you think I'm not being serious now?"

"Because you're not thinking about Mama."

'mama should come with me to Shenyang," Min Li said, finally ending the argument. But she knew that would never happen. Zhang Zhi Hao, her father, would never allow it. He looked forward to his retirement, a time for having nothing to do. He'll be sixty years old and will think that he earned his spot on a stool at the local wine shop. He won't work to save his own life, and he'll expect his wife and children to do everything for him. Min Li lived in Shenyang, so she would only have to come around on certain holidays. Hong Qi lived on the other side of the village with her husband, so she was off the hook. Xiong Yong worked hard at the quarry. That left Lian Min and Hai Tian to be her father's new servants. Min Li felt sorry for Hai Tian and her mother.

Hai Tian walked out to the pump with a small towel and a bar of soap.

"Here, make yourself more presentable. Mama and Papa will be home soon. Mama left to meet him at the bus station an hour ago."

Min Li filled the bucket again and removed her clothes while Hai Tian guarded the gate. She had grown used to the modesty imposed upon those who live in a big city and felt a little subconscious bathing in the garden. The three walls protecting the garden blocked the view from neighbors, and the gate faced the field assigned to her family. She stood among tomatoes, squash, and cucumbers while she bathed herself in the hot afternoon sun, except for her feet. She could stand nowhere without standing in mud or dirt, so her feet would have to wait until she could sit at the stoop.

Min Li wasted her energy trying to dry off because of the high humidity, but at least she was dry enough to don a fresh skirt, blouse, and undergarments. She had brought enough things for two days and had used the next day's set of clothes. *Bad planning*, she thought to herself. Her other clothes included a dress and high heels which she would wear for her father's banquet planned for the next day.

After cleaning her feet on a stool near the door, she entered the house with Hai Tian. Min Li had forgotten that the house had only hard-packed earth for a floor and immediately regretted not donning her shoes.

"You've been in the city too long, Jie Jie," Hai Tian said.

"If I had any sense, I"d still be there."

Min Li came to Shangguang only for the weekend, to celebrate her father" sixtieth birthday and retirement. She intended to spend no more time in the village than absolutely necessary and was only satisfying her customary obligation as her father's oldest daughter.

The family home had changed very little since Min Li last visited. For that matter, it had changed little since she was born. Against the back wall was the kang, a raised wooden platform that served as a bed, large enough for four or five people and heated in the winter by a bucket of coal embers underneath. To the left of the door was the stove, simply nothing more than a brick and mortar contraction formed in a circle covered by a large wok, rising in the back to form a chimney through the roof. Where a bench once occupied the center of the room used for eating now stood a folding table and four folding chairs. Upon the table, Hai Tian had piled a half of batch of dumplings next to a ball of dough and a bowl of stuffing made from minced pork, leeks, and garlic. Four shelves occupied the righthand wall, filled with various knickknacks, a few books, and cooking supplies.

A smaller room next to the stove was used for storage and as a bedroom when her father was home during the New Year holiday. Min Li wondered what the arrangements would be now that he was home permanently until she saw that it contained a new double bed covered with a bamboo sleeping mat. *I guess he'll be here to stay,* Min Li thought.

Min Li helped Hai Tian finish making the dumplings, which she knew her father would be expecting when he arrived home.

"I'm not so sure I'm excited about Papa coming home," Hai Tian said.

"I know I'm not."

"You don't even live here. How will that effect you?" Hai Tian asked.

"I don't have to live here to know what it will do to Mama."

"You don't think she misses her husband?"

"He's hardly been a husband. He's never been here except during the New Year holiday."

"He came home while you were taking the *gao kao* after you graduated high school. He must have care about you."

"If he cared so much, he would have been here more often," Min Li argued. "Besides, the only reason he came home then was to marry me off to Cao Hong Bo. He did that for himself."

"What do you mean? It is a parent's duty to find a suitable spouse for their child. I understand that Cao Hong Bo was well connected."

"Yes he is. His father is Cao Hong Li. At the time, he was just some low-level village official. Now he is the lieutenant governor of Liaoning Province."

"Just think what your life would be like now had you married him. You"d be living in a top-floor apartment with seven rooms and two bathrooms if you didn't run away," Hai Tian imagined.

'maybe, but I"d be the wife of a no account scum who had no regard for the rights of women. That is not what I want for my life. You don't remember who that guy was. You were too young to know what was happening back then."

"All I remember was Papa coming home from the bus station limping, calling you all sorts of bad names, how ungrateful you were, and how you got on a bus before he could talk sense into you."

"Talk sense into me? Is that what he told you? You don't know why he was limping?"

"No."

"He caught up to me at the bus station, but talking is not what he wanted to do. He beat me and told me I was going to marry Cao Hong Bo, that I would do that instead of going to the university. If I married him, then maybe his father would recommend Papa for membership in the Chinese Communist Party and his life would be different, not our lives. Our lives never mattered to him; otherwise, he would have sent money from Panzhihua. He never sent any money. Everything was on Mama. Nobody was going to make me marry some boy who tried to rape me twice. And Papa knew about that too. It didn't matter to him."

"Rape you?"

"You don't remember. I can't forget."

'so what does that have to do with Papa limping?"

"I stabbed him in the leg with a pen," Min Li said matter-of-factly, "at the bus station. I left him squirming on the bus station floor and hopped the bus to Shenyang before he could get up and come after me again."

"Then you got that nice job teaching English in an elementary school. Why did you quit that?"

"I didn't quit. Most of the faculty only had high school diplomas. That's all you needed in those days to be a teacher. But the government needed to do something about the high unemployment rate for college graduates. One June it announced that all teachers in the province must have a college degree. By the following September, half of our staff were out of work."

"Is that why you didn't marry that American teacher?"

"Oh Peter. No that's not the reason. We talked about getting married because we loved each other so much. He really wanted to, you know. I wasn't so sure it could work out for us. He wanted to go back to school to earn his master's degree, so he would have to return to America. If I went with him, I"d have to work to support us. As a Chinese woman recently arrived in America, my chances of making enough money would be slim. We thought it would be better to just put things on hold; then we lost touch."

"It's a good thing, too. Otherwise, you"d be living in America, and what would I do without my jie jie?"

"I still miss him though."

"No matter," Hai Tian said, trying to cheer up her big sister. "At least you're married now."

"At least."

"Why didn't your husband come?"

"He had to stay home and watch the shop. We've got over twenty accounts now, you know."

Min Li and her husband, Wang Jing, owned a small commercial janitorial service in Shenyang. When Min Li lost her job at the school, thet invested their entire savings into equipment and supplies, including an electric floor buffer, as well as a modified bicycle to carry everything to their clients' businesses. The bicycle had two wheels in the front which accommodated a platform of about three feet wide and four feet long, with stake sides approximately ten inches high. It was the same sort of contraption used by produce peddlers. In fact, they had purchased it from a retiring melon vendor.

Because Wang Jing was already unemployed, having been so for nearly the entire ten years of their marriage, nothing prevented his full-time involvement in the business. His greatest contribution, however, was the ability to pitch their business's services to potential clients, and their list of clients included banks, insurance offices, travel agencies, and one government agency, the marriage bureau. Wang Jing spent the day out canvassing for new clients, which he used as an excuse to avoid the work involved in actually providing the service. Min Li grew accustomed to her husband's absences during the working hours of the night. She assumed he spent the evenings sleeping in their home, a reasonable assumption given that he was pounding the pavement by day drumming up business. By now, they had three employees helping with the cleaning duties, whom Wang Jing supervised in Min Li's absence.

"Twenty accounts, you must be rich!" exclaimed Hai Tian.

"Not by any stretch of the imagination. We're making a little money, but not enough."

"Any money is more than I have," lamented Hai Tian. "I'll be stuck in this village for the rest of my life with nothing."

"Like I told you before, Mei Mei..."

Hai Tian interrupted, "I know. I can always go to Shenyang with you, but Papa said he has somebody he wants me to marry."

"Who?"

"He didn't say."

Three

Xiong Yong gripped the iron pry bar tightly with both hands, pulling back with all his weight to give the bar a slight arc. Cleaved into a fissure of a granite boulder the size of a small car, the pry bar offered no hope of rendering the boulder as Xiong Yong had hoped. Xiong Yong and the boulder sat at the base of a quarry, about 200 yards long and 80 yards wide. The steep sides of the quarry bore marks of other boulders being clawed away, or blasted, and sloping piles of debris rounded out the corners where the quarry's walls met its floor.

Shirtless workers teemed the quarry, their bodies covered in the tackiness of dust and sweat. Some, like Xiong Yong, broke boulders into workable sizes. Others hauled the smaller boulders to a mechanized rock saw that sliced them into smooth wafers, while others worked polishers that gave each slab a dull shine before they were loaded onto truck. These slabs then traveled to other cities where they became the floors of hotel lobbies, headstones, ornate building facades, or even kitchen counter tops in America.

Xiong Yong earned 800 yuan a month for this backbreaking, dangerous work, typically working ten hours a day with an hour off for lunch. Nobody worked Sundays. The next day, though, Xiong Yong would be taking Saturday off so that he could tend to his father" sixtieth birthday and retirement party. Xiong Yong thought that this would be his last day anyway, that is if he asserted his legal right to take his father's job in Panzhihua. He still had to think about that.

China set the mandatory retirement age for men at sixty, fifty-five for women, in order to help reduce the high unemployment rate. Certain critical jobs allowed men to work longer, as evidenced by the average age of seventy for the men serving on the Politburo Standing Committee. Xiong Yong's greatest concern about taking his father's job was whether he would have to start out as a common miner or if he would take over his father's office job as scheduler. It was no secret that the most dangerous job in China was underground mining. He would rather work in an open pit granite quarry than to work in a coffin hundreds of feet underground. The year before, 5,798 people died in underground mining accidents in China. Xiong Yong refused to become one of those statistics.

At noon, a loud bell clanged followed by the clanging of dropped shovels, pickaxes, and pry bars. Xiong Yong headed with his coworkers to the shaded break area and grabbed his *fanbao,* a square metal bucket with a matching lid held on with clasps. He removed the lid and picked up the chopsticks laying atop a large helping of tepid steamed rice. Next to the chopsticks were a cube of stewed pork, a small helping of steamed spinach, and a tablespoon of a mixture of chili sauce and soy sauce.

Xiong Yong finished his lunch quickly then found a shaded spot on the ground to take a nap, hoping to restore his energy for the afternoon work period and to avoid the sauna-like heat. He didn't count on his friend Lao Dong sitting next to him.

'so when's the big party?" Lad Dong asked, interrupting Xiong Yong's nap.

"Tomorrow. Coming?"

"It depends. What time?"

'six o"clock. You'll be off by then."

"Oh yeah. Tomorrow's Saturday and we get off by three. So, you excited about your old man coming home for good?"

"As excited as anybody I guess. It's not like I'm used to him being around," Xiong Yong answered. Things will be different at home."

"That shouldn't affect you much if you take your father's job in Sichuan."

"I'm still thinking about that."

"It's got to be better than working in this death trap," Lao Dong reasoned. "You know three guys died last month."

"That's not so bad. It was only one incident when that boulder broke loose from the northwest wall and nobody was paying attention. You won't get hurt here if you pay attention. In those underground mines, you can lose three hundred people because of a spark."

"But your father works in an office. You won't be underground. What's safer than an office?"

"I'm not sure I'll be in an office. It's likely, though, because it isn't all one company anymore."

"What do you mean?"

"Before it was one state-owned company that did everything. A couple of years ago, the government split it up. Now the government owns the company that manages the mine and contracts with private companies for the underground workforce. That way, the government won't be responsible for paying all those death benefits for the miners. The private companies will have to take care of that."

"Then if you take your father's job, you'll be working for the company owned by the government. Sounds like you'll be safe. Maybe you just don't want to fix your own lunch."

"I can manage," Xiong Yong said defending himself.

"If I were you, I'd walk away from this job now."

"They pay us today at the end of the shift. I need the money."

To Xiong Yong's relief, Lao Dong left to use the outhouse, allowing another chance for a nap. No sooner had he closed his eyes again, the bell clanged marking the end of the lunch hour. Xiong Yong peeled himself from the ground and fruitlessly padded his backside to knock off the dust he had collected while lying on the ground. It didn't matter, though, as his body was covered in a paste-like layer of rock dust and sweat, the only skin showing on the hands that he washed before he ate. He grabbed a ladle of water from the pump and headed back over to the boulder he had been working on before lunch.

He did not notice when he stepped on the snake. The poisonous *duanwei* snake instantly wrapped itself around Xiong Yong's ankle and sunk its teeth into his work boot. With his free foot, Xiong Yong stomped on the snake's mid-section, scraping it from its coil around his ankle. The fangs never touched skin, but Xiong Yong injured himself with his own foot, causing him to audibly wince in pain.

"You alright?" a coworker asked as he approached from behind. "You better go to the doctor. That bite could cause you to lose your leg."

"I'm fine. But I gave myself a nasty bruise, I think."

"Good thing. If that snake had bit you, you'd be out of a job."

Xiong Yong thought about that for a second, how a life could change because of one incident. China did not have a good worker's compensation law. If somebody was hurt on the job, the worker's employer simply reimbursed medical expenses but did not pay compensation for lost wages. In the case of death on the job, a worker would receive a stipend depending on the prevailing wage in the area where the worker lived. In Xiong Yong's case, if an accident at work killed him, his family would receive about 4,000 yuan, at the time worth about $450. He had to be more careful. Always looking overhead for falling boulders and for careless workers, he never thought to keep an eye out on the ground for snakes.

Xiong Yong thought, *I won't have to worry about falling boulders or snakes on the ground in an office in Panzhihua.*

Four

Min Li brushed the flour dust off her hands and clothes after she and Hai Tian made the last dumpling. While Hai Tian placed the dumplings in a bamboo steamer basket suspended over the boiling water in the wok, Min Li went into the garden for some fresh air. She stood at the gate and looked over the expanse of knee-high corn in the field beyond. She remembered when she was small and how this one field filled up hundreds of acres with its single rows that stretched for the horizon. She imagined seeing her mother with the production team in the distance bent over a hoe chopping at weeds. Now, this same expanse looked different. It still supported the single crop of corn, yet the field was marked off in patches with former members of the production team managing a single plot competing with the other plots.

Each plot, mostly rectangular in shape supported each farmer for a year. Somewhere, Min Li had a plot, although she wasn't sure where. She didn't know why it had been assigned to her as a member of the village, because she was never a member of a production team. Her name must have been on some list when they divided up the land. Her mother knew where it was, because she grew corn there, giving the family two acres instead of one on par with some of the families who were assigned an acre for each the husband and the wife. Lian Min's plot, by some stroke of fortune, abutted the gate where Min Li stood.

That day, few farmers worked their plots because it was so stifling muggy, although Min Li could see one old man a few hundred yards away, his head sheltered by a wide, conical straw hat, which disappeared from time to time below the tops of the corn plants. He still wore the faded blue Mao suit that so many elderly Chinese in the village wore, although the requirement to wear them had ended twenty-five years earlier. Min Li never owned a Mao suit. As a child, she wore the blue pants but a white blouse. She also sported the red neckerchief of the Young Pioneers until her grandparents fled the country ahead of arrest for being capitalist roaders. That's when her family was reclassified as a "black" family, making life even more miserable than normal for a family in the Chinese countryside.

Min Li looked back at the house, which had changed little over the years except for the decaying whitewash on the walls and chipping paint on the windowsills. But those windows were not even there before Min Li went away to high school. Xiong Yong had installed them sometime while Min Li was living in the dormitory at the Huludao Number Six High School. The squares for the windows had been there, but they were covered variously by plastic, newspaper, cardboard, or wooden planks, depending on the time of year and the availability of covering materials. The bench that once served as the family's dining table leaned against the left side of the house next to a pile of wood scraps used as kindling for the coal fires under the wok and kang.

The same outhouse stood in the corner of the yard farthest from the house. Made from mud bricks with a wooden frame, the outhouse remained the same as it always had with a hard packed dirt floor and a deep hole over which one squatted. The hole would fill up from time to time and the contents would be shoveled into a wheelbarrow for use as fertilizer in the garden and fields. Villagers wasted nothing. Before, during the time of the production teams, this unpleasant task seemed never to be a problem, as production team members often raided the village outhouses to fertilize fields in an attempt to meet production quotas.

It wasn't much of a home, and Min Li didn't miss it. She lived in a rented apartment in a big city and considered herself a success because of it. She"d spent the last fifteen years using countless cosmetic products to erase the permanent tan that marked her as a peasant, as did half of the other women in Chinese cities did. People wanted to do business with sophisticated, cultured people, and they did not want to do business with peasants whom they could not trust. Peasants are poor, and poor people steal. That was the general idea, anyway. Some families rejected potential suitors of their adult children simply because their skin was too dark.

Min Li thought how absurd it was that a nation founded on the principals of equality and rule by the working classes should scorn the majority and the working classes. China today was no different than it was a thousand years ago. Hong Qi interrupted her thoughts.

"Hey big sister," Hong Qi yelled from outside the gate. "I see you made it back for Papa's big day."

"I'm here. Where's your husband and son?"

"Han Bao Sheng went to fetch Han Wan Li from school. They'll be here in about an hour." Hong Qi always referred to her husband and son by their full names, customary in China in most families. It sounded strange to Min Li, because it was not the custom in her own family.

"Goodness, it has been a while. Since I was here last Wan Li hadn't started school yet. What grade is he in?"

'second, and he's already number one in his class in math and science. He's taken after his *da yi*."

'math and science were never my strong suit," Min Li argued.

"Nonsense, you nearly aced the *gao kao*, and certainly you were tested in math and science."

"That was fifteen years ago. I've forgotten all that stuff by now."

"You're being modest. It's too bad you couldn't go to college."

"No sense in going there. When are Mama and Papa supposed to be here?"

"They're not here already? They should have been here an hour ago. Maybe they stopped by the cemetery. Papa likes to go there when he comes back home."

'since when? He never did before."

"I don't know. The past couple of years, I suppose," Hong Qi explained. 'maybe because Papa is getting older."

The Shangguang cemetery sat on a small hill on the north side of the village on Cemetery Road about a thousand yards from an old Catholic Church, which had later been converted to the village agricultural planning office. The government converted the church to an old folks home when it abolished collectivized farming. Later, the village mayor had somehow acquired ownership of the church building, evicted the residents, and rented it out for social functions. Most of the time, the church remained unused.

Min Li never remembered the old church being used as a church because she was merely an infant when the government took over the building, forcing the retirement of the elderly priest, Father Wang. Father Wang remained in the village until being sent to prison without a trial, where he remained for about ten years. When the government released him from prison, he returned to Shangguang and resided in the old church with other retirees. He passed away shortly before the mayor evicted the other residents.

In past years, whenever somebody in the village died, people would gather in front of the old church, despite it not being a church anymore, and they would carry the coffin up Cemetery Road to the cemetery where the corpse would be placed in a family tomb. In recent years, however, the government required that all deceased persons be cremated by law, except for Muslims, who successfully petitioned the government for an exemption to the cremation requirement.

Zhang Zhi Hao and Zhou Lian Min sat in the unkempt grass near the front of the Zhang family crypt. Zhang Zhi Hao had just washed the front of the tomb marker with fresh water and had placed a bouquet of yellow chrysanthemums at its base. Inside the tomb, among others, lay the bones of his grandparents, an uncle killed during the Second World War fighting for the Chinese Nationalist Army, three cousins killed in the Korean War at the battle of Chosin Reservoir, and the cremated ashes of his parents who passed away while living in California.

"I suppose I'm the head of the family," said Zhang Zhi Hao.

"You've been so since your father died," Lian Min reminded him.

"Yes, but now I'm back home. It's hard to be the head of a family when you're nearly 3,000 kilometers away. Now I'll have no problem being in charge."

"Tread carefully, Lao Gong."

"What do you mean?"

"It's just that nobody will be used to you being around. Xiong Yong was only four years old when you left, Min Li was just an infant, and Hong Qi and Hai Tian were both born while you were away."

"Nonsense, I've been back every year like clockwork."

"Yes, for the Spring Festival, and only for two or three weeks at a time. Nobody is used to you."

"Then they better get used to me, because I'm back and that's that."

"They'll get used to you. Just give them time."

"Except for Min Li, I suppose. She has trouble with family loyalty," Zhang Zhi Hao complained.

"She has her reasons, Lao Gong. Leave her be."

"Well, she better be here this weekend. That's all I have to say. If she's not, I'll lose face."

"She'll be here. Chances are she's at the house now waiting for us."

"And Xiong Yong?"

"He'll be there after the end of his shift at the quarry."

Zhang Zhi Hao stood up and wiped the grass from his pants and began down the path toward the road leaving Lian Min sitting. Lian Min thought for a second how nice it would have been if her husband offered her a hand getting up, but they never had such a relationship. She lifted herself from the ground and trotted after Zhang Zhi Hao and caught up to him as he reached the road.

When they reached the old church, they stopped in to have a word with the caretaker. The found him asleep on the back in a back room. The church had at one time been divided into rooms for various offices. Later it more walls were added to allow for the housing of elderly villagers. Since the mayor acquired the building, most of the walls had been removed leaving a hardwood floor, marked in the many places where walls had been. Stacks of folding chairs lay stacked along the back wall next to a stack of folding tables. Zhang Zhi Hao looked worried.

"Hey old man!" Zhang Zhi Hao yelled for the caretaker, waking him from his nap.

"What? Who? Oh, Zhang. How can I help you?"

"Will this place be ready for tomorrow evening?"

"Yes, of course. Why do you ask?"

"It doesn't look like you started getting it ready."

"Why should I? Your party is tomorrow. There's no reason to get it ready today. "Don't worry, Zhang. It'll only take me an hour to set up. It's too hot to do anything now."

"It'll be hot tomorrow, too. I don't want any screw ups. Let me tell you how I want it set up."

"Your wife already told me."

"I'm in charge of my family. I'll tell you how I want it set up," Zhang Zhi Hao scolded the caretaker. First, I want the head table over here against the back wall."

"Are you sure? The late afternoon sun will be in your eyes."

"Hang shades on the windows, then."

"Can't."

"Why not?"

"Don't have any."

"Well, then set the tables over here on the south wall."

"Can't."

"Why not?"

"Then you'll be facing north. That's bad feng shui. You won't want to start your retirement out with bad feng shui do you?"

"That's superstitious."

"It's your retirement."

"Then where should we place the head table?"

"Your wife and I decided to put them near the north wall. Then you"d be facing south and the sun won't be in your eyes."

"Okay. Place the head table on the north wall. Then we'll need maybe seven tables out here."

"Can't."

"Why not?"

"We only have six more tables."

"What if we have too many people for the tables?"

"Invite fewer people."

"This is ridiculous. Are you sure there are no more tables?"

"I can have some brought in," the caretaker offered.

"Good. Bring in two more just in case others show up we didn't invite."

"No problem. I can have them here by Monday."

"But the party is tomorrow."

"I can't have more tables by tomorrow. If you want more tables, you'll have to wait until Monday."

"Why do I have to wait until Monday?"

"Because the mayor has them out his house, and he won't be home until Monday."

"Then what should we do?" Zhang Zhi Hao asked, exasperated.

"Invite fewer people."

Zhang Zhi Hao threw up his hands and headed toward the door. "We'll be back tomorrow at five. Please have everything ready by then."

"Isn't your party at six?"

"We'll want time to get ready."

"I'm glad you told me," said the caretaker. I would have started setting up at five."

Zhang Zhi How glared at the caretaker as he pondered something else to say. As he could think of nothing pleasant to say, he left it at that, then passed through the door into the late afternoon sun, again leaving Lian Min behind him. "Come on, Lao Po. Let's get home. I have my children to see."

Five

The three sisters so involved themselves in their conversation that they didn't hear their parents enter the gate. Their parents caught them laughing and sipping the tea that Min Li had brought with her from Shenyang.

"Good tea?" Zhang Zhi Hao asked from the door, surprising his daughters.

"Oh! You're home, Papa. We didn't even hear you come up," Hai Tian explained.

"What kind of tea is that?" their father asked.

"Tieguanyin," replied Min Li. "Would you and Mama care for some?"

"I don't know. We village folks aren't used to such nice things," he answered sardonically.

"Please have some."

"A kilo of that tea costs more than I make in a month," Zhang Zhi Hao commented. "Your business must be doing very well."

Min Li could see that her father had some grossly exaggerated ideas about her income and might have already been working on some kind of a plan. The tea had been the gift of one of her clients, a large bank. Actually, the bank manager gave Min Li the tea as a reward for calling him at home one night when she was cleaning the floors to report the auxiliary vault door ajar. The vault contained a fresh shipment of American one hundred-dollar bills. She could have explained this to her father, which would have caused him to dismiss whatever plans were formulating in his head. Instead of arguing with her father, Min Li fetched two more teacups from the shelf and poured tea for her parents. As custom required, she only poured them a half cup each.

Lian Min took the seat at the table offered by Hai Tian. Hong Qi offered hers to her father, but he remained standing, chugging the tea while his wife sipped.

"You wasted your money on this expensive tea," he proclaimed.

Min Li resolved to say nothing.

"It's not any better than Huangya."

"Huangya is expensive, too, Papa," Min Li said.

"Well, that's what I'm used to," her father lied. As soon as he said it, he realized his mistake. For more than two decades Zhang Zhi Hao had lived and worked in Sichuan, and by his account was making a decent salary. Yet during that entire time, he never sent any money home. Even on his annual visits at New Year, he left no money in the family coffers. The arguments were old, and they never changed. He claimed he had expenses, that he had a status to maintain, and he had countless other reasons why he had shared none of his income with his family all these years. Lian Min did it all with her meager corn crop every year, which she used to pay for food, clothing, school fees, and other essentials for her children, as well as covering the cost of growing the corn, including seed and fertilizer.

Lian Min, now in her late fifties, looked at least ten years older due to the rigors of Chinese farming. Lian Min farmed by hand, using hoes, rakes, shovels, and sticks to plant the seeds. At harvest time, she picked the corn by hand with neighbor farmers, most of whom helped each other out to bring in the crop in time. After the harvest, Lian Min was on her own again, now lately with Hai Tian's help, who had finished middle school only a couple of years before. Lian Min would cut down the exhausted corn stalks, bundle them, and carry them into piles, which she would later burn. Next came the chopping of the ground and stalk roots to prepare the ground for the winter.

Thinking about her mother's farm work reminded Min Li of something her former American boyfriend Peter had said. He came to her after teaching an English class one day at the local college. Most of his students were the offspring of farmers from throughout Liaoning Province, some beyond.

Peter liked to create role-playing situations for his students to improve their English conversation skills. That day he told them to act out the resolution of a simple problem: imagine you are the child of a farming family and are ready to leave the village for college, but the tractor breaks down, and you need your tractor to bring in that season's harvest; otherwise, the crop will go to waste. Your family only has enough money either to fix the tractor or to pay your first year school fees. Talk out the solution. He then broke the class into groups and assigned roles to various students. One student played the part of the student, another the father, another the mother, and two others were grandparents. The groups then role-played their solutions in English in front of the entire class.

Peter's perplexity resulted in the fact that every group ignored the tractor, maybe mentioning it only once in passing. The solution of every group was to send the kid to college and leave the tractor dead in the field. "Don't these kids realize how important a tractor is?" he questioned Min Li.

"Peter, they don't even know what a tractor is," Min Li replied. "They've never seen one. I grew up on a farm and the only tractors I've seen are in pictures in books. The tractor represented an insignificant loss. Besides, if those are farm kids in college, they did not get there by chance. They worked themselves to near death to get into high school and did it again to get a high enough score on their *gao kao* to get accepted at a university. Their families put up everything they had and borrowed from friends and relatives to pay for their children's school fees. They have staked everything on these kids, because that is the only way the farmers have to change their family history."

Min Li suddenly grew remorseful. She thought about how she had failed to change her family's history. All through school, Min Li knew that it was her destiny to change her family's history. She would have, too, had she attended Beijing University. Then she reminded herself that it was not her fault she did not attend college but her father's. He wanted her to marry Cao Hong Bo. He"d even take the money from Cao's father. Had she married Cao Hong Bo, she could not have attended college, because universities only admitted unmarried students. She would not allow herself to marry Cao under any circumstances, so she ran away, and no university would admit her without her father's authorization. On the bright side, however, she's not a farmer. But her mother and two sisters were still farmers, which concerned Min Li greatly.

"How's business?" her father asked as if nothing had ever passed between them.

"Picking up."

"I see you left your husband behind. Is he too good to celebrate my sixtieth birthday and retirement?"

"He had to look after the business, Papa."

"It's your business," Zhang Zhi Hao argued. "You can stop whenever you want and take a few days off."

"Business doesn't work that way, Papa. My employees can take off on holidays, birthdays, graduations, and even retirement parties. I can't. My customers expect us to do the job they paid us to do, or will not pay us, and they don't care of the owner's father or father-in-law is having a birthday."

"Then you should get some more understanding clients."

"That doesn't make any sense. What do you know . . . ?" Min Li cut herself off. She knew better than to get into an argument with her father. She knew an argument would do nothing more than to sour everybody's mood. She knew she"d walk out again and go straight back to Shenyang, party or no party, but she also knew her mother would lose face if she did. So she bit her tongue. "Excuse me. I have to call my husband."

Min Li crossed over to her bag laying on the kang and rummaged through it looking for her telephone. While there, she found the carton of cigarettes she brought for her father.

"Oh, I forgot. These are for you," Min Li said, handing the carton of Chunghwa cigarettes.

"Nice smokes," Zhang Zhi Hao commented. "They must have set you back a lot. I can sell these and buy ten cartons of my regular brand."

What did I expect? Min Li thought to herself, then continued back to look for her phone. Her search became more frantic, and she reached all the way to the bottom, fishing around for anything the shape of a telephone. She never found it.

"I have to use a telephone," Min Li announced, angry with herself for leaving her phone behind in Shenyang. Suddenly she felt isolated in Shangguang, in the house with her father in it.

"We can walk over to Han's Market," offered Hai Tian. Han's Market had the only telephone in the village, other than the two telephones in the mayor's office and the police office. Faced with no other choice, Min Li accepted Hai Tian's offer with a grunt and the two departed as soon as they donned their shoes.

The sky grew dark as the two sisters walked from the house, despite the fact that it was only 7:30 in the evening in June. Liaoning is in the northeastern part of China, which has only one time zone. Because China is so large, the sun sets early in the east in the summer but not until late at night in the west. However, even with the darkening sky, the air remained warm and humid. Large thunderheads loomed ahead, darkening the sky even more.

"I think it's good you left your phone in Shenyang," Hai Tian offered.

"How is that? I have a business to run, and I need my phone to do it."

"Your husband can look after things. Besides, I saw the tension in your face back at the house."

"Was it that obvious? I'm trying really hard to be nice to Papa."

"We can all see that. Maybe he's not as bad as you remember him."

"That whole thing about the tea, did you even notice that?" Min Li argued.

"I noticed. I'm sure everybody noticed. I know Mama noticed. I don't think she ever tasted tea so good. None of us did. And I'm sure Papa hasn't either. But then again, I don't really know. Who knows what life Papa led in Panzhihua?"

"It's like he's a distant cousin we barely knows," Min Li continued. "He visits his family once a year; then he acts like he's the lord of the roost. He has no idea how we suffered all these years, how hard Mama works, how little we had. He never offered even one *fen* for my school fees, or yours or Hong Qi's. He completely ignored Xiong Yong unless he was boasting to his friends about his prodigal son, and his daughters, he treated us like livestock to be sold to the highest bidder. How much did he fetch for Hong Qi?"

"You mean her bride price? I don't know. He never said. He married her off four years ago New Years, just a few days after you left. I know we never saw any of the money. He took it back to Panzhihua with him."

"Do you know how much Cao Hong Li paid for me?"

"No."

"Only ten thousand yuan. It should have been closer to fifty thousand."

"Why so low? You had just finished high school."

"That doesn't matter. They didn't want me for my brains, that's for sure. Papa took a lower amount in return for Cao Hong Li sponsoring his membership in the Communist Party," Min Li explained. "I had a full scholarship for both Beijing and Xinhua Universities. Can you believe that? Do you know how life would have changed for our family if I graduated from one of those universities?"

"Quite a bit, I'm sure."

"A lot. But Papa was only thinking about himself. He didn't think about the family. The family is nothing more to him than a potential source of income."

"Well one good thing is that Xiong Yong will be taking Papa's job."

"Yeah, and Papa is making Xiong Yong pay him ten percent of his salary."

"But Xiong Yong has a right to that job. It's in the law."

"Only until the end of the year. Starting next year, sons won't have the right to inherit their father's jobs. But Papa has to do the paperwork. He told Xiong Yong he would only do the paperwork if Xiong Yong paid gave him ten percent of his salary."

"That's Papa."

"Now he plans to sell you. Do you even know to whom?"

"Not yet."

People yelling and loud banging noises from inside a nearby house interrupted Min Li and Hai Tian's conversation.

"What's going on in there?" Min Li queried as she stopped to look at a rather new, two story building which seemed out of place in the village.

"That's Cao Hong Bo's house," Hai Tian said, as though that was explanation enough.

'so?"

"They're always doing that."

"Doing what exactly?"

"Fighting. Cao Hong Bo is in there beating his wife. Whenever you see her on the street, she usually has a black eye or two and something bandaged. Last winter he broke her arm."

"Broke her arm? Why?"

"Who knows? Maybe he didn't like her dumplings. Maybe she spent too much time visiting her mother. He's always beating her up for the slightest reason. Last year he beat her up after making her pregnant because he learned the baby was going to be a girl; then he dragged her to a clinic in Huludao to have an abortion."

Min Li shuddered to think what her life would be like had she married Cao Hong Bo as her father insisted. Then she wondered why any woman would marry that man. But whomever he did marry probably had no choice.

They reached Han's Market on Liberation Road only to find somebody else using the telephone and two people ahead of them waiting. The telephone set on a perch near the door of the small market so that people on the phone would not disturb any shoppers. The village people who used the phone always tended to yell, as though their voices reached the other end of the line by the energy they projected into the mouthpiece. Instead of waiting on the street in the humidity, Min Li and Hai Tian went into the market to browse.

Most of the essential items for sustaining life in a village home crowded the shelves of Han's Market. By Shenyang standards, Han's Market was miniscule. The shop might have been fifteen feet deep and only eight feet wide, but somehow Mr. Han had managed to arrange it to allow for two aisles. Near the cash register stood a small freezer chest with sliding glass doors on top stocked with an assortment of frozen fruit bars and ice cream bars. The most popular confection was a simple *bing gun er*, a long piece of fruity flavored ice stick, which sold for only a half a yuan.

Han's Market didn't exist when Min Li ran away to Shenyang fifteen years earlier. Shangguang had no market then, and anybody who needed to purchase something at a store needed to take the bus to Huludao. People were always able to get rice, flour, and corn meal at the rice shop, open every day now but only once a week long ago. Min Li had never even seen a *bing gun er* before she went away to high school. To Min Li, Shangguang benefitted greatly by the addition of Han's Market.

Villagers tended to talk only briefly on the telephone, and they tended to tabulate the cost of their calls as they talked. Every *fen* counted for people of such poverty. Min Li had only to wait in Han's Market for about five minutes before the telephone was available. As soon as she dialed the number in Shenyang, Mr. Han started a stopwatch. Min Li listened to the ringing tone at the other end, her husband's cell phone, but he never answered. Finally, she reached a recording produced by China Mobile indicating that the party she was trying to reach was not answering and to call back later. In frustration, Min Li hung up the phone.

"That'll be one yuan," demanded Mr. Han in his Zhejiang accent.

"One yuan, for what?"

"You called Shenyang. That's long distance. Rates are higher, minimum one yuan."

"But my call went unanswered. There's no charge for that."

"One yuan, please."

Min Li would rather pay the one yuan than to argue with Mr. Han, so she reached into her purse and handed over a one-yuan coin before starting for the house with Hai Tian. "Come on, Mei Mei," she said. "I want to get back to the house before Xiong Yong gets there."

Min Li and Hong Qi crossed the street and began their walk back to the house. As they passed by Cao Hong Bo's house, Min Li could still hear the screaming, banging, and crashing that she heard before. She wanted to do something about it, but she could do nothing. The big city and the little village in that regard were the same. Mindy often saw women on the streets of Shenyang with two black eyes, large bruises, scrapes, and even plaster casts, and she knew these were mostly the result of angry husbands. If somebody should call the police because of a man beating his wife in the neighborhood, the police would not even respond, except perhaps to keep the peace because the noise was too loud.

Even under these conditions, a woman will rarely leave her husband. The incredible loss of face in being divorced far outweighs having to suffer an occasional beating.

Six

Min Li awoke the next morning to the sound of her father snoring. She looked over at where Hai Tian slept on the kang only to realize that Min Li was alone. Through the door to the small room, she could see that her father was alone. Min Li pulled her shoes on and headed out to the outhouse and saw both her mother and sister in the field hoeing weeds. A pang of guilt shot through Min Li. She knew that her mother and sister must work like this every day, but Min Li avoided the backbreaking work on the farm because she was either away at school, studying for exams, or living the past fifteen years in Shenyang.

Min Li quickly donned the clothes she had worn the day before from Shenyang and tied back her jet-black shoulder length hair and walked out into the field to join her mother and sister. Lian Min stood up as she saw Min Li approaching, placing one hand on her hip and wiping her brow with the other while tilting her head slightly to the side. Lian Min wore her faded blue Mao suit while Hai Tian wore a pair of surplus army fatigue pants and a T-shirt. Both wore straw hats to keep the sun off their necks.

As Min Li approached near enough so that her mother would not have to shout, Lian Min said, "What brings you out here?"

"I saw you two working, and I thought I could give you a hand. You know, be useful while I'm here."

"That's nice of you, but there really is nothing you need to do," Lian Min said as Hai Tian continued chopping at weeds. "We're just doing a little weeding."

Nearby stood two piles, the first pile of dandelions and the second of other assorted weeds. Min Li looked at the dandelions when she remarked, "Hey, I remember eating those sometimes, but it wasn't until I went away to middle school, and we occasionally ate them in the summers.

"Before you went away to school, the farm was collectivized," Lian Min explained. Everything belonged to the collective, including the dandelions. I couldn't bring anything home then."

"Not even the dandelions?"

"Not even them. Sometimes folks would sneak out into the fields at night and pick them, but that was always such an awful risk. I don't think we were ever hungry enough for me to risk us losing our home and me being reassigned to the salt farms. But they're ours now. I'll make a big salad from them for the party tonight."

While Lian Min and Hai Tian continued to hoe, Min Li fetched a large wicker basket from the yard and carried it back out to the field. She loaded the dandelions into the basket then watched her mother and sister work. After a while, she convinced Hai Tian to give up her hoe so that Min Li could give her a break. With Min Li's first strike, she hit a rock and the hoe bounced at an odd angle causing a spark to fly. Lian Min and Hai Tian both laughed. Min Li ignored the others and tried again, this time sinking the hoe well into the dirt but missing the weed.

"Let me have the hoe back, Jie Jie," Hai Tian demanded. "We'll be out here all day waiting for you."

"I've got it. Take Mama's if you don't want a break," but Hai Tian continued to stand there watching her big sister's feeble attempt at farming. Then she froze. What passed for maybe two seconds seemed like a minute before Min Li let out a sharp scream. A *duanwei* snake had slithered by on the other side of the row of corn and had coiled itself when nearly struck by Min Li's hoe.

Min Li remained frozen both out of fear and out of not knowing what to do. The snake's coil tightened and its tongue continuously kissed the air as it stared directly at Min Li. Then it leapt, springing toward Min Li's left shin, it's journey interrupted halfway when Lian Min severed it in two with her hoe.

"Be more careful, Xiao Min," Lian Min said casually before returning to her work, using the nickname "Little Min" just as she had with Min Li was a small child. And Min Li felt like a small child trying to imitate big people, which embarrassed her. She handed Hai Tian the hoe and walked back to the house.

Just as Min Li walked in the door, her father came to the door of the small room scratching his back side through his pajama pants. "Where's your mother?" he asked without evening saying "good morning."

"Out in the field hoeing with Hai Tian."

"Then you can fix me breakfast," he ordered before heading for the outhouse.

Zhang Zhi Hao's command stunned Min Li, but she was hungry anyway, and, thinking about her mother, she didn't want to cause any more friction in the household. Min Li started a fire under the wok, went to the pump, and brought in some water to boil. She then dropped in some rice, and when the mixture began to congeal, added a few pieces of diced pork and a few sprigs of spinach. She made enough for four people.

"Your breakfast is ready!" Min Li yelled out into the yard for her father. He didn't answer, so she yelled again. Still no answer. She looked out, saw the outhouse door ajar, and walked out past the gate. She looked up and down the dirt track in front of the house, and even out in the field where Hai Tian and her mother were working. Her father was nowhere in sight.

Waving a white towel over her head, Min Li attracted the attention of her mother and sister and waved them over. When they were in earshot without having to hell, Min Li asked if they were hungry, and indeed they were. Min Lin then asked, "Have you seen Papa?"

"I saw him go out the gate about five minutes ago," answered Hai Tian.

"Where did he go?"

"He went off in the direction of Hong Qi's house."

"I thought he wanted to eat breakfast," said Min Li slightly piqued.

"No doubt that's why he went to Hong Qi's," Lian Min explained. He started doing that a couple of years ago after she moved in with her husband."

"But he told me to make breakfast."

"You have to remember, Xiao Min. He's not used to being around family."

"It has nothing to do with family. He must not be used to being around people."

"They must do things differently in Sichuan, dear," her mother said, continuing to find excuses for her husband's lack of civility.

"No problem," chimed Hai Tian. "There's more for us."

'save some for your father, Sweetheart," Lian Min warned.

"Why? He went to Hong Qi's."

"He'll be back soon."

"How do you know," Hai Tian asked.

"Hong Qi and her husband are out in their field," Lian Min explained.

True enough, no sooner had the three woman washed their hands and sat down to eat, Zhang Zhi Hao came back into the house, sat at the table, and scooped himself out about half of the porridge, leaving the three women to divide the half that remained.

"I could use some of that tea you brought with you," Zhang Zhi Hao said looking at Min Li.

"Anybody else?" Min Li asked.

"I'll have a little," her mother responded, mostly out of politeness.

'me too," said Hai Tian.

Min Li filled a kettle with water from the pump while Hai Tian retrieved four tea cups from the shelf and set them on the table. Zhang Zhi Hao picked up his cup and handed it back to Hai Tian. "Give me that one," he said, pointing to a large mug with a handle.

Min Li took the boiling water from the stove and added some tea leaves, then set it down to seep. Zhang Zhi Hao arose and went into the small room, returning with a small bottle in his hand. Min Li then poured the tea, filling her father's mug nearly full, assuming that his choice of cup was because he wanted more.

"Too full," he said, then swished some of the tea from his mug to the floor. He set his mug back onto the table, twisted the lid from his bottle, and poured in a little *bai jiu*, liquor made from sorghum.

"That might be something you do with cheap tea, Lao Gong," said Lian Min.

"Tea is tea," he said.

When he finished his tea, Zhang Zhi Hao announced that he was leaving so that the women could get women's work done and said that he would meet them at the party at six o"clock. Lian Min indicated that they had some food to prepare for the evening's celebration. They expected between thirty and forty people, but Lian

Min wasn't sure. Hong Qi offered to prepare some of the food, as well as one of the neighbors. Considering the lack of money in the village households, the food would not be very fancy, but there would be some favorites, such as dumplings, twice-fried pork, chicken and snow peas, various vegetable dishes, boiled chicken and duck eggs, and, of course, long noodles which are served at every birthday dinner to represent longevity.

The three women cleaned up the breakfast dishes and started to work on the various dishes.

'mama, why did you ever marry that man," Min Li asked.

"I don't understand your question."

"It's a simple question, Mama. What made you decide to marry Papa?"

"You know the answer to that as well as I do. My marriage was arranged by our families and our work unit."

"Your work unit?"

"Don't you remember how it used to be. Every aspect of our lives was controlled by our work units. I was on Production Team Number Three and your father was assigned to the tree-cutting team. Our parents agreed on our marriage and had to get approval from our respective work units. My production team leader wanted to say no at first, but your father's father, your Ye Ye, made some kind of an arrangement, so finally my team leader relented. He was afraid it would cause the quality of my work to suffer."

"But you were on an agricultural production team. How could a marriage make your work suffer there?" Min Li asked.

'my production team leader wanted to marry me, too, but his family had nothing for a bride price."

"And Papa's family did? I thought nobody had anything back then."

'mostly people had nothing, except some of the leaders. Everything was on a work credit basis. Ye Ye and Nai Nai had some gold stashed somewhere, which was enough to bribe people at the agricultural planning office to assign us this house and to apply pressure on my team leader to approve."

"That doesn't sound like a true socialist way of doing things," Min Li said sarcastically.

"That doesn't mean we had it any easier than anyone else. In fact, it became hard for a while. Various village leaders assumed Ye Ye and Nai Nai had more gold, so they came around all the time looking to hand out favors, in exchange for a little gold. Ye Ye and Nai Nai tried to convince them that there was no more gold, but for a long time people didn't believe them. Somebody even got the bright idea to reassign them to harder work assignments, hoping that that would induce a bribe to be assigned back to where they were. It didn't work, though. Both Ye Ye and Nai Nai had friends in the Agricultural Planning Office, so the reassignment didn't last long."

"But they did have more gold," argued Min Li. "They gave you some to pay for my college fees, but when I ran away to avoid marrying Cao Hong Bo, you gave it to me to set myself up in Shenyang. In fact, when the local government found out they were hording gold, they were reclassified enemies of the proletariat for being capitalist roaders, so they had to secretly flee the country in the middle of the night."

"That's true. And they used some of that gold to pay their way out of the country."

"That's when life for us became horrible. I was kicked out of the Young Pioneers and lost my standing in class in grade school. They wouldn't even let Xiong Yong go to middle school. That was the worse time for our family."

"Not the worse time. You were born shortly after the worse time," Lian Min added.

"Really?" Hai Tian chirped in. "Tell us about it."

"It's too long of a story," Lian Min protested.

"We've got nothing to do but make dumplings, noodles, and rice balls for Papa's party. Please tell us," Hai Tian begged.

Min Li and Hai Tian readjusted their seats and looked forward to Lian Min's long story. They had never heard tales from their parents' early days of marriage. They always assumed there was nothing to tell.

Seven

Zhou Lian Min and Zhang Zhi Hao married April 1, 1960, at the People's Marriage Bureau's office in Yangzhangzi. None of their friends or relatives traveled with them for the occasion, as none of them were allowed time off from work for such a bourgeois activity. Once there, Zhang Zhi Hao handed over the signed permission forms from his and Lian Min's work unit leaders, as well as the maroon booklet, the *hukou*, that served as his family's household registration document.

The marriage itself consisted of the filling out of numerous forms and the issuance of two red marriage identification booklets, one for each the groom and the bride. This booklet allowed the two to reside together, to register together in the same hotel room, and to sleep together in the same bed. With proof of their marriage, the newlyweds were able to obtain a new *hukou*, thereby establishing their family.

Few people in the area owned bicycles, and Zhou Lian Min and Zhang Zhi Hao were no exception, so they had to walk back to Shangguang, which took them nearly three hours on the unpaved road. They arrived at their new home shortly after dark, tired and hungry. Both sets of their parents were at the house waiting for them with candles, blankets, a wheelbarrow of coal, a wok, a teapot, two pairs of chopsticks, two bowls, one bar of soap, and two towels. Zhang Zhi Hao's mother also brought a half a kilogram of rice, two turnips, and about two tablespoons of salt. Those were the only household items the couple had to start their marriage.

The house is the same house in which the family continued to live until Zhang Zhi Hao's retirement, the only change being the addition of the small room on the side of the house after Min Li was born and the installation of the two windows on the front of the house. Electricity came in 1970 about the time Hong Qi was born.

Lian Min's father lit a candle and set it on the bench in the middle of the room giving Zhang Zhi Hao and Lian Min the first glance of their new home. Only one shelf hung on the wall to the right of the door as you entered, and Zhang Zhi Hao's mother placed the few items that had been brought upon it, except for the one candle burning on the bench. The only food in the house was the rice and the two turnips, more food than most houses had in the village.

Zhang Zhi Hao's father lit some pieces of coal under the wok in the stove, while his mother brought some water from the pump, then she filled the teapot with water to make tea.

"Why bother?" asked Lian Min's mother. "There's no tea."

"Ah, but there is," responded Lian Min's mother, and she reached into her pocket and pulled out a white cloth folded into a ball. She unfolded the cloth revealing a small wad of dark green oolong tea compressed to the size of a ping pong ball. Carefully, she pulled off a few leaves of tea and dropped them into the tea pot.

"Where did you get that tea?" Lian Min's mother demanded to know.

"We've been saving it for a special occasion. We hoped to do more for our son's wedding, but this is all we could manage to do. We would have bought a pig if we could find one for sale."

People throughout the village went to bed hungry every night. Everyone was poor, but that didn't matter. Poor or not, there was no food to be purchased. People didn't have money anyway. They purchased their food with coupons which they earned in their respective work units. The most important food staple, rice, could only be purchased one day a week, and on those days the line would stretch for up to a half a mile. People at the end of the line often went home empty handed and would go a week without rice. They could purchase other staples, such as corn meal, wheat flour, and sorghum, but they needed rice.

Despite the fact that Shangguan was a farming, producing mostly corn, little if any of the corn remained in Shangguang. The administrators at the agricultural planning office always reported higher yields than the village actually produced in order to make themselves look better to the officials in Huludao. The officials in Huludao likewise over-reported regional yields to provincial officials in Shenyang, who likewise over-reported provincial yields to Beijing. Beijing in turn "Taxed" the province for a percentage of the reported farm yields, which tax often exceeded the amount of grain actually grown. Demands for the grain then trickled down to Shangguang from Beijing by way of Shenyang, then Huludao. The agricultural planning officials in Shangguang then required all the grain to be turned over to Beijing, through the various local and provincial agencies, in order to support their earlier claims. The result was that there was no grain left for the people of Shangguang.

Although the farming cooperatives had been originally set up so that the workers supported themselves, sending a portion to the national government which it would use to trade to other Communist countries for hard goods, the result was that people at the village level starved. Some of the peasants on the production teams became desperate enough to try to steal grain in their pockets, but sometimes they were caught due to frequent inspections of workers' clothing at the end of work shifts, and were shot on the spot. For most of the villagers, despite the fact that they prepared the fields, planted the seeds, tended the plants, and harvested the grain, they never tasted the corn they grew.

Then there were times when the rice shop had no rice. People stood in line for hours only to learn that they could purchase sorghum and wheat, but their coupons would not allow them to purchase enough to provide food for themselves and families for the whole week. People might run out of food three days into the weekly food cycle and have to go without for four days. Some starved to death. In fact, the year Lian Min and Zhang Zhi Hao married, China's starvation rate was so bad that there were ten million fewer people than the year before. The following year, an even greater number of people died by starvation.

This high rate of starvation forced some people to more desperate measures, one in particular encouraged by the central government. One day, after Min Li's parents had been married a little more than a year, a team of scientists arrived in Shangguang and called a big meeting at the village's largest public outhouse. Once the people had gathered, one of the scientists went into the outhouse with some tools and a metal tray while another scientist explained that he was collecting the green substance that grew above the fill line of the pit. When the first scientist emerged with the tray half full of green stuff, he and a third scientist showed how to clean and heat it while the second scientist explained that they were converting it to edible protein.

When finished, they offered some of the green gook to some peasants standing nearby, who obviously had not eaten well in the past few months. Despite their hunger, the peasants turned down the offering. As a display of good will, all three of the scientists devoured the green goop in front of the crowd, which acknowledged having witnessed the act with various oohs and aahs, a few negative comments. One comment in particular drew the ire of the local officials when somebody in the back yelled, "Now see what the government is having us eat!"

Lian Min's production team worked later in the evenings during the autumn in order to harvest the corn. One evening, Lian Min was particularly hungry. She had gone to work without eating all day, she and her husband having eaten the last of their cornmeal the day before. She planned to eat again the next evening, which was the day that the rice shop would be open and she would be able to exchange some work credits for rice. Those production team workers who volunteered to work past the regular 8:00 p.m. autumn schedule would be rewarded with preferential placement in the rice shop line.

Her hunger consumed her every thought throughout the day, and by nightfall her stomach hurt even more from being empty so long. She thought she smelled meat cooking. She pushed the thought out of her mind and continued plucking ears of corn and throwing them in a burlap bag strapped to her back. But the though persisted. But soon, a worker on the next row said, "What's that smell? It smells like meat cooking."

Lian Min and her coworker peered through the moonlit semi-darkness toward the village, but no chimney spewed even a hint of smoke.

"It's not coming from Shangguang," Lian Min remarked.

"The breeze is from the south, so it must be coming from Xiaguang on the other side of the hill," her coworker rationalized.

"Where did they get meat?"

"Probably a baby swap. I heard a rumor that there hasn't been a girl baby registered on anybody's *hukou* over there in almost a year."

"What are you talking about? What's a baby swap?"

'some people are so beside themselves with hunger that they resort to cannibalism. A woman gives birth to a girl, which is the last thing a family needs these days. They don't want to eat their own child, even if she is just a girl, so they swap her with another family for their baby daughter. That way, they end up eating somebody else's daughter."

"That's horrible!" Lian Min cried. She had been trying hard to have a child. She couldn't image giving one up to be eaten, even if it was a girl. Just the thought of eating human flesh appalled Lian Min. She had seen many people die from starvation, and she was sure they didn't even think if eating another human, even a baby girl from another village. People were so hungry that they ate clay, which took away their hunger pains, but the clay eventually killed them by stopping up their digestive system.

"Of course, it's just a rumor," the other woman said, interrupting Lian Min's thoughts.

"You can't believe rumors."

"But we do smell meat cooking, and that's not a rumor."

'maybe somebody caught a rabbit," Lian Min rationalized.

"When's the last time you saw a rabbit?"

Lian Min went to bed hungry nearly every night. Her typical meal consisted of a bowl of hot water with a few kernels of rice, or maybe a little corn meal. If they were lucky, they found dandelions growing wild, and they could eat those for their greens. She couldn't remember the last time she ate meat, although she was sure she had in the past. After having existed on the verge of starvation for so many months, it's no wonder she couldn't conceive.

Both Lian Min's parents and her husband's parents regularly urged Lian Min to have a baby, to have a son. Lian Min also wanted a child, but the time couldn't be worse. Considering the large numbers of people starving to death and the deplorable conditions in which they lived, having a baby now could not have been good, but she tried anyway. Her malnourished body just wouldn't allow it. Finally, she had confided to her mother-in-law that she didn't think she could ever have a baby. Her menstrual cycle had ceased six months before, and she was so week from hunger that she thought she would die soon. And if she did manage to get pregnant, it was likely the baby would never develop in her womb.

A few days after this confession, her in-laws started coming by her home in the evenings after their work shifts had ended. Each night they brought food with them, soup at first, not the thin soup she had been eating consisting merely of boiled water and a few grains of rice. The soup had real vegetables, carrots, green beans, turnips, and even a small piece of meat. They also brought a cup of steamed rice each night.

"Where did you get all this food?" she asked the first night, incredulously.

"Don't ask, Sweetheart," her mother-in-law responded. "It's better you don't know. Let's just say that the trick is knowing the right person to bribe." And that was that. Lian Min never asked again, and she continued to eat well for the next few months.

After only a few days, Lian Min's energy returned, and her skin took on a normal hue. Her hair stopped falling out, and after two weeks added a little weight. One of her co-workers noticed.

"Why do you look like that?" asked her co-worker suddenly.

"Like what?"

"Have you been gaining weight?"

Lian Min's clothes hung loosely on her, still too big, but not as loosely as before. "No, I don't think so."

"You do too. What have you been eating?"

"What I've always been eating, rice gruel, corn meal soup. We also share a sweet potato once a week, just like you."

"That can't be," argued her co-worker. "You've been eating something else. You're gaining weight. Your skin has more color. Your hair is fuller. And you're on your period."

"How do you know that? I haven't had my monthly visit in seven months."

"Because you're bleeding."

Lian Min looked down and saw a spot of blood in her pants, just at the inseam in her crotch.

The next day Lian Min's production team leader told her to report to the agricultural planning office. The officials there wanted to know why Lian Min had gained weight. They accused her of being a capitalist roader, of not working as hard as her co-workers, of being a spy. Lian Min protested, but nobody believed that she had not been eating secret food. Three people on her production team had died within the last week, yet she was getting fat. She had to be working for the counterrevolutionary forces hiding on Taiwan.

Lian Min cried, but her protests would not ameliorate her accusers, and she did not want to get her in-laws in trouble. Then she remembered the three scientists from Beijing, how they had shown people to convert the green slime in the outhouse to consumable protein, and how none of the villagers would eat any of it.

"Comrades, I have been eating the same thing everybody in the village has been eating. With my husband we share one *jin* of rice, one *jin* of corn meal, and one sweet potato every week, as well as the protein the people from Beijing taught us to make."

"What protein are you talking about, peasant?" demanded on of the party cadres interrogating her.

"You mean you forgot?" Lian Min asked. "You didn't trust our comrades from Beijing when they taught us to make protein from the green slime in the outhouses?"

"Oh that protein," her interrogator responded. "Of course I trust the Party's scientists. I eat it myself," he lied, as he patted his slightly large belly. "You know, if other people ate that stuff, we wouldn't have such a problem here. Production is down because the workers are sick or dying. We must make sure people eat that stuff. It's for the good of the country. It's for the good of the Party."

Thus six workers were pulled from various work units in the village to form a new team responsible for converting the green outhouse slime to edible protein. To make it more palatable, they dried it in the sun, then pulverized it, turning it into a green powder that they called sustenance tea. The lot was packaged in dried corn husks tied and distributed with the weekly rice rations. People had no idea what it was, but they mixed it with hot water and drank it like broth.

The sustenance tea had only little effect, but fewer people died once they started drinking it regularly. When people noticed that Lian Min continued to gain wait and become healthier, she was ordered to stop making the sustenance tea for herself because the green slime belonged to the people and from now on somebody would be by each week to collect from her home's outhouse. Lian Min did not object.

When her periods stopped again, Lian Min grew worried. She told her mother, who worked for the village doctor. Her mother looked at her, felt her breasts and her belly, and declared Lian Min to be pregnant. She told Lian Min by declaring, "It's going to be a boy."

"How do you know that?"

"Well, from the medical evidence I can tell you're pregnant. I can confirm it with a test, but we'll need a rabbit, and I haven't seen a rabbit in three years."

"How do you know it will be a boy?"

"Because I'm your mother, and I just know."

Zhang Zhi Hao learned of his wife's pregnancy three days later. His work unit was camped fifteen miles away near the remnants of what was once a small forest. In the two and a half years Zhang Zhi Hao had been on the timber-cutting unit, he felt as though he personally cleared over a hundred acres of trees by himself. By the time he"d been assigned to the unit, already every tree in Shangguang had been felled, and the unit had already worked its way half way up Pàotǎ Shān. It was grueling work. Many of the workers on the unit had volunteered in order to get out of working the fields, but they soon regretted it.

The tree-cutting unit provided wood for the village forge, which had been set up four years earlier as the village's own contribution to China's iron production. Mao Zedong wanted to reduce China's dependence on the Soviet Union for iron, for which China traded enormous stores of grain in exchange. He declared that if there were enough small forges in China, China would not need to buy iron from the Soviet Union. China would become more independent and would have more food to feed its own people. Iron ore from nearby Fushun County fed the forges, but these forges required extremely high heat and consumed prodigious amounts of timber, keeping Zhang Zhi Hao's work unit working constantly.

Most of the time the tree-cutters made it home evenings, but now they were working further from the village, having cleared the land surrounding the village for miles. Where they worked now, their ability to return home in the evening depended upon space on the truck that hauled the cut trees back to the village. The men on the tree-cutting team cut trees all day, sawed them into stackable logs, and from time to time stacked them on a truck, which hauled them to town. At the end of the workday, they stacked the last load of cut logs onto the truck, then climbed aboard on top of the stacked logs, twelve men precariously perched on an unstable load. What kept them off at times was not the apparent safety issues of men riding on top of an unstable load of cut wood, but the fact that the added weight of the men placed too much of a strain on the truck's engine. Even without the men onboard, the truck strained under the heavy weight of the wood to crest even the smallest of hills. If me were riding on the load, they would often need to jump off and push the truck up the hill and the engine whined in first gear.

At times, there would be so much wood stacked on the truck that the truck wouldn't budge even on a flat surface with all the men onboard, so some of them had to stay behind. Zhang Zhi Hao stayed behind two nights because of this. Staying behind had its advantages, though. Those left behind created lean-tos from tree branches to protect them from evening rain, and built fires to keep warm, but more importantly they hunted small animals. In those days, hunting proved fruitless for most people, because so much of the wildlife had already been killed off by starving peasants. But as the wooded areas became smaller and smaller, what wildlife remained became more concentrated in the small patches of woods left uncut. So the tree-cutters left behind almost always ate meat, usually a rabbit but sometimes a large bird. They learned to catch snakes, skin them, and cook the meat. One of the men said how much they tasted like chicken, but another asked how he could know that, since it had been so long since anybody tasted chicken.

Word of his wife's pregnancy reached him after his second night camping with his co-workers, so Zhang Zhi Hao made sure he was on the last truckload that night. He helped stack the wood onto the truck, tied it down, and pulled himself up with four other men to the top of the load. The team leader sat in the cab with the driver above and slightly behind the vehicles single front wheel, a feature that added to the load's instability on turns. Large patches of rust obscured most of the truck's pale blue paint, and the mud tread of the solid rubber rear tires were sliced and pitted from the rough terrain over which the truck drove between the road and the tree-cutting sites. The back, a simple wooden flatbed with an iron frame, had deteriorated so much that the first layers of cut wood were laid in order to reinforce it.

Zhang Zhi Hao made the fifteen-mile journey to Shangguang in three hours, which required some two hours of "push" time by the men riding on top of the load. They arrived at the village forge around eight that evening, and spent twenty minutes unloading the wood and stacking it. The forge, actually a collection of five cylindrical furnaces made from yellow brick, blackened by the constant fires that burned within, never rested, and the acrid black smoke they produced fouled the air around the clock. With the unloading and stacking finished, Zhang Zhi Hao walked to his home, normally a ten-minute walk, but news of his wife's pregnancy allowed him to have the energy needed to make it in only seven minutes.

"Is it true?" Zhang Zhi Hao asked as he burst through the door of his small home.

"It is indeed," Lian Min beamed.

"This is wonderful. We really must celebrate. I have proven myself a man. This will be great for my reputation."

"Celebrate now? I'm only pregnant. We'll celebrate after the baby is born and has been alive for a hundred days, just as everybody else does," argued Lian Min. "We don't want to jinx anything by forgetting our customs."

"But it's nearly New Year. We have reason to celebrate."

"Then we can wait ten more days for the beginning of the New Year festival. We'll celebrate then. I don't want to bring outside attention to this house."

Eight

The following October found Lian Min harvesting corn when her water broke. She failed to notice the moisture running down her legs at first because she was working hard and it had been horribly humid again. Then she noticed the mud forming under her feet. She stared at her mud-splattered feet, not sure what had just happened, when a co-worker near her saw what had happened.

"Your baby is coming!" yelled her coworker.

Suddenly, a cramp seized hold of Lian Min and she doubled over, more out of surprise than pain. Then another cramp forced her to sit down on the damp ground.

"What's happening here?" bellowed the production team leader. "We've another hour to work before break time. Get up and get back to work!"

'she's having a baby, you moron," explained the co-worker.

"It's comrade to you, you insolent peasant."

"Excuse me. She's having a baby, Comrade moron."

"I'll fine you a half-week's rations for your insubordination, I'll..."

"Do you mind? I think I'm having a baby here in this field," interrupted Lian Min.

"Not in my field, you aren't," said the production team leader. "You two men," he yelled, pointing at two men working further down the row, "get over here and carry Comrade Zhou to her house. You," looking at Lian Min's insubordinate co-worker, "I'll deal with you later. Do you know her mother?"

"Yes."

"Then go fetch her and send her to Comrade Zhou's home. Do it now."

Whereupon, the two men so tasked picked up Lian Min, one holding her two legs on either side of him with his back toward her, and the other with his hands under her arms, his fingers interlaced to keep his hands together. They walked, half trotted, through the picked corn stalks toward Lian Min's house, and the woman told to fetch Lian Min's mother ran down the row she had been working. Halfway across the field she realized that Lian Min's mother would not be at home but was likely at the doctor's office where she worked, so she cut a slight angle through three rows of stalks to readjust her arrival in the village to come out of the field closer to the doctor's office on Liberation Road.

The two men gently lifted Lian Min to the kang, one of them bringing water from the pump and the other lighting the coal under the wok. Both were fathers and had done this before. One of the men, the one that had carried Lian Min by the feet, asked, 'should we get back out to the field?"

Surprised, the other man said nothing at first and only looked at his co-worker.

"Well?" the first man insisted.

"If we go back out to the field, we'll be picking corn for another eight hours. If we stay here, nobody will blame us. We can relax a little bit and help Comrade Zhou if she needs us."

'she looks fine. Let's go."

"Are you nuts? Sit, relax, maybe drink a little water. We're all that's here to help until her mother shows up."

"That's what I'm afraid of."

"Oh. I see. I didn't take you for the squeamish type. Don't worry. Her contractions aren't that close, so it will be awhile. My wife took more than six hours with our first-born."

Lian Min cried in agony as a cramp overcame her. The first man bolted upright.

"Are you sure? She could have that baby any minute, and I don't want to be here for that."

'so what if she does. Somebody will need to be here. Tell you what, if the time comes and her mother isn't here by then, you can step outside. I helped deliver all four of my children. I can figure out what to do."

With that, the first man sat down on the bench in the center of the room and watched the water boil in the wok. The second man found the teapot, which still held some cold water from earlier and offered Lian Min a drink, which she eagerly accepted. Then another cramp seized her. "How long was that?" he asked the first man.

"What?"

"How long since the last cramp?"

"I don't know, a few minutes."

"What, five? Six?"

"Less I think. Maybe four."

"It won't be long then."

"Are you kidding me?" the first man asked in surprise. "You said it will be a while."

"I guess the baby wasn't listening."

Fortunately for the first man, Lian Min's mother flung the door open as she entered and rushed to the kang. "How far apart are her contractions?" she asked to both of the men.

'maybe four, more or less."

"Good, I'm here in time. You did well, Comrades."

Lian Min's mother and the woman who had brought her to the house remained and shooed the men away, disappointing them, one because he wanted to again witness the miracle of birth, both because they would prefer not to return to harvesting corn. Within an hour, Lian Min gave birth to Xiong Yong, a name suggested by the co-worker because it means strong as a bear. Depending on how it is written, it could also mean tempestuous. Either meaning seemed to fit, because the baby was strong, stronger than most babies born in Shangguang anyway, and he was loud, sometimes as loud as a summer storm.

Zhang Zhi Hao cast his eyes upon his son three hours later, having missed Lian Min's ordeal. The proud father looked at the sleeping baby for at least twenty minutes before he spoke. "I must name him."

"Well, we have a suggestion for a name," Lian Min said, referring to herself and her mother. "We like the name Xiong Yong."

"I am the father," Zhang Zhi Hao asserted. "It is my responsibility and privilege to name our children."

'so it is, which is why we selected a name which you yourself would choose."

Zhang Zhi Hao thought for a second, then said, "Xiong Yong means troublemaker. Is that the name you want for our son?"

"You have ascribed the wrong meaning, Lao Gong. Xiong Yong means strong as a bear, like his father."

"Hm. Okay, but there are other words that have the same meaning, Lao Po."

"True, but those words are common. Our son is certainly not common, and he is born during turbulent times, times that will require his strength. So Xiong Yong works best. Besides, the name is unique and people will remember it."

'so it is. As soon as I have a chance, I will go to the police station and have his name registered on our *hukou*. Xiong Yong will occupy the first space for our many children."

Xiong Yong's birth heralded the end of an era for China. The central government had learned that agricultural production reports were greatly exaggerated, which caused the greatest famine in human history resulting in the death of more than thirty million people. It issued new policies that punished false reports, which allowed more food to remain in local control. People ate better, and they stopped dying. But the farming collectives remained, and life remained harsh in rural China. The cities fared better, as urban dwellers were able to buy food and other goods. Life returned to normal, if one could call normal everybody wearing the same clothes and having no choice as to occupation or dwelling. It was still better than before.

By 1966, Chairman Mao thought that people were too soon forgetting the purpose of the Revolution and were becoming counterrevolutionary, sympathizers of the old regime, and capitalistic in nature. He condemned the way people thought and wanted to encourage them to keep the fires of the Revolution burning. His wife, Jiang Qing, or Madame Mao, suggested that the way to rekindle the ideals of the Revolution was to control culture itself, and she prevailed upon Mao to name her the Minister of Culture.

Officially named the Great Proletarian Cultural Revolution, Jiang Qing began by banning everything derived from western culture, including art, literature, and even science. Everything would be Chinese, but nothing old. The old was out, because the old represented China's ties to its feudal past, so even traditional Chinese opera was outlawed. Jiang Qing, a former actress of no importance, fancied herself to be the most knowledgeable person in China with regard to the arts. She wrote four modern operas for the pleasure of the people, intended to re-teach them the ideals of the People's Revolution.

All radio programming in China changed practically overnight, and the radio stations in China's cities became nothing more than repeater stations for the single programming out of Beijing. People had no choice of listening to only one station, which carried the continuous message of the Chinese Proletarian Cultural Revolution. The only music programming were Jiang Qing's operas and a few patriotic songs extolling the virtues of the Great Helmsman, the Rising Sun of the East, Chairman Mao Zedong. The song "The East is Red" was played more often than any other, which was an obvious metaphor for Chairman Mao.

Loudspeakers were installed in villages throughout the country too small to have a radio, or too remote to receive a signal. These loudspeakers served various purposes, the primary purpose being to repeat the message of the state to the people several times a day, the other to announce struggle meeting.

The worst change was the birth of the Red Guard, made up mostly of college and high school students who, leaving their studies behind, flocked to Tiananmen Square in Beijing to see the Great Helmsmen himself. There, Mao instructed the students to go out and make revolution, that they were the bright stars of China's future, and it was up to them to weed out the evil and corrupt elements of society. They were, according to Mao, to continue the revolution, "a great political revolution carried out by the proletariat against the bourgeoisie and all other exploiting classes." They were to seek out and remove the blemishes of China's socialist society who were the capitalist-roaders, counterrevolutionaries, spies of the nationalist government in Taiwan, foreign agents, and traitors. After only a few years, Mao announced that intellectuals were likewise class enemies, and the Red Guards directed their attacks against teachers, effectively closing all of China's schools.

The Red Guards terrorized the cities, arresting anybody they believed belong to any of the categories of class enemy, confiscating their property, forcing them to attend struggle sessions, publicly humiliating and beating them, then imprisoning them. Red Guards traveled freely throughout the country, taking trains and buses without having to pay for their passage, and even causing the police and the military to hide in the shadows. Hundreds of thousands of Red Guards soon divided into factions and often competed with each other for the loot taken from people's homes. After only a few years, after exhausting the spoils of the cities, they turned to the countryside and terrorized villages until finally an edict from Chairman Mao disbanded them.

Min Li's birth ushered in the beginning of the Cultural Revolution in 1966. Min Li, whose name conveys the strength of the people, grew up listening to the loudspeakers in Shangguang, the singing of "The East is Red," and the daily quotations from the *Little Red Book*, a collection of the sayings of Mao Zedong. She thought she live in the greatest country on Earth, that the Chinese Communist Party cared only about her and the people of China, and America was evil and that American children had no food to eat. Everything changed after she turned six when the Red Guards came to Shangguang.

By then, because China's population continued to grow to unmanageable levels, the government encouraged the work assignments of married couples in different provinces. The anticipated result would be that China would suffer fewer births if married couples only saw each other once a year. Zhang Zhi Hao volunteered for the assignment, though, because it meant having a salary in lieu of food credits, and the family, like any family, sorely needed money.

Because he had the luxury of choice, Zhang Zhi Hao discussed the job in Sichuan at length with Lian Min. They would be apart most of the year except during the New Year holiday. Zhang Zhi Hao would live in the worker's dormitory and eat in his work unit's mess, keep what money he needed for himself, and send the rest home to help his family and, more importantly, pay for the children's school fees. That was the plan, but once he was in Panzhihua, Sichuan, Zhang Zhi Hao developed new needs. He learned that he could curry favor with his supervisors by hosting dinners and drinking bouts in local restaurants, by lavishing them with gifts, by providing them with women, and by acting important himself. For this, he would need to live outside of the dormitory in his own apartment, which he rented. He never had money to send home, and his trips home served no purpose other than to remind his family that he was the head. On two occasions, he managed to father two more daughters, Hong Qi, meaning red flag, named by Zhang Zhi Hao during one of his patriot moods, and Hai Tian, whose name Lian Min chose meaning the sweetness of the sea.

Lian Min remained home throughout the years tending to the family's small plot, barely earning enough money to keep the family fed and struggling to pay her children's school fees. There never would be enough money to pay for the children's high school fees. When Min Li qualified to enter high school, those fees were paid by her father's parents, Ye Ye and Nai Nai.

Nine

"Why have we never heard this story before?" Min Li wanted to know.

"Because it's not important," her mother answered.

"It certainly tells a lot. Was Papa always the way he is?"

"Your father is a hard-working man who had goals and tried to achieve those goals despite adversity," Lian Min said defensively.

"But all that he achieved he did for himself. We have nothing to show for it.," Min Li continued.

"We have each other," Hai Tian interrupted.

"Of course," Min Li answered, "but look where we are. You and Mama live in this hovel where we all grew up. I had a chance to go to the university with a full scholarship, but Papa tossed that idea when he wanted me to marry that rat Cao Hong Bo, just so that Papa could join the Party and with no regard for my future and how I could have brought fortune to this family. Nobody else was able to go to high school, and only Hong Qi attended middle school. She was married to another farmer, so her life will not change, and who knows what will happen to you. Whoever Papa wants you to marry will no doubt benefit the family, only Papa in some way. And look at Mama. She's old before her time and has had to maintain this family all these years without Papa's help. But at least we have each other," Min Li added sarcastically.

"He's still your father," Lian Min scolded. "Have respect."

"Hmpf," was all Min Li could say, and she went back to rolling out dough for more dumplings.

"Let's finish up," Lian Min suggested. We still have to get ready for your father's party and get this food to the old church."

"What exactly is a church?" Hai Tian asked, more out of wanting to change the subject than any curiosity about the building where they planned to have her father's party.

"It's a place where Christians meet," Lian Min answered. "That's pretty much all I know."

"Are there no more Christians?" Hai Tian asked.

"I'm not sure. There was a small group of them who met at the church every Sunday. The government closed the church when I was a child and forced the priest in charge to retire. What was his name?" Lian Min wondered out loud.

"Father Wang," Min Li answered.

"That's right. I haven't seen him in years. He used to play mahjong with Ye Ye and that dear old man who owned the gift shop."

'mr. Li," Min Li answered again.

"That's right. It was Mr. Li. Both he and Father Wang went to prison the night the Red Guards came to the village."

Lian Min's remembrances conjured up memories long forgotten by Min Li of the bitterly cold night the Red Guards called a meeting and all the village witnessed Father Wang and Mr. Li being criticized for being counterrevolutionaries and capitalist roaders. They had been airplaned, that is their hands were tied behind their backs and a long piece of wood slid between their arms and their backs. They were beaten, humiliated, and trucked away. That is the first time Min Li ever saw anybody killed when the Red Guards summarily executed a man and woman for having an extramarital affair. Min Li was only six. The only other time she saw somebody killed was later that night when a local teenage boy was shot for pillaging the remnants of Mr. Li's gift shop after it had been ransacked by the Red Guards. Min Li wanted to change the subject.

'shenyang has churches, and Christians still meet there. Or I should say they meet there again."

'really?" Hai Tian asked with real interest. "What do they do there."

"I'm not really sure. There are two kinds, Catholic and Protestant. I heard that they have secret churches too, but I don't know anything about those. I almost went to one of the services once with Peter. I'm not sure whether it was a Catholic or Protestant church, but it was a service for foreigners and a policeman at the door wouldn't let me in."

"Foreigners? They have enough foreigners in Shenyang for them to have their own church?"

"They don't have their own church, just a special session for them at one of the Chinese churches. They have foreign priests or ministers for those sessions, which is why Chinese people can't go."

"Why not?"

"Government policy."

"I've never seen a foreigner," Hai Tian said. "Have you, Mama?"

"No, dear."

"There are many foreigners in Shenyang, Koreans, British, Russian, Japanese, and even some Americans," Min Li explained.

"Peter is American, isn't he?" Lian Min asked.

"Yes. Most of the Americans and British in Shenyang are probably teachers, although there are a few there on business, and of course there are foreign consulates there."

"I want to see a foreigner," Hai Tian said excitedly.

'maybe you can come back to Shenyang with me after Papa's party."

'may I, Mama?"

"You better ask Papa," Lian Min cautioned.

Min Li protested, "For Hai Tian's entire life Papa has only been here for a week or two every year, and now she has to ask him?"

"He's here now," Lian Min answered calmly.

"And she's 26 years old. There's no reason she should have to ask Papa if she could come visit me in Shenyang."

"It's a simple matter of respect, Xiao Min."

"I understand respect, Mama. I understand family loyalty. But how does Papa deserve any of that. He never even respected you as his wife."

"But he's here now."

"You said that."

"And he's still here. Please have respect."

Min Li realized that any argument with her mother with regard to her father would be fruitless. Obviously, she believed that things would change now that her husband was finally home for good. She never complained for having to bear her family's burden while he was gone. Once the most beautiful woman in the village, Lian Min, now 56, looked like a woman in her late sixties. Her skin, darkened by years working in the sun, and her prematurely white hair bespoke a life of hardship and despair. Still strong, she moved more slowly now. She sacrificed her entire life for a man who acknowledged her only during his annual pilgrimages to satisfy a familial duty, to reassert his role as the dominant member of the family. Even if she didn't think things would change, she really had no choice.

The women wrapped up their food preparation, finished steaming the dumplings, and cleaned themselves up for the party.

Min Li wore the dress she brought with her from Shenyang, a traditional *chi pao*, mint green with blue orchids embroidered overall with the Chinese symbol *fu* for good fortune. She wrapped her long black hair into a large, loose bun held together with black enameled chopsticks. To compliment her dress, she fastened a fake blue orchid in her hair and wore a matching necklace and bracelet of light green jade beads. Hai Tian wore her best white shirt and blue jeans adorned in a modern way with rhinestone rivets running up the outer seams. Lian Min donned her cleanest blue Mao suit pants and a white colored blouse with long sleeves, her best clothes. Min Li accented her mother's outfit with a fake yellow carnation in her short, straight hair.

Lian Min looked in the mirror. "This flower makes me look like a prostitute."

"Hardly. It's pretty, Mama, leave it in," Hai Tian suggested.

"Wait," Min Li said. "I have something else for you, "whereupon she produced an eight-inch pearl necklace from her suitcase and draped it over her mother's head. Now you look beautiful."

Lian Min stared at herself in the mirror. She had never worn a necklace before and was admiring how it changed the way she looked. She looked like she was about to cry as she fondled the pearls below her neck. She was about to say something when Xiong Yong burst through the door.

"Hey, ladies," he shouted, then flung his arms around Min Li, saying nothing more than necessary to make her feel welcome.

Min Li pushed Xiong Yong back in feigned anger. "Why didn't you come by last night?"

"I didn't want to interfere with your reunion with Papa."

"Liar. You just didn't want to visit with Papa."

"Well, I admit that I was savoring my time away from him, but really, I was just too tired. I went home with Lao Dong for a beer and I fell asleep on his floor."

"Why didn't you come by earlier today?"

"What? And interfere with your dumpling making? I didn't want to be responsible for ruining tonight's party."

"Another lie."

"Okay, I did stop by the old church to see how things were going there."

"Were the tables set up?" asked Lian Min.

"No."

"Did you talk to the caretaker?"

"No."

"Well, why not?"

"He wasn't there. At least I don't think he was there. The doors were locked shut and I banged on the door awhile. He never answered."

"Could you at least look inside so see if the tables were set up?" Lian Min asked.

"All the tables were stacked against the other wall. There was one leaned up against the outside wall, as well?"

"That's a little relief," Lian Min responded.

"Then we better get over there and get things set up," Xiong Yong offered.

"That won't do us any good if the doors are locked," Min Li said.

"No problem. I used to get in there at night when it was the agricultural planning office. Remember when I brought those two 25-kilograms of rice home a long time ago?"

"I'd rather not," his mother said.

They all resolved to take the food to the old church as soon as possible. They had roughly an hour before the party started, and other people were likely to show up with the food they promised, so they gathered up the dumplings, long noodles, hard-boiled eggs, and steamed buns stuffed with red bean paste and headed toward the old church. They had to walk about three blocks to Liberation Road, turn right, go another block, then turn left on Cemetery Road and start up the hill. The old church was about a hundred meters up Cemetery Road.

When they arrived, everything was just as Xiong Yong explained. They peered through the dirty windows for any sign of the old man taking care of the place when their neighbor, Gao Bai Yun arrived with her contribution to the party, corn fritters and cold boiled spinach with peanuts. "What's happening?" she asked.

"We're waiting for the caretaker to open the doors," Hai Tian answered.

"Where is he?"

"We don't know."

"I'll take care of it," reassured Xiong Yong.

"Don't do anything stupid, Xiong Yong," his mother admonished.

"Did you already pay the fee for using this place?" he asked.

"Yes."

"Then you have nothing to worry about," he said as he excused himself from the group and walked around to the back of the building. Three minutes later Xiong Yong opened the doors from the inside, allowing his mother, two sisters, and Mrs. Gao into the converted meeting hall. As they poured through the door, Xiong Yong grabbed the folding table leaning against the outside wall and dragged it through the door as Hong Qi and Liu Yuncun showed up. Within ten minutes, the group had all the tables set up and arranged with the head table near the north wall and the other five tables arrayed in front of it with two along the west wall, two along the east wall with the windows, and one in the back.

Min Li suggested to use the back table to place the food, and they would have people serve themselves there, although the usual arrangement was to have the food divided between the tables. She had seen it done this way at a hotel in Shenyang that catered to foreigners, and they seemed to like it because it promoted mingling with each other and stimulated conversation. It also made cleaning up easier.

As they placed the last of the folding chairs at the table, the caretaker came into the room from one of the back rooms. He yawned, stretched, and said with surprise, "What are you people doing here?"

"What do you mean, what are we doing here?" Lian Min fired back. We rented the place for my husband's birthday and retirement celebration."

"Zhang, right?"

That's right, Zhang Zhi Hao. I paid you a week ago and we stopped by only yesterday to check on things. You promised you would have it set up."

"It looks set up to me," answered the caretaker matter-of-factly.

"That's because we did it," Hai Tian added.

"Zhang, Zhang, Zhang, let me see. Isn't that tomorrow night?"

"No. It's today, Saturday, June 23."

"Today is Saturday? Hey! Where did you get the sixth table?"

"Go back to your nap, old man," Xiong Yong suggested. "We'll let you know when we're done."

The old caretaker mumbled to himself as he departed the room, something about it being Saturday or not. Xiong Yong's friend, Lao Dong came then, with his mother and father, as did Lian Min's mother who arrived by pedicab, a contraction built on the frame of a large bicycle with two wheels in the back that served as a modern-day rickshaw. She brought a basket of steamed buns shaped like peaches, and a plate of candied plums. More people came, and soon every seat was taken but one, the seat at the head table belonging to Zhong Zhi Hao. Lian Min looked worried.

Lian Min, Xiong Yong, Min Li, Hai Tian, Hong Qi, and Liu Yuncun sat nervously at the head table. The empty seat noticeably sat between Lian Min and Xiong Yong. The guests were seated at their tables, laden with small glasses for each guest and two bottles of *bai jiu,* as well as larger glasses for the numerous bottles of beer. The guests talked amiabl as some of them, mostly the men, began to drink. Lian Min worried about what she would have to say at six o"clock regarding the absence of the guest of honor, but a minute before six, Zhang Zhi Hao showed up, walking around the room greeting his friends and neighbors. The look of relief on Lian Min's face was obvious. He then sat next to Lian Min, and she could smell the *bai jiu* on his breath.

"It seems that the old man didn't let us down," Zhang Zhi Hao said as he surveyed the room's set up. See, it's easy to trust people."

Lian Min raised her eyebrows but said nothing.

Zhang Zhi Hao stood up with a glass in his hand, filled with *bai jiu,* and welcomed all the guests to the celebration of his most honored event, his turning sixty years old. He said a few words about doubting whether he would live this long, making the guests laugh, and mentioned that it could only have been made possible by the fact that he spent his winters in a warmer climate, except for his brief annual sojourns for New Years. A few people laughed. He announced the beginning of festivities, sat down abruptly, and told Lian Min to bring him food.

Min Li brought her father a plate of long noodles and a whole, steamed fish, the noodles representing longevity and the whole fish representing prosperity. Hong Qi brought him a plate of sticky rice balls wrapped in bamboo leaves, representing a rich, sweet life, and Hai Tian brought him a dish of garlic, which stands for eternity, and a whole chicken for family unity. Lian Min remained sitting at the insistence of her daughters and enjoyed the same dishes as her husband, being served second. Zhang Zhi Hao never noticed as he dove into his food with gusto, washing it down with large mouthfuls of beer.

When everybody had filled their stomach, they lined up at the head table, Xiong Yong followed by Min Li heading the line, and each pulled out a small red envelope, a *hong bao*, and presented it to Zhang Zhi Hao. Decorum required that Zhang Zhi Hao refrain from looking inside the *hong bao* while the guests were present, but he couldn't resist. Xiong Yong had given him five thousand yuan, a substantial sum for any villager and which must have taken Xiong Yong a long time to save. Min Li's *hong bao* contained ten thousand yuan, which Zhang Zhi Hao happily announced to the full room of guests, causing some embarrassment. Most of the people, poor villagers with little cash, had given fifty, or sometimes a hundred yuan, with the exception of Xiong Yong's friend, Lao Dong, who had given five hundred yuan.

Zhang Zhi Hao counted his take while still at the table and seemed pleased that he had racked up more than eighteen thousand yuan, which he considered as net profit, since Lian Min had paid for the use of the old church from her own funds. He folded the money, stood up and slid it into his front trousers pocket, and left the old church. He reached the door, then turned around as if he forgot something, and returned to the table.

"Lao Po," he addressed Lian Min, "I'm going to Huludao. I'll be back late so don't wait up for me." Then he left.

The invited guests assumed Zhang Zhi Hao went to the outhouse and would be back in a moment. An hour later, most of the guests had drifted away, leaving Lian Min and her children to pack up things and clean up. Lao Dong walked his parents home and returned to help.

"Where did your old man go, Xiong Yong?" he asked.

"Huludao."

"Why?"

"To have a good time, I guess. Don't worry about it. He'll be back before morning. He usually is."

Usually, but Zhang Zhi Hao did not return until long after the sun had risen the next day. Lian Min and Hai Tian were out in the field working, and Min Li was busy packing her suitcase for the trip back to Shenyang when he came into the house.

"Good, you're still here," he said without even a greeting.

"I see you've returned as usual," Min Li replied with somewhat of a bite. "Did you have a good time?"

"For most of the night until my luck turned. I don't suppose you can lend me some money."

Min Li looked at her father. She remembered the time when she was little and her grandparents had given her a little money, the first money she ever had. She went to bed with it to keep it safe, but her father found it in the middle of the night. She remembered the crystal monkey, the closest thing she ever had to a toy, a valuable gift from Mr. Li, and how her father had taken that from her and sold it. 'sorry, all I have is enough for a bus to Huludao and a train to Shenyang. Maybe I can send you some."

'sure, that"d be nice. Thanks for thinking of your father. You are a good daughter."

Hardly, Min Li thought to herself. "I'll say good-bye to Mama and Hai Tian on my way," and with that she grabbed her suitcase and slammed the door on the way out.

Ten

Min Li arrived at her fourth-floor walk-up apartment around seven o"clock. Clothing and papers had been strewn about and the bed remained unmade. At least the sink wasn't filled with dirty dishes, which didn't surprise Min Li as her husband never cooked for himself. An overfilled ashtray rested precariously on the arm of the sofa in the main room, and another, also full, sat on the table next to the bed. The smell of stale cigarette smoke and dirty laundry permeated the room, so the first thing Min Li did was to open some windows to let in the cooler evening air. She found her cell phone underneath some newspapers on the dining table in the main room and saw that she had missed forty-seven calls.

He could have at least answered my phone while I was gone, Min Li thought to herself. One of the calls was from herself while she was in Shangguang, but strangely, three of them were from her husband. *He didn't even know I left my phone behind. From the way the apartment looked, Sun Donyu spent a lot of time in the apartment, but how could he have not been here at least some of the times when my telephone rang?*

Min Li decided now was a good time to call him. He was likely out supervising their three cleaning crews, as Sunday was their busiest night, and eighteen of her twenty clients required services then. But he didn't answer his phone. Frustrated, Min Li called the most senior member of one of her crews.

"Wei? Ni hao," answered the woman when Min Li called.

"This is Zhang Min Li. How are things going tonight?"

"Everything is fine. I think I'm going to run out of floor wax before we finish the lobby at the China Merchant Bank. Can you bring some?"

'sure, when do you expect to be at the China Merchant Bank?"

"In about an hour, more or less."

"Have you seen Sun Dongyu?"

"Not yet. I tried to call him about the wax, but he didn't answer."

"Okay. Do you need anything else?"

"A raise."

"You're funny. I'll see you in an hour."

She called the second crew and learned that they were a little behind schedule. The night watchman at the marriage bureau wouldn't wake up when the crew arrived, and somebody had to walk around the back and bang on a window to get his attention. Min Li thought about how similar that was to the situation at the old church in Shangguang. She promised to stop by and check on them later. That crew had not heard from her husband either. Nor had the third crew heard from him that evening.

Min Li went into the second, smaller bedroom where they stored their cleaning supplies, grabbed a three-liter can of liquid floor wax, and headed for the door. Sun Dongyu returned at the same time, flinging the door open just before Min Li grabbed it.

"Oh, you're home. Good," Sun Dongyu said by way of greeting.

"Where've you been? None of the crews have even seen you."

"I was at a meeting with Hui Xijing. He wants to buy our business."

"You mean my business. Don't forget, I had this business going before we married. And why are you talking to our competitor about selling my business?"

"Right, well, I've helped you build up this business, you know."

'maybe to some extent, but after we were married a year, you quit your job. I've been giving you a salary ever since. So it's still my business. Tell me why you're talking to my competitor."

"That's a technical argument. I had a meeting because Hui Xijing called and asked for one."

"Hui Xijing had your telephone number?"

"That's beside the point. Do you want to listen or not?" Sun Dongyu half-answered.

'so what's he offering?"

"A half a million *renminbi*."

"That's a liquidation value. I'm sure it's worth a lot more."

"Just think what we can do with that much money. We can buy a better apartment and start another business, a more reputable business."

"You mean start over again. There's no reason to start something new and have to build it up over many years, just to get where we are today, simply for the sake of starting something new."

"We can do something that allows us to sleep at night like normal people," Sun Dongyu argued.

"But you already sleep at night."

"And we can have the kind of business people respect."

"People respect my business."

"We're nothing but janitors."

"What's wrong with that? I have my own business, a successful business, which I built up from scratch. It has a good reputation, and it continues to grow. Nothing can be more respectable," Min Li reasoned.

"You just don't get it. Why do I even bother?"

"We'll talk later. Right now I have to get this floor wax over to the China Merchant's Bank. See you," Min Li said as she departed.

Over the next few months, Min Li poured herself into her business and even managed to pick up three new clients, taxing the workload on her three crews. She contemplated adding another crew or maybe expanding the size of the crews, enabling them to complete each client site quicker, in order to handle the extra workload.

Sun Dongyu fashioned himself as some sort of fancy rainmaker for the business and would often invite various business owners to lunch and dinner, complete with private parties at some of the many local karaoke lounges. His efforts typically provided no more result than making himself feel important and tended to drain some of the business's profits. Min Li allowed him to keep up the charade for two reasons, it made him feel good about himself, and it kept him from interfering with the day-to-day activities of the business itself. *Who knows?* she often wondered to herself. *He might actually hook a big fish.*

Min Li's life had become routine, and she was glad of that. Each morning she awoke at eight, dressed, ate breakfast, and visited her clients to make sure they were happy with the work done by her crews the night before. She would then go home, prepare a light lunch, then take a nap until four in the afternoon when she would wake up and prepare dinner for herself and, if he was home, her husband. She would then call each of the crew leaders at six to make sure they were aware of their assignments and any special requests and to make sure there would be no problem picking up the carts in storage nearby her home. If one of the crew leaders were sick or otherwise unable to work that day, she would meet the crew at the storage site and give instructions to the assistant crew leader. Upon occasion, Min Li would serve as a crew leader. Throughout the evening as her crews worked, assuming Min Li wasn't supervising a crew herself, she would visit each of the crews to verify attendance and compliance with quality standards and client work orders. Sun

Dongyu, when he wasn't entertaining potential important clients, simply complained about how boring his life had become.

One evening in late December, Sun Dongyu returned to the apartment moments before Min Li was about to leave. Excitedly, he told her that he had picked up a big piece of business.

"Who's the client?" Min Li asked.

"Ran Peng Fei."

"Who's that? Which business is his?"

"He doesn't have a name for his business, I don't think, and he doesn't have any set location."

"Then what are we supposed to clean?"

"Nothing."

"Nothing?"

"Right. Nothing. All he wants us to do is to deliver packages from time to time. They'll be within the neighborhoods where our crews work. One of the crews will pick up the package on the way to one of their work sites and drop it off near another work site. It's perfect. And the money is good."

"What kind of packages? This sounds too good to be true."

"I don't know. He didn't say. I'm assuming something small enough to fit on the equipment carts."

"You're assuming, and are you assuming what might be inside these packages?"

"He didn't say."

"Did you ask?" By now Min Li had grown particularly suspicious.

"No, I figured it wasn't important."

"How do we know this is a legitimate enterprise?" Min Li asked.

"I don't know. I'm sure it's all on the up and up, though."

"Where do you know this Ran Peng Fei from?"

'my brother introduced us."

"You promised you wouldn't allow your brother to have anything to do with this business. He just got out of prison for burglary. If any of my clients find out about him, they'll cancel their contracts."

"They won't find out. Besides, all my brother did was introduce me to this guy."

"How does your brother know him?"

"Eh, I think they were cellmates."

"Forget it. He's probably *heishehui*, organized crime."

"How do you know that?"

"I don't know, but I'm not taking any chances."

"I already told him we"d do it," Sun Dongyu pleaded.

"Well tell him you changed your mind."

"I don't think that's possible."

"Why not?"

"He didn't give me his phone number. He said he'll contact me after the first delivery to pay us."

"When is the first delivery?"

"Tonight."

"Then he'll probably see you tomorrow. You can tell him then why we didn't make his delivery for him."

"But..."

"But nothing. We're not doing it and that's final."

Min Li left the apartment to check on her crews. Five minutes later, Sun Dongyu also left and walked five blocks to the intersection of Fengtian Street and Shifu Road where he approached a vendor selling mandarin oranges and bananas from a cart made from a converted bicycle, just like Min Li's equipment carts.

"I'm from Pretty Office Cleaning Company," he told the fruit vendor.

Without saying anything, the fruit vendor reached under his cart and retrieved a brown cardboard box, about ten inches square, sealed in tape from the China Post, and handed it to Sun Dongyu. Sun Dongyu then walked back south on Fengtian Street, carrying the one kilogram package with him, and turned left on Qingzhen Road, famous for its Hui, or Chinese Muslim, restaurants. He went up the right side about half a block, entered Ma's Lamb Restaurant, and delivered it to the manager. The small restaurant could only fit five tables, each with four chairs. The walls might have been painted white at one time, but years of greasy air and cigarette smoke had stained them a greyish tan, darker in some places. The dull matte of grease and dust partially obscured a painting of sheep in a meadow, and some blue Arabic writing over the kitchen door was similarly soiled. Two men wearing white circular caps eyed him suspiciously from the table where they were sitting near the door. Sun Dongyu suddenly grew thirsty and licked his dry lips but decided not to buy a beer. He turned and left without saying anything.

When Min Li returned home that night around midnight, she found Sun Dongyu sitting at the small table in the main room drinking a beer and smoking a cigarette. She left him there and went to bed.

As usual, Min Li woke up at about eight the next morning, cooked breakfast for herself, bathed, and dressed. When she approached the door to leave, she noticed a small white envelope on the floor, just inside the door. She picked it up and saw her husband's name on it, so she walked it into the bedroom where he was still sleeping.

"What's this?" she asked waking her husband.

Sun Dongyu sat up and rubbed is eyes. "What?"

"This envelope. I found it under the door. It has your name on it."

Sun Dongyu took the envelope from Min Li's hand, opened it, and pulled out seven one hundred-yuan bills. He noticed Min Li looking at the money and said, "It was easy. Not bad for less than an hour's work."

Min Li said nothing and left the apartment.

When Min Li returned after visiting her client's, she found herself alone. Sun Dongyu returned around four that afternoon wearing new clothes.

"I see you found a use for that money already," Min Li said with a sour look on her face.

"I needed new clothes. Maybe tomorrow I'll buy you something nice."

"Don't."

"Why not?"

"I don't like where you're getting your money."

"It's okay. It was easy. Pick up a package here and drop it off there."

"Nothing that easy comes without risks," Min Li cautioned.

"Nonsense. What can happen?"

"You can go to prison. Worse, you can make me go to prison. I'll lose my business."

"That won't happen. I'll make sure of it."

"How can you make sure of anything? You don't have any control here. Who knows who will rat you out to save their own skin? Who knows if your next delivery isn't into the hands of an undercover policeman? None of that matters anyway. It's wrong. I don't want you doing anything wrong."

"I'll be alright."

'stop it now. If you make another delivery I'm changing the locks on the apartment."

"You're serious."

"You bet I'm serious. This isn't worth it. We'll make our money the honest way, and there's no way you can convince me otherwise."

"Okay. I won't do it again," Sun Dongyu relented.

"And don't let them near our home again," Min Li said as she walked out the door.

The next day Min Li woke up alone. That in itself wasn't too unusual, as Sun Dongyu would sometimes spend the night out with his friends and be too drunk to come home. She slowly set her feet on the cold floor, feeling around for her house shoes. She opened the bedroom door to head for the bathroom when she saw her husband again sitting at the table smoking. He and the two men sitting on the sofa had waited for her to wake up.

She froze in place and rubbed her eyes, not believing that there were two strange men in her home at eight o"clock in the morning. She looked toward her husband for an explanation, but he only shrugged. She looked again at the two men, both dressed in black slacks and black shirts, one a button down with long sleeves and the other a black T-shirt. The man in the T-shirt was missing half an earlobe and the little finger of his left hand. The other man wore a gold chain around his neck drooping to the middle of his chest, a gold bracelet, and a gold watch, from the distance what looked like an Omega.

"Honey," Sun Dongyu said, breaking her spell, "This is Ran Peng Fei."

"Who"

"Ran Peng Fei. You know, the man with the packages."

Suddenly Min Li realized her hunch was correct. "Why are they here? I told you to stop with the packages. I told you to keep them away from our home. I told you . . ."

'shut up and sit down," Ran Peng Fei demanded.

Min Li sat down at the table across from her husband. She glared at Sun Dongyu.

Ran Pen Fei spoke first. "I thought we had an arrangement. You didn't pick up the package last night."

Min Li felt absurdly relieved; then she said, "I told him not to."

"And I told you to shut up. I'm talking to your husband."

"We just thought the risks were too great," Sun Dongyu answered.

"You should've thought about that before we revealed our operation to you," said Ran Peng Fei. "You placed me in quite a bind."

Sun Dongyu raised his eyebrows.

"You see," continued Ran Peng Fei, "we have arrangements with other people who likely have arrangements too. It's not good when our arrangements don't do as promised. Things like this don't go unnoticed."

"I'm sorry," Sun Dongyu explained. "We have too much at stake, too much to risk."

"That's too bad, but it's not up to me. I work for people who don't take kindly to broken promises."

'so, what are your going to do?" Sun Dongyu asked, glancing over to see the frightened look on his wife's face.

"Were it up to me, the matter would have been resolved while you were sleeping. But it's not up to me. Frankly, I don't know how this matter will be handled. I was just told to bring you and your wife."

"Bring us?"

"To my boss. I suppose he already has a plan. He doesn't like it when somebody messes with his plan. That's why we're going to take a little ride."

"I have to go pee," Min Li said.

"Then go but leave the door open."

"No way," she protested.

"Then you're not going pee."

Min Li acquiesced and sat on the toilet, draping her nightgown around her as much as possible to preserve her dignity. While she sat in the bathroom, she grabbed a nail file with the hand farthest from the door, sliding it under her bra strap before standing up. She had no idea what she would do with it, but she took it nevertheless. It was the only thing she could grab without being noticed, and it was at least something.

When she finished in the bathroom, Ran Peng Fei opened the apartment door and motioned for Min Li and her husband to exit, warning them not to alert anybody. He and his friend Lang would be right behind them, and Lang was fast and accurate with a knife. Min Li wanted to pee again, but thought twice about saying so.

Min Li's section of the building opened out on an alley, where Ran Peng Fei had parked his black late model Audi 500. Ran Peng Fei opened the back door and Lang pushed the couple in, Sun Dongyu banging his head on the doorframe. Min Li followed her husband into the car and sat behind the driver's seat. Lang snickered, slammed the door closed, and sat behind the wheel while Ran Peng Fei sat on the passenger side in the front seat. Min Li wondered why the 'muscle" was driving; then she realized that maybe only he knew how to drive. So few people in China knew how.

They drove through the city, narrowly missing two collisions with taxis speeding through red lights. As they drove west on Guanquan Road, they nearly ran into a donkey cart near Dongwan Street, then turned onto Shenping Highway and started out of town toward Qipanshan Reservoir. As city became countryside, Min Li became more nervous. She thought these guys would be less likely to hurt them in a city full of potential witnesses. But then again, her neighbors were not particularly good at reporting incidents in the neighborhood, despite there being a police substation on the first floor at the other end of her building.

After thirty minutes, Lang drove the car up a dirt road and stopped. A cornfield, fallow for the winter, lay to their right. To the left stood a rusty bulldozer, a front-loader, and a road grader, also sitting out the winter, as well as a temporary wooden construction shed. Next to the shed lay some tools, some shovels, gravel rakes, and at least one pickaxe. The nearest people besides the four were on the highway a hundred meters behind them speeding by at sixty miles per hour.

"Is this the right road?" asked Lang of his partner.

"I don't know. I've never been out here. I thought you've been here before."

"Yeah, twice, but this is the first time I drove it."

"You got a map?" asked Ran Peng Fei.

"In the glove compartment."

Min Li saw her chance as Ran Peng Fei rummaged through the glove compartment. She pulled out the file, showed it to her husband, motioned for the door to her left, and jammed the file in Lang's right ear, driving it in at least three inches. Lang's scream distracted Ran Peng Fei enough that both she and Sun Dongyu had time to jump out of the left-side passenger door and make a break for the construction shed. Ran Peng Fei ran after them, but the distraction caused by Lang's screaming put him twenty seconds behind Min Li and Sun Dongyu, giving time for Min Li to grab the pickax and run behind the shed with her husband. Ran Peng Fei didn't notice the pickax until he rounded the back of the construction shed and its dull rusty point split his skull open.

Min Li realized how much colder this part of Liaoning was in the winter than Shangguang. She stood there shivering, still in her nightgown and house shoes looking at Ran Peng Fei's lifeless body. Although Sun Dongyu was fully dressed, he had no coat.

"Can you drive a car," Min Li asked her husband.

"No."

'me neither."

"What do you want to do?" he asked her.

"Get warm. Go to police. Let's see what's in the car."

Because they were in the apartment and immediately the car, neither Ran Peng Fei nor Lang had worn coats, adding to their tough guy persona, Min Li figured, but they likely had coats in the car, and she was correct. They had winter coats folded neatly on the front seat between them. Min Li quickly chose the smaller of the two, the one belonging to Ran Peng Fei, noticing that it was lined in sable. Sun Dongyu donned Lang's coat, a surplus army long coat—warm but ugly.

Min Li's feet remained uncovered, so she pulled the socks off Lang's dead body, but before she could get them out of the car, their odor overwhelmed her. She threw them on the ground and headed back to the construction shed and yanked Ran Peng Fei's socks off his feet and put them on hers. He wore Italian leather lace-up boots, which she slid onto her feet and laced them tightly. The shoes fit her loosely, being five sizes too big, but at least she could keep her feet warm and walk on the dirt road.

After walking back to Shenping Highway, they had to wait only fifteen minutes for a police vehicle to come by, which they waved down. The policeman allowed them to sit in his heated Volkswagen Santana while Min Li explained what had happened to them. The policeman sat, mouth agape, during the story, not even taking his eyes off Min Li to write notes. He spoke briefly on the radio, asked for backup, and told the ratio dispatcher where to find the dirt road off the main highway; then he waited for backup.

Within fifteen minutes, six more police cars had swarmed the area, including one unmarked police car from the Shenyang Organized Crime Task Force. Min Li and Sun Dongyu showed them the car and the bodies, and the man in the unmarked police car said, "I know these guys. Good job."

The other policemen looked confused, so he explained.

"These are the hatchet men for the Wang crime syndicate. You two are lucky. Nobody ever walks away from their countryside meetings. Usually we find their victims, if we find them, chopped up in pieces and scattered throughout some farmer's field for the crows to pick at. Really lucky."

After spending another five hours in the police station, another police car dropped Min Li and Sun Dongyu off at their apartment. When they got inside, Min Li said, "You can keep the apartment."

"What are you talking about?"

"I'm not staying here after what happened today. Who else knows where we live."

"I'm sure it'll be safe."

"You were sure about a lot of things. One thing I'm sure about, though, is that I no longer live here and you and I no longer live together. If you want to stay here, that's fine by me, but I'm leaving and you're not coming with me."

Min Li called three women who worked for her and made arrangements for them to come help her pack for some overtime pay. She then called a trucking company, one of her clients, and arranged for a truck to pick up the furniture and cleaning supplies. Next, she called an ad she found in the newspaper laying on the table. The ad was for a new guard-gated apartment complex in Shenyang's Heping District. Sun Dongyu sat on the sofa, stunned, but said nothing.

Eleven

Min Li continued looking over her shoulder for the next month and a half when she had to decide whether to return to Shangguang for the lunar New Year holiday. Most of her clients had suspended service for a week or two for the holiday, anyway, and all of her employees wanted the time off to be with their families. About half of her employees claimed Shenyang as their hometown, so if she needed to, she could call a skeleton crew together for odd cleaning projects. The other half of her employees hailed form towns and villages within an hour or two of Shenyang, and those employees, without exception, would be back in their hometowns for the holiday. Min Li really had no compelling reason to stay away from Shangguang, other than wanting to avoid her father. If she chose to go, it would be to see her mother and sisters, and likely Xiong Yong would be there from Sichuan, too.

  She called Hong Qi and talked about it. She hadn't firmly decided, so she thought it would be better to talk to Hong Qi rather than her mother or Hai Tian, just in case she changed her mind. She also knew that her mother would twist her arm to go and remind her of her family obligation.

  Having grown accustomed to living in a city in an apartment with hot running water, a flush toilet, and a shower, Min Li didn't look forward to the deprivations of village life. She didn't mind sleeping on the kang, because she was used to sleeping on a hard bed, but this time of year was so bitterly cold. And there was no place to take a shower unless she took the bus to Huludao. She became used to that luxury quickly since she moved out of her last apartment. Before, she would take her showers at the bathhouse a half a block from her apartment. For five yuan, she could spend all the time she wanted soaking in the steam, luxuriating under the warm running water, and gossiping with the other ladies who were there for the same reason. She missed that and had twice visited the bathhouse after moving into her own apartment. But the convenience of taking a shower at home had proven itself to be worth the added cost when she upgraded to an apartment in a gated compound, although that was not the reason she chose to live there.

    Min Li finally decided to take off for two weeks and so informed her employees and clients. Somebody would be around to handle emergencies, and Min Li vowed not to forget her cell phone again. She would leave for Huludao by train in four days, then take the bus to Shangguang. The only problem would be in acquiring the train ticket. One can only buy the ticket no more than seventy-two hours before the trip, so she had to wait until the next day.

    Min Li hadn't taken the train to Huludao during the lunar New Year for five years, so she had forgotten what trouble it could be. When she arrived at the train station the next day to buy the ticket, she couldn't believe her eyes. Typically, she wouldn't find people in line at the ticket counters, each looking like the object of a swarm of bees, with more persistent travelers making their way to the window, and the ticket clerk dealing with multiple demands and hands sticking under the glass with money, but today, a single line had been roped off with the head of the line racing for the next available window. This process only maintained itself for so long as the railroad police, helped by the Shenyang city police posted officers every twenty feet or so along the line. Line jumpers were dragged away and forced to the end of the line. The line itself was more than a thousand meters long and wrapped around a side street.

Min Li couldn't believe her rotten luck. She called the client with whom she had a lunch appointment and cancelled after explaining the circumstances, which the client understood well, having just purchased his train tickets the day before. But the line moved, mostly, usually about a half a step a second, which gave Min Li some relief. Within two hours, she stood before a ticket clerk.

"I'd like a soft seat to Huludao on Thursday morning," Min Li said.

The clerk said nothing but picked away at her computer keyboard. '*meiyou*! Sold out," she finally said.

"How can that be? That's three days from now."

"That train is sixty-eight hours from now. Other people bought those tickets. Do you want a hard seat?"

"Okay."

'*meiyou*. Do you want to go somewhere else?"

"No. I want to go to Huludao on Thursday."

"There's a train at 2:34 in the afternoon Thursday."

"Good. Let me have a ticket for a soft seat on that train."

"Can't."

"Why not?"

"You can't buy tickets sooner than seventy-two hours before departure time."

Min Li looked at the clock on the wall behind the clerk and saw that it was 2:32 p.m., seventy-two hours and two minutes before departure time, so she needed to stall the clerk for two minutes. "How about a ticket to Jinzhou and a ticket from Jinzhou to Huludao?"

"Let me see. Okay. I can sell you a ticket from Jinzhou to Huludao, but there are no more tickets to Jinzhou. Maybe you can take a bus."

"What about another time," Min Li asked for the sake of stalling, which worked, because the clerk was typing several permutations on her computer.

"I can sell you a ticket to Jinzhou for 11:54 p.m. on Wednesday and a ticket from Jinzhou to Huludao Thursday at 1:15 p.m. Will that work for you?"

The minute hand on the clock reached 2:34. "Look at the 2:34 again Thursday from Shenyang to Huludao."

The clerk double-checked the time, confirmed that it was indeed late enough to sell tickets for the 2:34 to Huludao on Thursday, and punched her computer keys. 'm*eiyou*."

"What do you mean *meiyou*? They just went on sale this minute."

'sorry," the clerk said, "but they sold out."

"How?"

'some people have connections," offered the clerk.

The clerk spoke true. Train tickets during holidays, especially the New Year holiday, are hot items that sell well. Many scalpers, government officials, and railroad officials have connections with the office of China Rail that is in charge of selling tickets. More popular routes are sold or promised before the law allows them to be, defeating the purpose of the law, which is to prevent scalping. Nevertheless, if Min Li wanted a ticket to Huludao for Thursday, she would have to leave the line and find a scalper. They were easy to find, because they typically canvassed the line trying to sell their tickets, often for twice or three times what they paid for them.

Sometimes a scalper would be arrested, but it was because the scalper didn't pay the police officer making the arrest. If the police officer wanted more than usual for whatever reason, he would keep the scalper in jail overnight. The scalper would pay extra to get out of jail to avoid being stuck with out of date inventory. Min Li approached one of these scalpers, and after waiting for the scalper to finish his conversation with a police officer, offered to buy a ticket to Huludao for Thursday.

"Hard seat or soft seat?" the scalper asked with the police officer looking on.

'soft."

"That'll be 350 renminbi."

The regular price was 128 renminbi, but Min Li gladly handed over the money. At least she had a seat on the train. Many people would have purchased a platform ticket, which will get the train without a seat, then once on the train would buy a ticket from the conductor for the regular price. If there were no seats available, the passenger would stand all the way to their destination. During the holidays, there would be no seats available.

Now that she had her ticket, Min Li had shopping to do. The next day she took a taxi to Wu Ai, a large clothing wholesale market serving Northeast China. There she could find designer clothing and accessories, real and fake, for wholesale prices, as well as dishes, objects d"art, and household goods. She would be traveling alone, and the train would not have baggage compartments, so whatever she purchased she would have to carry.

At Wu Ai, Min Li purchased a silk *chi pao* for each of her sisters, a porcelain tea set for her mother, Levi look-alike jeans with matching jackets for her brother-in-law, a silk robe emblazoned with an embroidered golden dragon for her father, and a New York Yankee's Starter jacket knock-off for her brother. Remembering that Hong Qi was recently pregnant with a son, Min Li also purchased some powder blue baby clothes and warming blankets. She also purchased some large red, white, and blue striped zippered bags made of plasticized fabric with carrying handles in which to pack everything for the trip, the same kind of bag that half the passengers on the train would be using.

Min Li found a note taped to the door of her apartment when she arrived home and pulled it down before hauling her purchases into her living room. She opened the note and saw that it was from Hui Xijing, the owner of a competing office cleaning company with whom her ex-husband had spoken before about selling the business. The note simply asked her to consider his offer again and to give him a call. Hui Xijing gave her his private cell phone number. Min Li left the note on the table next to her kitchen, another addition to her life since moving, not because she planned to keep it, but because she was too preoccupied with her recent purchases and her pending trip to Shangguang.

The next day, Min Li bought an elegant bottle of Motai *bai jiu* for three hundred yuan, the most popular yet expensive brand of Chinese liquor. She planned to give the bottle to her father so he would have that to drink rather than the stuff he usually buys for twenty yuan. After all, it was the holidays, and people will be drinking. Min Li never developed a taste for *bai jiu*, which is the most popularly consumed liquor in the world, an easy task when you consider that it is the most common form of liquor in China given China's large population. She occasionally tasted it at formal events, such as weddings, and in restaurants with friends, but she had never purchased a bottle before. She had to ask the clerk for advice on which brand to buy.

Two days later, Min Li found herself again in Shenyang's north train station in a large waiting hall for her train. The room was massive with a vaulted ceiling and had seating for at least three hundred people, but at least seven hundred people were there waiting to board one of two trains using the same hall. Some people had already lined up at the gate leading to the trains, despite the fact that the train would not arrive for at least forty minutes. They sat on their luggage or stood next to it, jealously guarding their place in line. Because she had a ticket with a seat, Min Li would ordinarily not worry about the crush of people waiting for the same train, but because she had her suitcase and the two large bags filled with gifts, she worried about whether she would find a place to stow her things once on the train. She decided not to take her chances and filed in at the end of the already long line.

It didn't matter. As soon as a dark blue uniformed female railroad agent began announcing the arrival of her train, the people in the hall swarmed the gate. Two railroad agents checked tickets at the gate and did everything they could to get people through the turnstiles quickly, but anybody could see how frustrated they were. People pressed against those in front of them, and Min Li found herself in the center of a large living mass pressing around her. She couldn't budge an inch. Finally, she grabbed her bags and started pressing too, and eventually found herself at the turnstile thrusting her ticket in an agent's face.

Once inside the turnstiles, people ran for the train, and Min Li found herself walking at a fast pace and ignored the narrow straps of one her bags cutting into the palm of her hand. The other bag was propped up on her suitcase, which she pulled behind her with its telescoping handle and two wheels. This arrangement worked well until she reached to the top of the stairs that took her down to track level. She hoisted the second bag off of her suitcase, grabbed both bags with one hand, and picked up her suitcase with the other in order to maneuver down the fifty or so steps, nearly being knocked over once by a young man running with a backpack.

Once at track level, Min Li stopped for a moment to decide which way to go to find her car, which caused two people to bump her from behind. Once she found her car, she jumped into the doorway but was stopped dead. The soft-seat car, slightly more comfortable and roomier than a hard-seat car, was designed to hold about forty-five people, but it was packed with at least twice as many, most standing, some trying to get their suitcases into the already packed overhead racks, and some struggling to get to assigned seats.

The train started to move and Min Li was still at the door, which had already been closed behind her. Her seat was near the other end of the car, and she had to squeeze her way through the other passengers to get to it, an endeavor that she finally managed to do in about twenty minutes, well outside of Shenyang. By the time she made it to her seat, the train had just passed the last of the concrete machine gun bunkers left over from the Japanese occupation 57 years earlier.

The bench-like seats faced each other, and small pullout tables attached at the bottom of the window separated the facing seats from each other. Min Li had a window seat, so she had to crawl over two other people to get it. But somebody was sleeping in her seat.

"Excuse me, sir," Min Li said politely.

No answer.

"Excuse me, sir!" Min Li said more loudly.

Still no answer.

Min Li reached over and shook the man's shoulders lightly. He pretended to be asleep and rolled away from her. Tired and frustrated, Min Li was in no mood to go five hours on a crowded train without sitting down in the seat that she paid for. In desperation, Min Li lied, 'sir, if you do not remove yourself from my seat, I will call my father and have you arrested at the next stop."

Without saying anything or even looking in Min Li's direction, the man lifted himself from his seat and stepped out into the aisle, leaving his suitcase on the floor under the small table. Min Li had her own bags to deal with. She crawled over to her seat, placed one of the striped bags under her seat, kicked the man's suitcase into the aisle, and set the other striped bag and her small suitcase in its place. She sat down, happy in her victory, and saw her five seatmates staring at her. The old lady across the small table from her offered her an apple. The man sitting to her left stood up and moved into the aisle, and a thankful pregnant woman sat down holding her ticket tight in her hand. Her ticket indicated that she had been assigned to the seat next to Min Li.

The sun set about two hours before Min Li's train pulled into the Huludao station. Much smaller than the station in Shenyang, Huludao's train station was no less chaotic. The passengers for Huludao grabbed their things and squeezed themselves off the train. Min Li noticed the man that she kicked out of her seat hovering, waiting to stake his claim on it again as soon as she removed herself and her things.

Min Li exited the door behind her, which was much nearer than the door she came in, pulling her suitcase and two bags through the people standing between the cars, then hopped onto the platform. Then she followed the crowd through a short tunnel which opened out onto the square in front of the station, thereby avoiding the crowds inside. Going through the exit gate, Min Li once again showed her used ticket to the railroad agents standing there for that purpose and was pushed through the gate by the humanity behind her. Heading toward the taxi stand, Min Li stopped when she heard her name called.

'min Li! Over here," Xiong Yong yelled after her.

Pleasantly surprised, Min Li smiled and half-walked, half-ran to her brother and gave him a big hug. He had come in from Sichuan earlier in the afternoon and waited at the train station for her.

Twelve

Min Li and her brother discovered everybody awaiting their arrival at the house, her mother and father, Hong Qi and her husband Liu Yuncun, and Hai Tian, as well as her putative fiancé Yang Lin. Neither Min Li nor Xiong Yong knew about Yang Lin, this being obvious by the way they glanced at Hai Tian. She would talk to Hai Tian about him later, following the pleasantries. Min Li lifted her suitcase onto the kang to get it out of the way, Xiong Yong also placing Min Li's other two bags and his own bag atop each other on the kang.

Xiong Yong reached into his bag and pulled out a carton of Chunghwa cigarettes for his father and a box of oolong tea for his mother. "I"d wait, but I thought these would come in handy now," he said by way of explaining the early exchange of gifts. Both parents were equally pleased, and Zhang Zhi Hao opened the carton immediately and took out a pack to exam it to determine whether it was genuine.

"This is my second carton of these in a year," remarked Zhang Zhi Hao, remembering the carton that Min Li had given him for his sixtieth birthday. 'maybe one day you can afford to bring me a carton of Hong He Dao," he added, giving the name of the most expensive cigarette brand that he knew, which sold for about a thousand renminbi per carton.

'someday, Papa," Xiong Yong answered. "If I get that promotion they're talking about, then I'll buy them for you. But for now, Changhwa is the best I can afford."

'm*ei guan xi*. I'm only joking. What promotion are you talking about?"

"Well, you know I took your old job in the scheduling office."

"You're lucky. You were supposed to go the scheduling office, but they made you a scheduler. You should have had to work your way up to that."

"The lower positions were filled. But the job suits me fine and I do it rather well. My efficiency was noticed by somebody in the operations office who happens to be the brother-in-law of the Technical Director who is the son of the company president."

"That sounds too confusing," Hai Tian interrupted.

'maybe it does, but the short version is that they want to make me the contract manager, or at least they're thinking about it."

"No kidding?" Zhang Zhi Hao was shocked. "That's a good job, and it pays well. Not only that, the contractors will pay you extra money and you'll have more gifts than you'll know what to do with. I think I will expect a carton of Hong He Dao next year."

"What's he talking about?" asked Min Li. "What's a contract manager do?"

"I'll try to explain. I work for what is now known as the Panzhihua Minerals Mining Company, which is a state-owned entity. That involves a lot of underground mining, as well as open pit mining, but mostly underground. That is very labor intensive, and the company has more than twenty thousand workers doing the digging. The company doesn't want to be liable for any of those workers, because it is such a dangerous job and so many are often hurt or killed. So they contract out the actual labor at the mines. That way, if there is a cave-in, it won't be on the company's hands, it'll be the responsibility of the contracting company."

'so, how does that make you rich?"

"There are many labor contractors in Panzhihua, and they all compete for these mining contracts. Each company will supply about three thousand workers, and we contract with six or seven at a time. Because these contracts are big, the competition for them is intense. They like to butter up the director of contracting."

"I didn't have to bribe anybody for my contracts," Min Li bragged.

"Your contracts are nowhere close in value to the mining contracts. If I get the job, I'll be able to get married."

"Any prospects, dear?" Lian Min asked.

'maybe, but you know how it is. It's easy to find women who will let you date them and buy them gifts, but they won't even talk about marriage unless you own a house and have money in the bank."

"There used to be other criteria," Lian Min said. "People these days only care about wealth, and with the shortage of women, they can afford to hold out."

This comment made Yang Lin nervously shift his weight a little bit. Yang Lin came from the nearby village of Xiaguang. Country boys had no money, and if they had a house, they might have received it as an inheritance from his grandparents, or their parents gave them the money to build one, a simple hovel similar to that in which Min Li grew up. Houses in the village were cheap. A home in a big city, typically a small apartment, might cost between sixty and three hundred yuan, depending on the city and the neighborhood. Xiong Yong looked at some small apartments, but in Panzhihua, he"d have to pay around two hundred thousand yuan, certainly more than he could afford now. But until he had his own home, the likelihood of him being married remained slim.

Xiong Yong's problem resulted from two different national policies. The first started with Deng Xiaoping when he demanded that China open up and allow more businesses to prosper with less central control by Beijing. The government closed poor-performing factories, giving them away or leasing them cheaply to Party members who then turned them into prosperous businesses, usually manufacturing goods for export. This allowed more people to be employed and brought foreign capital and investments into China, which allowed more and more Chinese entrepreneurs to get rich. Quickly, the foreign manufacturers of luxury automobiles and other goods found a lucrative market in China. These stories abound in China, and even non-Party members were getting rich. The largest sock manufacturer in Yiwu, Zhejiang Province, started out selling cheap socks on the side of the road. China's economic policies created several million millionaires, and pretty, single women wanted to marry one.

The other thing that effected Xiong Yong's ability to easily find a wife was China's family planning policy that went into effect in 1989, which only allowed a married couple to have one child. Soon, expectant parents learned that they could determine the sex of their unborn child with an ultrasound examination, and the abortion rates skyrocketed. Couples needed to have a son, and if they learned that their unborn child was to be a girl, many aborted and tried again. This caused an overabundance of males and a shortage of females, allowing young marriage-aged women to be more selective.

Zhang Zhi Hao regretted not realizing this until after he allowed Hong Qi to marry; otherwise, he could have forced Hong Qi to be more selective so he could get a higher bride price for her. This also explains why Hai Tian, now 26, had not yet married. Zhang Zhi Hao was holding out for better offers, and it didn't look like poor Yang Lin would be able to pull it off. He wanted to marry Hai Tian, but his family did not have enough money to satisfy Zhang Zhi Hao, who suggested that they borrow more from relatives.

For Hai Tian, living in Shangguang with her parents at the age of 26 did not bode well for her chances to marry a rich man. She already looked like she was in her mid-thirties, having spent too much time in the field with her mother. Although she completed primary school, she did not go on to middle school to finish the compulsory nine years of education. Her mother couldn't afford the school fees, especially because Hai Tian would have to live in the dormitory, which more than doubled the costs, but mainly because Hai Tian saw no need for it. She never saw anything more in her future than being a wife and living in the village, Shangguang or another. Min Li had managed to do well living in a big city, but Hai Tian believed she wasn't cut out for living the fast life. She liked life simple.

Hai Tian had three other suitors, all from the village, none of whom received Zhang Zhi Hao's blessing. They moved on and married other women in the village, leaving Hai Tian waiting for another suitor and her father's blessing. She planned to plead with her father to take whatever Yang Lin's family had to offer, because she would soon reach an age where nobody would want to marry her, if she hadn't already passed it. So Yang Lin was more nervous than he needed to be.

"Of course, some people have no respect for the institution of marriage," Zhang Zhi Hao interjected, obviously referring to Min Li's recent status as a divorcee. In fact, Min Li is the first person in the history of the family to have ever been divorced. "It is the wife's responsibility to preserve the marriage and to keep the family intact for the sake of posterity and dignity." Zhang Zhi Hao had begun his lecture. "I understand that big cities are starting to see more divorces, but as far as I know, the only women that I have ever known are those whose husbands refuse to wear a green hat." Contemporary legend has it that men who wear green hats allow their wives to sleep with other men.

Min Li bit her tongue.

Zhang Zhi Hao continued, "Good women know that they have an obligation to remain faithful to their husband and to bring children into the world, sons especially, even if their husbands are unfaithful. This is, of course, to preserve the purity of the bloodline."

Min Li thought to herself, *He's speaking as though his grandchildren are royal progeny that will inherit his family fortune and prestige. Any wealth his grandchildren have will be from their own making.*

"Wives are to be subject to their husbands as servants are subject to their masters."

Min Li glanced at her mother who sat quietly looking at the floor. *Is that what you believe?* Min Li thought about her mother.

Lian Min had heard this all before and would say nothing. She knew that so long as somebody didn't argue with Zhang Zhi Hao, he would soon stop and everybody could get on to what they were doing before. The only person who listened with rapt attention was Yang Lin, but a stern look from Hai Tian caught him by surprise and he shrugged his shoulders.

Min Li wondered if she shouldn't have stayed in Shenyang for the holiday, but her mother wanted to see her, and she offered to help get things ready for supper. The table only set four people, but eight people in the cramped room needed to be accommodated. Min Li knew her mother would refuse to eat until everybody had eaten, and custom dictated that the men should eat first, so Min Li set four places at the table for her father, brother, brother-in law, and Yang Lin, while Lian Min and Hai Tian steamed the dumplings and cooked the vegetables. Hong Qi served rice, while her father uncorked the *bai jiu*. Xiong Yong started for the glasses on the shelf, but Min Li was quicker and had the glasses on the table before Xiong Yong even got out of his seat.

The men ate noisily while the woman sat on the kang waiting their turn. Min Li brought them up to speed on the changes in her life. Business was still good, she had a new apartment which she described in detail, and she had no idea what her ex-husband was up to. Hong Qi would give birth sometime in March, and Hai Tian really wanted to marry Yang Lin. He would make an okay husband and didn't seem like the type to beat her much. Lian Min said nothing was new with her.

"Mama went to the doctor last week," Hai Tian said out of the blue.

Both Min Li and Hong Qi looked at Lian Min for an explanation.

"It was nothing, just a checkup," Lian Min told them.

"What made you go?" asked Min Li.

"No reason. I'm nearly sixty years old, and I just figured I'd get a checkup. That's all." Lian Min refused to make eye contact with her daughters.

Several days passed, and Min Li couldn't get her mother to say anything more about her doctor visit. She told herself not to worry about it, that people go to the doctor all the time for routine checkups, some out of routine. But Lian Min had never visited the doctor, not even to give birth, and had only found herself in the village clinic on those rare occasions that one of her children was hurt. For the rest of her time in Shangguang, Min Li didn't think about it, at least not until the day she left Shangguang. Dr. Zhang noticed Min Li walking past the village clinic on her way to the bus station, so he came out to talk to her.

"Your mother didn't show up for her appointment Tuesday," he informed Min Li.

'she had an appointment?"

"Just a follow up. I wanted to go over her test results with her and set a course of treatment."

"Treatment for what?"

"For her cancer. She has cancer of the pancreas."

'really? Can that be cured?"

"No, but we can at least prolong her life and make her feel better."

"How long do you think she can live?" Min Li asked.

"Three to six months without treatment. With treatment, I have no idea. That's not in my area of knowledge." Dr. Zhang wasn't trying to be evasive, as he wasn't a real doctor. He had come to the village many years ago during the Cultural Revolution as one of China's "barefoot" doctors, people selected to administer to the health needs of China's villages who had no formal education in medicine. Mao Zedong believed that the best way to learn anything was to do it, so after imprisoning or sending to reform through labor camps most of the nation's physicians for being members of the intelligentsia, one of the class enemies of China, he started this on the job training for people like Dr. Zhang. After doing his job for almost thirty years, Dr. Zhang knew a thing or two, but he didn't know anything about treating cancer, something he left for the real doctors in Huludao.

Thirteen

Min Li threw herself into her work after returning to Shenyang, trying to take her mind off her mother's diagnosis. Naturally, the first thing she did after boarding the bus to Huludao was to call her mother by way of Hai Tian's cell phone. Lian Min had no phone of her own and the house never had a landline. Min Li learned that her mother's cancer was unresectable and metastatic, having already advanced into her lymph nodes. Without treatment, her actual chance of survival would be three to six month, less than what Dr. Zhang had said.

Min Li also learned the reason her mother had missed the follow-up doctor's appointment. Because so many people were around for the holiday, Lian Min couldn't go to the doctor's office unnoticed, so she simply refused to go. Min Li prevailed upon Hai Tian to get her mother to the doctor no matter what and to call her as soon as she returned home from the doctor, which instructions Hai Tian obeyed to avoid the wrath of her *jie jie*.

"We're back from the clinic," Hai Tian informed Min Li over the phone.

"What did the doctor say?"

'mama still has cancer."

"Are you being glib? Please be serious. What about treatment?" Min Li impatiently demanded.

"He wanted to know who was going to pay for it?" Doctors and hospitals will not treat anybody without payment in advance or a guarantee of payment. Some institutions have their own hospitals with doctors, such as schools. In this case, teachers go to the teachers' hospital in their city where they can receive treatment for minimal co-payments or for free. Farmers and other villagers had not such medical coverage and had to finance their own medical treatment.

"I'll pay for it. What kind of treatment and how much?"

"Dr. Zhang said that he can continue the treatment, but Mama would have to go to the hospital in Huludao where they will develop a treatment plan. That will cost about five thousand yuan, more or less. If the doctors in Huludao want to give Mama medicine, she would have to go to the doctor each time to get it, but she can get it from Dr. Zhang, and that will cost about 500 yuan each time, two or three times a week."

"Are there any other options?"

'maybe. Dr. Zhang said something about radiation, but if she needed that, she would have to go to the hospital in Jinzhou because they don't have that in Huludao."

"How soon can you see the doctor in Huludao?"

"As soon as we can get there, but we don't have money for the bus or the doctor," Hai Tian explained.

"Don't worry about it. I will send you some money today, about 15,000 yuan. That should cover the bus, the time in the hospital in Huludao, and the initial treatments. Let me know what you need after that."

"Okay, *Jie Jie*. I'll call the hospital in Huludao and tell them to expect us day after tomorrow."

Min Li walked to the bank as soon as she hung up with Hai Tian. She wished she could be with her mother now, but she had to keep her business going, especially if she would be paying for her mother's medical treatments. She wondered why people like her mother became seriously ill. Lian Min was a good person, never hurt anybody, and did so much to raise a family the best she could under the circumstances without help from Zhang Zhi Hao. *Life isn't fair*, she thought to herself. She didn't mind helping her mother. After all, she was her mother's oldest daughter, and it was her obligation, or at least she tried to convince herself. The real obligation belonged to her father, but she knew there would be no help from him. Lian Min had done so much for Min Li; it was Min Li's turn to give back.

Lian Min went straight to bed when she returned home from the hospital in Huludao. The medicine given to her made her feel sick and week. She had little appetite, but Hai Tian did everything she could for her, making her thin soup and tea. Spring planting was still about six to eight weeks away, so there were few chores to do, all of which Hai Tian could do without help. She worried about the planting, though, because her mother would be unable to help her, and she wasn't sure whether her father would pitch it. She had never seen him do anything remotely resembling a chore, other than repair a broken leg on a chair. She thought that Yang Lin might help some, but his own family counted on him, although he did have two younger brothers.

Hai Tian walked her mother to Dr. Zhang's office two times her first week back from Huludao, and the plan was to go three times a week after that. By the end of the second week, though, Hai Tian needed to call Min Li.

"We're out of money?"

'so soon? I thought I sent enough to last at least two or three months."

"There would have been enough, but um . . ."

"But what?"

"Papa found it."

"Are you saying Papa took Mama's treatment money?" Min Li was beside herself with rage. "How did you let that happen?"

"I had it hidden in the outhouse," Hai Tian said in her defense.

Min Li remembered how she had hid her crystal monkey there when she was a child and how she once found a banned book of Tang Dynasty poetry there. She also remembered how her father had taken money from her when she was sleeping, and how he took the crystal monkey one night and sold it. Hai Tian would have been too young then to remember these things.

"Do you have a bank account?" Min Li asked her little sister.

"No. Why would I? I've never had enough money to put in the bank."

"Open an account today. I'll send the money directly to your bank account. Do not let Papa know about your account. He obviously knew you had money; otherwise, he wouldn't have looked for it. Do you understand me?"

"I understand."

By the end of Lian Min's second month of treatment, she had no strength to walk to Dr. Zhang's office, so he came by to see her three times a week. The treatments had no affect and her health deteriorated rapidly. Hai Tian spent most of her time at her mother's side, her father absented himself from the house most of the time, and nobody had planted the corn. Min Li talked to Xiong Yong and Hong Qi. Xiong Yong, still waiting for his promotion, had no money with which could help. Hong Qi, as poor as anybody else in the village, offered to help out at the house the best she could. Min Li suggested they hire some neighbors who had no fields of their own to plant the corn and Hong Qi and Hai Tian would alternately supervise the planting and taking care of Lian Min.

"Dr. Zhang says the treatments aren't working. They're a waste of time," Hai Tian reported to Min Li one day in April.

"Does he plan to stop trying?" Min Li asked. She immediately planned to make another trip to Shangguang, her third trip since New Year, to check on her mother. This time she would meet with Dr. Zhang.

"He said he talked to the doctors in Huludao. He can change medicines, but the other medicine is much more expensive. It comes from America."

"Let's do it," Min Li demanded without even considering it.

"It's very expensive."

"Doesn't matter. We'll find a way to pay for it."

"You're paying 1,500 yuan a week now. That has to be hurting you financially, but that's far less than the American medicine costs," Hai Tian explained.

"How much?"

"Dr. Zhang said it's 2,000 yuan per treatment. That's 6,000 yuan a week. Can you afford that."

"I'll find a way."

Min Li had no way of paying the 6,000 yuan a week. Already, her mother's treatments had completely drained her cash reserves, and she was now relying heavily on the income of her business to keep things afloat. To make matters worse, one of her clients had been arrested for corruption and his business closed up shop, causing her net revenue to drop. She needed a lot of money fast and fretted over that for a couple of days. She tried to pick up some more business, but that wasn't easy to do quickly. Then she remembered the note from her competitor, Hui Xijing. She called him.

"Wei?"

"This is Zhang Min Li."

"Who? Do I know you?"

"Are you kidding? I'm the owner of Pretty Office Cleaning Company."

"Oh yeah. I haven't thought about you for a while. What do you need? Ready to accept my offer?"

"No. Your offer is too low."

"I thought five hundred thousand was a fair offer. What did you have in mind?"

'my company has a better reputation than yours."

'says you."

'says everybody. And my employees are better trained and better disciplined than yours."

'says you."

"This is common knowledge. Are we going to argue about the obvious?" Min Li was slightly agitated now.

"How much do you want?"

"A million yuan."

Hui Xijing laughed. "Your business isn't worth that much. You're being ridiculous."

"Do you want to buy me out? Then make a serious offer or I'll take it to somebody else."

"Let me sleep on it," Hui Xijing stalled.

"As soon as I get off this phone, I'm calling somebody else. You have thirty seconds to decide if you want to buy my business or not," Min Li bluffed.

"I'll give you seven-fifty, but you have to give me a non-compete agreement."

'sold. I want to close our deal by Friday."

"That's a little fast. I don't think I can get it all together by then. There are many papers for the lawyers to write, and I have to move money around."

"Friday, or its no deal."

"You drive a hard bargain little lady," Hui Xijing condescended.

"One more thing," Min Li added.

"What's that?"

"Don't ever call me "little lady" again. Have everything ready by one o"clock this Friday."

'my lawyer will still be at lunch at one o"clock."

"Not this Friday. Make sure he knows."

Min Li wrote down the name and address for Hui Xijing's lawyer, then called Hai Tian to tell her she'll be in Shangguang the following weekend and instructed her to make the arrangements with Dr. Zhang. Lian Min will start the treatments with the new medicine the following Monday.

Next, she called her crew leaders and scheduled a meeting for Thursday afternoon. She needed to let her employees know that they would soon have a new boss. She agreed to not talk to her clients for fear of them jumping ship on hearing of the change of leadership, so she needed to brief her crew leaders on what to say. The crew leaders had no such prohibition from talking.

Friday afternoon, after closing the sale of her business to Hui Xijing, Min Li paid her rent for a year in advance, and deposited what she estimated to be a year's worth of service with the utility companies, electricity, water, and gas. She turned off service to her landline but kept her cell phone active. She did not plan to be gone for the whole year, but she would be coming and going from Shangguang frequently, and she did not want to have to worry about anything other than food. On Saturday, she met with the manager of her bank branch of the China Merchant's Bank and made arrangements to be able to easily withdraw funds from its branches in Yangzhangzi and Huludao, because Shangguang had no banks. After finishing her business at the bank, Min Li took a taxi to the Shenyang North train station and bought a soft seat ticket for Huludao for the next day. All she had to do was pack.

When Min Li arrived at her family's home, she found her mother in bed, emaciated, and jaundiced. Not wanting to disturb her sleep, Min Li stepped outside with Hai Tian.

'mama looks much worse. What's going on?"

'she won't eat or drink," Hai Tian explained. "I can barely get her to sit up."

"Have you mentioned this to the doctor?"

"Dr. Zhang says it's probably just the side effects of the medicine."

"Probably? Did he call the doctors in Huludao? Did you call the doctors in Huludao?"

"No. I just assumed Dr. Zhang knew what he was talking about."

"Come on, Hai Tian. You know Dr. Zhang better than that. He's not even a real doctor and you're trusting Mama's life to him. Give me the number for the hospital in Huludao."

Min Li called the oncology department at the Huludao Number One Hospital and explained her mother's symptoms. After a few moments she hung up and issued orders to Hai Tian.

"I'll get Mama dressed. You go find a car to get us to Huludao."

"There are no taxis in Shangguang. What should I do?"

"I don't know. Be creative. Flag somebody down if you have to. Just get us a car."

Min Li re-entered the house and roused her mother awake. She found some clothes for her, one of two Mao suits that she wore regularly, and slowly dressed Lian Min. She made a pot of weak tea and encouraged her mother to drink some while she waited for Hai Tian to return. Twenty minutes later, Hai Tian returned with Liu Tan Yi, the middle-aged man who owned the truck that took the villagers' corn to market. The truck was one of China's ubiquitous three-wheeled variety, painted standard blue with a flatbed and stake sides.

After lifting Lian Min into the cab, Min Li sat next to her by the passenger door while Hai Tian hopped onto the flatbed. They had to drive through Yangzhangzi where Liu Tan Yi filled up his fuel tank, paid for by Min Li. Their next stop was the Yangzhangzi branch of China Merchant Bank where Min Li withdrew what she thought would be enough money to cover her mother's hospital expenses in Huludao. An hour later, Min Li and Hai Tian carried their mother into the hospital up to the third floor, and down the hall to the oncology department. Their task would have been easier with a wheelchair, but there were none available.

The doctor glanced at Lian Min and knew immediately what was causing her trouble.

"Her bile duct is obstructed. That's why she can't eat and why she's so jaundiced. She needs surgery immediately. Do you have money?"

"I brought twenty thousand with me," Min Li answered.

"You'll need more than that. This is delicate surgery. I'm not taking out tonsils, you know."

"How much?"

"Fifty thousand. Come back when you have it."

Min Li and Hai Tian carried their mother down to the hospital's lobby where Hai Tian waited with her while Min Li took a taxi to the nearest branch of the China Merchants Bank. She came back twenty minutes later and the three repeated their trip to the oncology department. The doctor instructed Min Li to make the payment with the hospital's cashier and to take her mother to the surgery ward. He would call ahead to the ward to reserve a bed for Lian Min. Min Li made the payment, which served as a deposit against anticipated hospital expenses, and was given a receipt, which she took with her to the surgery ward where Lian Min and Hai Tian waited.

After settling their mother in a one of eight beds in the room, Min Li and Hai Tian watched the nurses hook up three different I.V.s, a saline solution to deal with her dehydration, glucose for her malnutrition, and something else, which Min Li assumed was some medication. One of the nurses told them that surgery was scheduled for eight the next morning, that they should go get some rest as their mother would like sleep until then.

"Let's go find a hotel," Min Li suggested.

"A hotel? I didn't bring a change of clothes."

"No problem. We'll do a little shopping and get what we need."

Min Li and Hai Tian arrived at the hospital the next morning a little after seven. Lian Min, awake, seemed a little bewildered by her surroundings but otherwise comfortable, but for the apprehension caused by knowing that soon she would be under the knife.

"Who is taking care of your father?" Lian Min asked.

Min Li and Hai Tian both realized that their father didn't even know where they were. He was out the day before, and the girls rushed their mother to the hospital without even telling him. She thought about calling him, but the house had no phone, Hai Tian's cell phone being the only way to communicate with the outside world, and her cell phone was in Hai Tian's pocket. Immediately, Min Li called Hong Qi to tell her what was happening. That's when Min Li learned that her father was with Hong Qi, having gone there for breakfast.

Relieved to hear that Hong Qi had fed her husband, Lian Min made both Min Li and Hai Tian promise to care for their father after she was gone. They both agreed and both assured their mother that she would be cooking for Zhang Zhi Hao for many years to come. Then the nurses came, transferred Lian Min to a gurney, and rolled her away. The two then walked down to the waiting room where they would sit for the next two hours while their mother was in surgery.

They briefly saw their mother again when she was wheeled out of surgery into the recovery room and had to wait another two hours. Meanwhile, her doctor told them that the surgery went smoothly, that the bile duct obstruction had been removed successfully, but there was another problem. The cancer had spread to Lian Min's spleen and liver, and the prognosis wasn't good. Her only chance of surviving the month would require that she be placed on intensive chemotherapy, which would require her to remain in the hospital for her treatments. The treatment was expensive but, if effective, would add a few more years to Lian Min's life. Without hesitation, Min Li said to do it.

Min Li and Hai Tian remained in Huludao during the entire course of their mother's treatment, visiting her every day and bringing in her meals from various nearby restaurants. Lian Min's appetite had improved, but not so much that she could tolerate the food prepared in the hospital's kitchen. She started losing her appetite after a few days, as well as her hair, the effects of the treatment, but Min Li and Hai Tian managed to keep her eating. On days she refused to eat, Lian Min drank protein shakes and tea.

Finally, after three weeks in the hospital, Min Li and Hai Tian took their mother home. They helped Lian Min into the house, weak but otherwise in good spirits. They sat at the small table while Hai Tian put water on for tea. Lian Min scanned the room and seeing it in some disarray, rose to tidy up.

"No, Mama. We'll straighten up. You just sit there and relax," Min Li demanded.

"But I have laundry to do. I've not been home for a long time. You father will want his clothes washed and ironed."

"Leave them be, Mama," Min Li scolded, "Hong Qi said she took care of everything. You only need to sit down and enjoy life."

"But what will I do?"

Min Li thought about that, *what would she do?* Lian Min lived in a small house with a dirt floor and no electricity. Outside she had a small garden and a field of corn seedlings that needed tending, but she would do none of that. Doing nothing would not lead Lian Min to happiness, unless she had some kind of diversion.

"Hai Tian, take care of Mama for a while. I'll be back in an hour or so," Min Li said. Then she donned her sweater and left the house, leaving both her mother and sister wondering what she was up to. She came back later with two men and a cart laden with electrical cable and tools and set them to working. The men ran some wires into the house, installed two sockets, hooked up a meter on the outside wall, and ran a cable to an electric pole fifty meters away. the wire to the pole sagged, coming to within a meter from the road, so they found a long board and propped up the wire about halfway to the pole, stabilizing the pole by making a makeshift tripod. The house that Min Li grew up in finally had electricity.

Min Li paid the men and left again for the bus station heading for Yangzhangzi. She returned two hours later with a small television set with a remote control and a rabbit ear type antenna. "You should be able to pick up the stations in Huludao, Jinzhou, and Shanghaiguan," she announced. "A better antenna will be installed outside tomorrow, but this will do for now. After today, you'll be able to catch stations from Shenyang, Tianjin, and Beijing."

Lian Min reacted like a small child tasting ice cream for the first time. She never had a television before. She pressed the red button on the remote, lighting up the TV's screen, then flipped through the channels. Without moving the antenna, she could almost pick up the Jinzhou station, but to tune anything in, she needed Hai Tian to turn the antenna in various directions.

"You won't have to do that after they install the aerial antenna tomorrow," Min Li explained.

"If I sit here watching television all day, I'll never get my chores done," Lian Min complained.

"You can't be serious, Mama," Hai Tian said. "You don't have chores anymore."

Zhang Zhi Hao returned home to find his wife and two of his daughters sitting there watching a news broadcast on the television. They didn't even notice him come in.

"Ahem!" Zhang Zhi Hao managed to get their attention. "I see you're finally home. Now I won't have to go over to Hong Qi's just to eat."

Min Li and Hai Tian didn't know whether their father was joking or not. "Aren't you glad Mama is home, Papa?" Hai Tian asked.

"Of course. Why is she wearing that rag over her head?" Zhang Zhi Hao asked, referring to the paisley head scarf tastefully tied on to the side by Hai Tian to cover her mother's baldness.

"Two reasons, Papa," Min Li answered. "One is that it looks nice. The other is that it helps Mama preserve her dignity for the loss of her hair."

"What did she do with her hair?"

"It fell out from the chemotherapy in the hospital."

"Don't those doctors know what they're doing? Can't they treat people for a simple illness without making their hair fall out?"

"Papa, you know better," scolded Min Li. "Everybody loses their hair from chemotherapy for cancer."

"Dr. Zhang didn't make her hair fall out. You should have let him treat her."

'she would have died in Dr. Zhang's care," Hai Tian yelled.

Zhang Zhi Hao looked at Hai Tian. "That is no way to talk to your father. You've been spending too much time with Zhang Min Li."

Hai Tian almost said something, but Min Li stopped her. They both knew any argument with their father would be futile. They also both knew that now that their mother was home, he would be expecting things from her. They both silently resolved to prevent that from happening.

Fourteen

Min Li returned to Shenyang after another week, leaving the sole care of her mother in the hands of Hai Tian and occasionally Hong Qi. Hong Qi would soon give birth and would be in no position to care for her mother, so Hai Tian tried to develop a routine to make it easier for her. She made sure she woke up every morning before her mother to make breakfast. Min Li had left enough money to hire help for the fields when needed, which seemed to have the negative effect of keeping Zhang Zhi Hao in the house.

It pleased Min Li to know that her mother had developed a short list of favorite television shows, and she managed to keep the control to herself during their broadcasts. At other times, Zhang Zhi Hao took over the control, which didn't seem to bother Lian Min much. She learned to sit through soccer and basketball games, but when it was time for one of her shows, game or no game, Zhang Zhi Hao relinquished the remote control, albeit reluctantly.

Min Li returned to Shangguang for one week every month. Her mother seemed to be dping well and kept her spirits high. During that week visit, Min Li and Hai Tian took their mother to Huludao to visit the doctor for a checkup. The doctor always seemed a little surprised at how well Lian Min was doing, despite her illness. He even once joked that they had beat the cancer, but everybody knew that couldn't be true.

For the other three weeks of the month, Min Li explored financial opportunities. She had nearly exhausted the money she made from selling the business and needed to come up with a way to make money. She hoped that her mother would not need more surgery, which would wipe out any remaining cash Min Li had.

One of her former crew leaders had quit the cleaning business and, resuming her former occupation as a hair stylist, opened up her own shop. Min Li visited her often, spending hours on slow days talking about her mother and her plans. While visiting, her friend had taught Min Li a few things about making women beautiful, and Min Li learned how to do facials and to apply makeup. It was never her intent to do this for a living, but it gave her something to do to help pass the time. She learned that she was good at it.

"You should get into this business," her friend, Tong Li Hua told her one day.

"I don't think so. There doesn't seem to be much money in it," Min Li answered.

"That depends how good you are and where you work. This isn't a good neighborhood, and not enough people know me yet. The business will pick up, I'm sure."

'still, even if you're busy, you"d have to be very busy and have a few people working for you before you can make good money," Min Li argued.

"True, but that's China. People don't want to pay for personal services. If you want to make good money, you have to leave China."

"I'm not leaving China. I want to stay close to my mother. Besides, where can somebody go to make a lot of money doing this?"

"America, Australia, Canada, the Middle East."

"The Middle East?"

"Yeah, like Kuwait, Dubai, or maybe Bahrain."

"Why those places?"

"I'm not sure. But that's what I heard. It's easier to get a visa to go there, and the women in those countries are rich. They go to the beauty shop often and pay well for it. I'd go myself, but I don't know English."

"English for the Middle East?"

"I suppose you can learn Arabic, too, but English is essential. Those countries have many foreigners living in them, so English is very common. Most of the Arabs speak English in those countries, or at least some English."

"I speak English, or at least I used to," Min Li corrected herself.

"Then you should go. One of my customers told me that her sister lives in Kuwait and sends back more than thirty thousand yuan a month. I'm sure she's keeping money to live on in Kuwait, so she must be making a lot of money."

"What does she do there?"

"I don't know, but she left China without any particular skills."

"It's out of the question. I can't imagine not living in China."

As soon as Min Li said this, she remembered that she once thought about marrying an American, Peter North, who she met many years ago while teaching English in Shenyang. Had she married him, which they talked about for a while, she would likely be living in America. She's glad that didn't happen, of course, considering her mother's cancer, but it did make her think again about leaving China. *If things were different*, she reminded herself.

As a matter of fact, Min Li has never been out of Liaoning Province, not even to visit her father in Sichuan or even to Beijing, her nation's capital, her sisters likewise. Like their mother, they had pretty much stayed in Shangguang, traveling to Yangzhangzi and an occasional trip to Huludao, or maybe even Jinzhou. Shangguang sat in a valley about thirty miles from the coast on the Bohai Sea, and she knew of nobody in her family who had visited the sea, other than her paternal grandparents who escaped China by sea in the early 1970s. She called up Hai Tian and told her that this coming weekend, they were going to the beach and to let their mother and Hong Qi know.

When Min Li arrived in Huludao the next day, boarded the bus for Yangzhangzi where she arranged to hire a car to take her mother and sisters to the beach the next day before taking another bus to Shangguang. The car picked them up in Shangguang at ten in the morning and drove them to Bijiashan on Liaodong Bay. This small port city serving the city of Jinzhou is named for a small island in shallow water about five hundred meters offshore. At low tide, people can walk to the island on a sand and gravel road, allowing access to the island twice a day between high and neap tides.

The car dropped of Min Li with her mother and two sisters on the road that ran along the beach shortly before low tide. Hai Tian ran out onto the beach, leaving everybody behind, and quickly bogged down in the deep, soft sand. She never walked on sand before and was surprised at how difficult it could be. She trudged back to her group and helped Min Li walk their mother out to the middle of the beach where they spread an old blanket, and Lian Min, already exhausted from the twenty-meter walk from the road in the soft sand, and Hong Qi, now eight months pregnant, sat down to rest. Min Li and Hai Tian left their mother and sister on the blanket to warm up in the mid-morning sun while they went to fetch grapes and strawberries, as well as a disposable camera.

When they returned, they found Lian Min and Hong Qi watching as the tide ebbed and the road to Bijiashan Island slowly appear. Other people, some vendors and some beachgoers, had already begun to walk down the road, accompanied by a pair of donkey carts, and advanced slowly as the tide continued to ebb. Somebody nearby told Min Li and her group that the tide would allow passage on the road for about thirty minutes, so if they wanted to walk to the island, they should go now.

Hurriedly, they gathered their things, rolling the blanket and packing their fruit into a backpack, and started for the road that grew out of the shore. After trekking about a hundred meters on the wet sand and gravel road, Lian Min grew exhausted and suggested they turn around. She didn't think she could make the other four hundred meters to the island before the waters rose again. Not wanting to miss this once in a lifetime chance to walk to the island, Min Li offered to carry her mother on her back. A year before, this might not have been possible, but Lian Min had loss so much weigjt, her skeleton frame weighed far less than Min Li.

Min Li carried her mother this way for another two hundred meters before she slowed from exhaustion. Looking to their rear, Min Li could see the waters already rising, the middle section of the road already submerging. She looked toward the island and saw they still had another two hundred meters to go; then she looked at Hai Tian who was carrying nothing more than the rolled backpack. To Min Li's relief, Hai Tian realized it was her turn to carry her mother and so offered, exchanging the backpack for Lian Min. Hai Tian carried her mother the rest of the way with energy to spare, and they all rested on a bench at the foot of the trail where the road met the island while watching the road completely submerge under the waters of Liaondong Bay.

After resting twenty minutes, they slowly walked up the inclined path on the east side of the island toward the crest and picked up a trail to take them to the south end of the island where stood a granite temple, complete with granite doors and windows. Lian Min, exhausted from the hike, remained on the first floor with Hong Qi and lit some incense while Min Li and Hai Tian explored the top floors while taking in the view of the Bohai Sea and the central coast of Liaoning Province northwest of Dalian.

They walked back to the north end of the island along the easier east trail, less scenic due to the long row of docks jutting out from the shore only fifty meters to their east. Here, they encountered numerous souvenir stands, soft drink vendors, and a makeshift BB-gun shooting gallery giving people a chance to kill allied invaders for only one yuan. Hong Qi spotted an unoccupied bench, and they rested some more before returning to the foot of the island nearest the shore. By the time they reached the wide trailhead, the road to the mainland was completely underwater and would be impassable for several hours. Instead, they hopped aboard a boat with an outboard motor, equipped to seat a dozen people, and for ten yuan each were taken back to the beach five hundred meters away.

The sun neared the western horizon as they reached the shore, so instead of returning to the sandy beach, they walked across the road to a restaurant, and Min Li treated her mother and sisters to a fresh seafood dinner, complete with crabs, shrimp, and other local catches. Lian Min, who still had little appetite, at least sampled each of the dishes, most of which she had never tasted before.

Lian Min smiled all the way back to Shangguang in the hired car, and the four women couldn't stop talking about what a wonderful time they had. They had never spent this much time doing nothing but having a good time together, and Lian Min said that it was the highlight of her life. Nothing could make her happier, unless Hong Qi gave birth before she died. Everybody stopped talking. They had forgotten that their mother lived on borrowed time, and that she could leave this world soon. They had no way of knowing when, because the surgery didn't stop the cancer. It only made it possible for her to eat and to avoid dying of starvation.

Soon, the conversation started again, this time talking mostly about the lack of rain and whether Hong Qi's baby will look like Hong Qi or her husband. Hong Qi said that she didn't care, so long as it was born with Lian Min's patience and Min Li's heart.

Fifteen

Min Li packed her things for her return to Shenyang while Hai Tian checked the fields. Zhang Zhi Hao wasn't home, as usual. Lian Min watched Min Li pack.

"I might not see you again, Xiao Min."

"Nonsense, Mama. I'll be back in three weeks."

"I won't be here."

"Why? Where are you going?"

"To visit my parents."

"Tomb Sweeping Day is past, Mama. Why would you want to go visit their tomb next month?"

"I won't be visiting their tomb, dear. I don't think I'm going to make it until then."

"But, Mama, you're doing so well lately. I think you added a little weight and your color is improving."

"I'm tired Min Li. I've never been so tired in my life. I can't do anything anymore. I can't take care of the fields. I can't even get the eggs from the chickens. Hai Tian or Hong Qi cooks for your father. He even acts as if I've already gone. I have no reason to be here."

'Mama, you can keep going. You are stronger than you think."

"You don't understand, Sweetheart. My time here is finished. I want to get ready, and I need your help."

"You want my help? What can I do? Mama, please stop talking this way," Min Li pleaded.

"Xiao Min, you can ignore the inevitable if you want, but I need you now. Please do as I ask whether you believe I'm going to die or not."

"What is it you want me to do, Mama?"

"Find me the perfect place."

"Perfect place?"

"For my body. When I die. You know."

"Won't you be buried with Papa's parents and his other family? That's what custom requires you know."

"If I wanted that, I wouldn't be talking to you now. Please listen to me. I've been married to your father for thirty-three years. I've done everything I'm supposed to do as his wife. I gave him a son and three daughters. He wanted more sons, but I'm glad we have what we have. I've put up with his occasional visits home and did my duty for him. I took care of the family, farmed our field, fed and clothed our children, paid their school fees, and did everything possible to help him keep face."

"Okay, but I don't really understand what you want."

"Daughter, I have no face. I don't want to be with him forever. I don't have to. I've done what I had to do already, and I don't have to do anything more. When I'm gone, he'll have the television and he won't have me. I will be happy again and at rest. I will be able to walk across to Bijiashan without anybody carrying me. I will have no burdens, unless you place my body in his family crypt. Don't put me there, please."

'sure, Mama. Where do you want to be, in your parents' crypt?

"No. I don't belong to them anymore. But if you find the perfect place, I can finally rest, and I can take care of you and your siblings."

"I don't understand."

"It's *feng shui*. I don't understand, either, but I know it. If you find me the perfect place, my spirit will have positive effect on my children. Things will change for the better."

"Things worked out well for me, Mama."

"You're fooling yourself, Xiao Min. Things did not work out for you. You did exceptionally well in school despite your grandparents being labeled capitalist roaders and despite their fleeing China in the middle of the night. You had the highest score on the national college placement test, but you didn't go to college. You were sold into a marriage that you didn't want, just like me. You tried to make things better yourself by running away, and it looked good for you when you got that job teaching English in an elementary school. But that didn't last because you had no degree. Then you started your own business and struggled with that for many years. You finally found a husband, but that didn't work out either. Now you have no college, no husband, and no business."

"Those were mostly choices I made, Mama, except for the college."

"You were forced to make those choices because of the circumstances. Your circumstances need to change, and that can only happen when there is a change in *feng shui*."

"What do you have in mind, then, Mama?"

"I need to be high, not too high, but high enough so that I can look down on this valley and see our home and our field. I want to be able to look out after Hai Tian and help her find a husband. Otherwise, your father will imprison her here for the rest of his life. I'll work on that a little bit before I go."

"How are you going to do that?"

"I'll simply tell your father that if he doesn't let her marry that nice Yang Lin boy, my spirit will stay here and haunt him the rest of his life."

'she'll go live with him in Xiaguang," Min Li pointed out. "Who will take care of your field?"

"Your father won't. That's for sure. He'll just let it go fallow and live off his pension. I've already signed it over to Hong Qi and her husband. She doesn't know it yet."

"I also want to see the ocean. Do you know Pàotǎ Shān north of here? I used to play there as a child before they cut all the trees down."

"I know it well, Mama. Most of the trees have come back, although I'm sure they're smaller now than they were when you were a child."

"Are there squirrels?"

"And rabbits and all kinds of other animals."

"I want to be there. There's a place with a large boulder behind a little clearing. From the top of that boulder, you can see the valley below and Shangguang, and you can see the blue waters of the Bohai from there. If you take me there, things will change. All the things that should have been will be, and I can rest knowing that my family will be better than now."

"I'll do that, Mama. I promise. In fact, I will go to Yangzhangzi today and buy a small crypt to place on top of that boulder. I can delay returning to Shenyang a day or two."

"You are a wonderful daughter, but please spend very little money on the crypt. I don't want to be noticeable. And there's one more thing."

"Anything, Mama."

"Don't tell your father."

"How am I to keep him from knowing about it? He'll have you interred in his family's tomb if I don't stop him."

"Let him do that. Later, you remove me from his family tomb and take me to Pàotǎ Shān. It will only be the perfect place if he knows nothing of it."

Min Li thought about that for a moment. She didn't like the idea of sneaking into the cemetery and stealing the remains of her mother from inside a large crypt full of the remains of many other people. But she promised, and she has already proven to herself that she can do anything she sets her mind to, so long as she has control over the situation. She would tell her siblings, of course, so long as they swore to keep it secret. Not only would her father not approve, but the government would not approve. Burials in China are highly regulated. Remains must be cremated, placed in approved containers, and only interred in registered locations, such as existing cemeteries. She stopped packing.

'mama, I'm going to catch a bus over to Yangzhangzi. I should be back in time for supper, so let Hai Tian know. I'll leave it up to you whether you tell her or Hong Qi about our plans. Otherwise, I'll tell them when needed, whenever that will be."

'soon," Lian Min reminded her.

Min Li simply shook her head, kissed and hugged her mother, and headed for the bus station.

Yangzhangzi's small size allowed Min Li to quickly find the granite shop, although she must have seen it many times before without noticing. She even walked past it before when she bought the television for her mother. The granite shop consisted of a small office, covered in white dust and a yard with various samples of cut granite, mostly head stones for cemeteries and small crypts. The crypts averaged a meter in height but varied more in width from a third of a meter to slightly more than a meter. All crypts were designed for the placement of a burial urn within it, and most were ornately decorated with various scrolls, Buddhist phrases, and Chinese axioms. Most were adorned with a pitched roof peaking in the center with various ornaments lining the eaves such as dragons, phoenixes, or lions, likely to ward off evil spirits.

Min Li found a crypt cut from white granite with a simple, yet elegant design. It stood just under a meter and a half a meter wide and had a rounded, peaked roof. The front had a double door with stone hinges that could be bolted or welded closed. A lion carved to one side of the door guarded the entry. On the other side of the door was carved a stylized cross, a unique feature on Chinese tombstones. Min Li liked it because it would blend in well with the limestone surroundings and its features, being less angular than the other crypts, would allow it to blend in with the natural curves of the landscape where she planned to leave it. Another feature that had attracted Min Li to it was a removable slab from across the top of the door that could be affixed later after carving in the personal information of the deceased. She didn't like the idea of having her mother's name carved on the crypt while she was still alive.

Min Li paid the three thousand yuan for the crypt, but when she tried to arrange for it to be delivered to Pàotǎ Shān, the granite shop owner asked if she had a burial permit.

"Why would I need a burial permit now? It's for my mother who is still alive," Min Li tried to explain.

"Then you should have plenty of time to obtain a burial permit."

"How long does that take?"

"A year, maybe longer."

"You mean people have to wait a year to bury their departed loved ones?"

"Or longer."

"I can't wait a year. Can't you just deliver it for me?"

"I don't want to get in trouble."

"Nobody will know, only you and me."

"I can't take that risk."

"I'll pay you extra, plus the delivery costs."

"Where's it going?"

"Just north of Shangguang on a hill called Pàotǎ Shān."

The shop owner pulled out a rare topographical map of the area and found Shangguang. "There's a hill here, but it has no name."

Min Li looked at where the man pointed on the map, studied it for a moment, turned her head to the side, saw that there were no other hills in the area, and said, "That's it."

"I don't see any roads."

"There's a road that runs past the hill, and over here is a trail wide enough for your truck. You can get to within a hundred meters or so of the spot."

"I'll need at least four men to deliver it and special equipment."

"How much?"

"Ten thousand."

"Now you're trying to take advantage of me and my special circumstances. I've already paid three thousand for the crypt and you want me to pay another ten for the delivery?"

"Do you have a permit?"

"Okay. You win. I want it done this afternoon."

'sorry. My men are busy. The earliest I can do this is next Monday."

"We can do it this afternoon or you can give me back the three thousand I already gave you and I'll get it in Huludao. There's at least five shops there where I can get a better price, and I bet I can have it delivered from Huludao for less, permit or not."

"Fourteen thousand and I can have the men and equipment ready before lunch."

"Deal. Leave the name stone here, and I will tell you what to engrave when it's needed. I trust I won't have to pay more for that."

"It's included so long as it's simple."

Min Li returned to Shangguang after seven that evening, covered in dirt after having ridden in the back of the granite delivery truck to and from Pàotǎ Shān. When she came into the house, her father was flipping through the channels on the television while Lian Min and Hai Tian sat on the kang talking. Hai Tian jumped from the kang to heat up supper for Min Li, who sat on the bed in Hai Tian's place.

"Is it done," Lian Min asked expectantly.

"It's done."

"I want to see it?"

"Now?"

"No, tomorrow. Can you take me there?"

"I suppose. I'll have to arrange for a ride, but can you climb up the hill? We'll bring Hai Tian with us so she'll know what's going on and help me if need be."

"I'll manage. If you can get me to the trail, I'll do the rest. Don't worry about it, but you can bring Hai Tian if you like."

Anxious to go to Pàotǎ Shān, Lian Min was ready to go by six the next morning. Min Li fetched the same truck and driver that took them to the hospital in Huludao, giving him a hundred yuan for his time and gasoline. They left the house while Zhang Zhi Hao slept, leaving him tea and porridge to warm up for his breakfast. They decided not to take Hong Qi because, as Lian Min determined, she was going to have her baby any time.

Min Li directed the driver up the trail when they arrived at Pàotǎ Shān and asked him to wait for them while they trekked up the hill.

"It's been nearly fifty years since I was last here," Lian Min said as she hiked up the narrow trail leading to the summit. "The trees seem a little different, but I guess that's to be expected. There were once pines here, but now they're mostly hardwoods."

Lian Min reached the boulder on her own steam and stopped, leaned against it, and soaked in the view. The view had changed little over the past fifty years, except the village below had a small number of newer buildings and she could see smokestacks in the distance that she had never seen before. Further to the south, she saw a blue horizontal strip between the barren brown rolling hills and the lighter blue sky.

"There it is!" she exclaimed. "You can see the Bohai from here just like I told you. Now, let me see the crypt."

The boulder upon which Min Li had set the crypt must have been four meters high, the near vertical face standing behind them like a wall as they looked toward the valley. The true size of the boulder couldn't be determined, as the backside remained buried in the soft dirt around it. Small trees grew along its side and on the back, almost enveloping it from three sides. The ground in front of the boulder had been gouged by heavy lifting equipment, and scuff-marks trailed up the front from where the crypt had been hoisted. Min Li led her mother around the east side of the huge boulder, and they found a small, inclined patch of dirt leading up to the back between the boulder and some elms. The exposed roots of the trees served as rungs for their feet and hands as they dragged themselves up the side of the boulder toward the back.

When they reached the top, Lian Min wrested herself from Hai Tian's helping grip and walked over to the crypt. It sat atop the boulder, about two meters from the edge facing the valley, snug up against the branches of the nearby elms. Lian Min stood in front of the crypt and looked south.

"The view is even more glorious here, and I can make out more of the sea. This place truly is perfect. Thank you, dear daughter." Then she looked more closely at the crypt, saw the space behind the small double doors where her remains would be placed, and looked pleased. "Let's go home," she said, and her daughters helped her down the small path which had taken them to the top.

During the entire ten-minute drive back to Shangguang, Lian Min smiled the same as she did when she had come back from the beach. She said only one thing on the way home, "It is the perfect place."

Sixteen

Hong Qi's baby decided to wait no longer, and Hong Qi gave birth that evening while she and her husband were visiting her mother. Everybody agreed that they had miscalculated Hong Qi's time of conception, because the baby was born healthy and fat at 3.4 kilograms, or 7½ pounds. Lian Min and Hai Tian congratulated themselves about being right that it would be a boy, which fact had been confirmed earlier in the pregnancy by a sonogram, but Lian Min had never trusted that. They named the boy Yuzhao, which would later be recorded on Liu Yuncun's *hukou* as Liu Yuzhao.

After Hong Qi had recovered from giving birth, they carried her and the baby back to her house, laid her on her kang, sealed up the windows and door, and left her alone with the baby for the next month. During that month, Hong Qi could receive no visitors, nor could she bathe, a custom aimed to protect the health of both the mother and the baby. After a month, if the baby was still alive, people could visit and the mother could take a break from the baby's constant needs. Min Li returned to Shenyang shortly after the birth, planning to return a month later with gifts for the baby. Shortly before Hong Qi's month of quarantine had ended, Lian Min passed away.

Xiong Yong's employer allowed him time off to return to Shangguang to fulfill his duties to mourn for his mother and to receive visitors. Traditionally, Lian Min would have been placed in a coffin and returned to her home for a period of time to be visited by friends and relatives. New regulations, however, required that she be immediately cremated, so visitors paid their respects to an earthenware urn containing her ashes. Xiong Yong, Min Li, and Hai Tian erected a large floral wreath and a makeshift shrine in the garden, protected by sheets of plastic over a wooden frame, providing a roof and three walls.

Lian Min had few relatives, her parents having passed before her. She had some female cousins who lived in other villages, all of whom came by to pay their respects. Within the Shangguang area, Lian Min was well respected, and many people came to visit, including nearly everybody on her former production team who were still alive. Xiong Yong's friend, Lao Dong, came and kept Xiong Yong company throughout the day and most of the evenings when he wasn't working. When the visits from people paying their respects had waned, Zhang Zhi Hao told Xiong Yong that it was time to take Lian Min to the family crypt.

Min Li thought about telling her father that her mother had made other plans, but she made a promise to Lian Min that her father could never know where she her permanent resting place would be. Min Lin had to go along with entombing her mother's remains in the Zhang family crypt in the Shangguang cemetery. The procession slowly walked from the Zhang family home through the streets of Shangguang and up Cemetery Road past the old church. Few people attended, which suited Min Li fine. The possession was led by Xiong Yong and his friend Lao Dong, followed by Zhao Zhi Hao carrying the urn. Following the urn were Lian Min's three daughters according to age, Min Li being first, then Hong Qi carrying her baby, and last by Hai Tian. Hong Qi's husband, Liu Yuncun walked beside her, and Yang Lin walked beside Hai Tian. Only Lian Min knew that Hai Tian and Yang Lin had secretly married only a week before Lian Min died.

The caretaker of the cemetery met them at the gate, handing the key to the family crypt to Xiong Yong with instructions to return the key by the end of the next day, giving the family an opportunity to mourn Lian Min at the crypt and to pay respects to their ancestors. When they reached the crypt, Xiong Yong cleared away some ivy that had overgrown part of the door, unlocked the bolt, and pulled open the iron door, creaking from its own weight on its rusty hinges. Inside, the walls on both sides bore several heavy shelves containing the urns of departed ancestors. On the back wall, on three shelves, wider than the others, lay five coffins bearing the bodies of more ancient ancestors.

Zhang Zhi Hao placed the urn on the third shelf on the left side wall, near the door, then stood in quiet reflection. Before leaving the crypt, he glanced around inside the crypt. It looked as though he was about to say something, but instead he slowly exited the crypt and asked Xiong Yong to close the door. Zhang Zhi Hao began walking down the pathway to Cemetery Road, and the others filed in behind him.

"I might as well give the caretaker the key now while we're here," Xiong Yong said to anybody who would be listening.

"Wait," Min Li said. "Let me have it. I'll give it back to him tomorrow. I'll want to visit again in the morning and bring flowers."

'Really? Do you want me to come with you?"

"No, but thank you. I'd rather be alone. You can come later if you like." Min Li didn't want to tell her brother what she had planned to do, later perhaps.

Xiong Yong handed her the key to the crypt and headed down the path. Min Li walked back to the crypt, placed her face near the door, and said, "I'll be back later, Mama. You can count on me."

The family went to bed late that night, spending most of the evening talking about Lian Min, how hard she worked, and how she sacrificed so much for her family. The three daughters told Xiong Yong about their trip to the beach at Bijiashan. It was all Min Li could do to keep from talking about the small crypt she had installed on Pàotǎ Shān. So far, only she and Hai Tian knew about it.

Min Li arose early the next morning and roused Hai Tian awake.

"What time is it?" Hai Tian asked groggily.

"About four thirty. Keep it down and get dressed. Hurry."

"Why? What are we doing? We can collect the eggs later." Hai Tian planned to sleep in as they discussed the night before, so she was confused by being awakened so early.

"We have to go to Pàotǎ Shān. Did you forget? Now get dressed and don't wake Papa and Xiong Yong."

Hai Tian dressed quickly, suddenly alert knowing what task lay before her. Before leaving the house, Min Li told her to grab a flashlight while Min Li grabbed the backpack they had taken to the beach. The girls made a quick stop at the outhouse then followed their footsteps from the day before to the cemetery.

The sun had not yet peaked the horizon when they reached the Zhang family crypt, so Min Li couldn't see the lock. 'shine the flashlight on the lock so I can open it," she demanded of Hai Tian.

Hai Tian couldn't get the flashlight to come on. "I think the batteries are dead."

"Take the batteries out and put them in again."

Hai Tian tried that, and the flashlight worked dimly for about ten seconds, just long enough for Min Li to get the key into the lock. Then the light went dead.

"Now what are we going to do?" Hai Tian asked.

"What we came here for."

"Our light stopped working."

"We don't need the light. We'll just feel our way in the dark," Min Li said.

"In there? Are you crazy? There are dead people in there. I'm not going in there without a light. It's bad enough with a light."

"You can't back out now, Hai Tian. I saw where Papa placed the urn, so it should be easy."

"You do it then."

"We're doing this for Mama. We promised."

"Then do it. You don't need me to lift that urn."

Frustrated by her little sister's cowardice, Min Li entered the crypt, the strange, stuffy smell being made more pungent by the morning air. She immediately felt for the shelves on the left side, used her hands to count up to the third shelf, then slightly swept her hands to the right until they touched the urn. Relieved that the urn she touched had no collection of dust, she assumed it was the correct one, grabbed it, and quickly exited the crypt. Outside, Min Li placed the urn inside the backpack she had been carrying, pushed the door closed, and locked it.

Min Li and Hai Tian quickly traversed the path to the roadway and didn't stop until they reached the old church where there was enough light to make sure they had the correct urn. They did. Min Li swung the backpack onto her shoulders and the two women walked down to Liberation Road, the main street in the village, and turned right toward the east. As they neared the edge of the village, the road turned north, and they hiked out to Pàotǎ Shān. The sun broke the crest of the horizon as they started up the trail to the boulder.

By the time Min Li and Hai Tian reached the boulder, the sun had fully risen, giving them the light they needed to climb up the side of the boulder. They stopped for a moment and looked at the crypt; then Min Li unshouldered the backpack and set it down gently before removing the urn.

"Here is your new home, Mama," Min Li said as she placed the urn inside the small crypt. She then closed the double doors, sealed them with the bolt and lock provided for that purpose, and turned to look at the valley before. The sun glimmered in the east as Min Li watched Shangguang come to life. The fields lay flat around the village in their haphazard quilt pattern, and the tall corn waved gently in the breeze. Soon, the farmers would be harvesting their corn and plowing their fields, changing the colors from verdant green, to yellow, and to brown, and by winter, these same fields would be a hard, grey, frozen, and lifeless.

Seventeen

Saddened by the loss of her mother, Min Li found it hard to motivate herself after returning to Shenyang. She forced herself to look for work. Down to her last forty thousand yuan, she knew she would run out of money soon, but she had no drive or ambition that would be necessary to start up her own business. She thought maybe it was time for her to be an employee for a change, but she needed something with growth in order to ensure her future because she had no husband or children.

Within a month, she landed a job as the office manager for the start-up Shenyang Electrical Appliances Company, owned by Shu Feng Ming, a member of the Chinese Communist Party and former deputy mayor of nearby Anshan. Impressed with her experience running her own business, the owner believed that Min Li could easily take charge of the day-to-day administrative operations for this small manufacturer. The company made mostly toaster ovens, rice cookers, electric teakettles, and countertop electric hotplates, which were quickly becoming more popular in China to replace the typical two-burner gas stovetops in most homes. She would receive a token salary of two thousand yuan a month with a bonus at the end of the year based upon the company's net income, a typical arrangement for many companies in China at the time. The owner of the company had hoped to take advantage of China's recent membership in the World Trade Organization and had planned to sell most of the company's products overseas.

Min Li dove into the job and quickly organized her employer's administrative functions to be efficient and productive. She supervised the company bookkeeper, two secretaries, accounts receivable, accounts payable, warehousing, inventory control, and distribution. Although the company was new, after six months with her heading up the administration, it had already turned a profit due mostly to domestic sales to the Shenyang regional market. The sales department then picked up a contract with Beijing Hua Lian, a large retailer with outlets throughout northern China, and production could barely keep up with orders.

Because of the briskness of sales and need to continue production, the company's owner asked all the employees to forego their lunar New Year plans in exchange for a cash bonus at the end of the year, to which most employees agree, including Min Li. Workers saw no bonus in December during the first year of operation because, as the owner worded it, the company hadn't yet seen a full year of operation, but they would be amply rewarded the following December. The workers seemed satisfied enough to await the end of a full twelve-month cycle, and they all could see that the company did well. Shortly after the New Year, the owner had purchased a new home, a villa in one of Shenyang's new executive housing complexes, and drove himself to work in his new Mercedes Benz S-600 automobile. He frequently hosted elaborate dinners in expensive restaurants and treated buyers and executives of retail chains to expensive parties. This encouraged the employees to work hard as they rationalized that such a lifestyle could only be supported by the company's excess profits, which they would all share when bonuses were paid at the end of the year.

Min Li soon achieved executive status, at least in title and responsibility, and often gave presentations to visiting buyers and communicated with various government agencies. She frequently visited the production floor and became familiar with the individual workers. Min Li knew all the workers by name, and could even relate to some of their personal stories. Because of her rapport with the workers, Min Li's boss added to her responsibility the job of intra-company communications. To make this job easier, Min Li created a small company newsletter in which she published company policies, revenue projects, and news of new markets. She also included tidbits on the lives of the workers, such as birth announcements, children passing the college entrance exam, and other personal information, all of which boosted morale and increased productivity.

In August, the company announced to its employees that they could purchase company stock. Most of the employees, seeing how well the company had grown, jumped at the opportunity to buy stock in the company that they helped build. At the time, the stock market was fairly new in China, and many Chinese talked about getting rich in stocks. Because they had not yet received their end of year profit share in the form of a bonus, those workers wanting to invest with no money of their own borrowed what money they could from friends and relatives, promising to pay the money back at the end of the year. Min Li also purchased stock with what money she had left from the sale of her office cleaning business, keeping ten thousand yuan in her savings account in case of emergencies.

December came to the jubilant employees of the Shenyang Electrical Appliance Company. All of them expected large payments as their share of the profit in the company's glorious beginnings, as well as quarterly dividends on the stock they had purchased only a few months before. As the days crept toward the end of the month, the employees grew restless, and many of them started to complain. They asked Min Li to find out when they would receive their bonuses.

Because Min Li had grown to managing the daily operations of the company, the owner rarely came to his office, leaving things up to Min Li. She would sometimes call him for decisions beyond her authority or responsibility, but she rarely saw the owner anymore, except on some rare occasion that the facility received a VIP visit. Min Li, just as anxious as the other employees, called Shu Feng Ming's cell phone and spoke to him.

"Is there problem you can't handle, Zhang Min Li?"

"Not quite yet," Min Li tactfully replied, "but the employees are growing somewhat restless with regard to their bonus payments."

'so?"

"Last year, they were promised payments on December first this year, but it is now the twentieth," Min Li explained.

"There's a problem with the audit."

"What kind of a problem?"

"I don't know. That's not my area of expertise. But the accountants tell me they have to make a few adjustments to the books before they can allow me to pay the bonuses."

"But the workers are growing impatient. How can I ask them to wait longer?"

"Ask them if they want to get all that they're entitled to. If we pay now, they'll get less money."

"They still won't be happy. Nobody received their profit shares last year, and they've been working very hard to ensure good profits since then."

"I don't understand your point," Shu Feng Ming said blandly.

"They will ask why the audit did not occur before the first," Min Li explained.

"We had unexpected expenses which needed to be calculated against net profits."

Min Li knew of no extraordinary expenses, especially since it had been one of her responsibilities to review and approve all expenditures, except for those expenses incurred by the owner himself.

"When shall I tell the employees to expect payment?"

"Before the end of the month."

Min Li then called a meeting of all the employees on the production floor and explained to them that they would receive their money at the end of the month. Nearly all of them expressed disappointment, some louder than others, but they all knew nothing could be done, that they were all, as usual, subject to the whims of those who controlled their lives. They accepted the bad news and went back to work, but few expended the same energy as they did before the meeting.

On the last day of the year, instead of going to their workstations on the production floor, the workers gathered in a large group outside the door to the administrative offices. Min Li, who had already been in the office for at least an hour, called Shu Feng Ming, but he did not answer his phone. She announced to the other employees that they should expect their money that day, as soon as the owner arrived, and that they should return to their workstations until then. She called again, but there was still no answer.

By eleven that morning, having fruitlessly called Shu Feng Ming all morning, Min Li took a taxi to his home to confront him. When she saw his car in the driveway, she assumed that he might have been out too late the night before, as was his habit, and he simply did not hear his telephone ringing. A servant answered the door.

'Shu Feng Ming is not home," the servant said, assuming Min Li was there to see him.

"Where is he?"

"Vancouver."

"What?"

"Vancouver, in Canada."

"Why is he in Vancouver? Why didn't I know he was going to Vancouver?"

"I'm sorry, but I can't answer those questions. He told me yesterday that he was going to Vancouver, and I am to stay here in the house until the trucks come to take his things."

"Take his things? You mean his furniture?"

"Yes."

"Why are they taking his furniture?"

"To ship to Vancouver. That's where he is."

"You mean he's not coming back?"

"Aren't you listening to me?" the servant asked sassily. "He lives in Vancouver now. He's not coming back."

Min Li realized that this could not have been a spur of the moment thing. A Chinese cannot simply pick up and move to Canada without prior planning. He would have needed a visa and a residency permit, which takes a few weeks to obtain. Then she realized that Shu Feng Ming had no plan to pay the employees their profit shares, so she hopped another taxi to the bank where the company kept its accounts. By a stroke of fortune, it was the same branch of the China Merchants Bank where Min Li kept her accounts for many years, so she and the branch manager were like old friends.

"Zhang Min Li, it's a pleasure to see you today," the manager greeted Min Li.

"Good morning, Lu Wei Yin. I'm here to check on some accounts."

"Your own or for Shenyang Electrical Appliances Company?"

"The latter. Would you please tell me the balances on the company's various accounts?"

"Certainly," the manager said as he pulled up a screen on his desktop computer. "That's strange."

"What's that?"

"All the accounts have been emptied as of, let me see, day before yesterday."

"All of them?"

"All of them."

"What about the payroll account?"

"Empty. Is there something else you need today?"

"How much do I have in my own account?"

"You have, umm, here we go, 14,390 yuan and some change."

Min Li thought she was going to throw up. Now she had to return to the factory and tell all the workers that they would receive no bonus and they would receive no dividends on the stocks they purchased in the company. Not only that, but they would receive no salary for December. Most of the employees had no money in the bank. Most of them had family, so their monthly expenses exceeded her own, and most received a salary of between five hundred and a thousand yuan a month. Next, she would go to the police and report She Feng Ming for embezzlement, but that turned out to be nothing but a waste of time. The police told her that since it was Shu Feng Ming's business, he couldn't be guilty of embezzling from himself. They also told her that the proper course of action is to file a claim with the Liaoning Bureau of Wage Enforcement, who would issue a finding and, if proven, would send a letter to Shu Feng Ming advising him that it is his duty to pay the money earned by his employees.

By three o'clock, Min Li left the office for the last time and took a taxi to her friend Tong Li Hua at her hair styling shop. Because it was Wednesday, there were few customers, giving Min Li the time to tell Tong Li Hua everything that had happened.

"Why did you let that happen?" Tong Li Hua asked her.

"I didn't let it happen. It just happened."

"You're too smart for something like that to happen to you. You must have been blinded by something. The whole thing sounded too good to be true. You should have known better."

Min Li thought about that for a moment and almost agreed with her friend. But the money was there. The company was doing well, it was filling orders, and money was flowing. She explained all this to Tong Li Hua.

"You looked at the money but not at the source. What did you know about Shu Feng Ming?"

"Not much."

"Because you didn't want to see him for what he was, a selfish rat who would just assume walk on the backs of those who worked for him without even being careful if he left bruises. You looked at the money."

Min Li had to agree.

"What are you going to do now?" her friend asked.

"I don't know. I need to work. I need to make money."

'start up another office cleaning business. It should be easier this time around because you already know the business so well and you would have no problem acquiring clients."

"I can't. When I sold the business I signed an agreement not to engage in the same business in Shenyang for at least ten years."

"You can work here doing facials when I'm busy."

"But you're never busy."

"That's true. But some day I will be."

"I can't wait for some day."

"Then leave China. Go to the Middle East. Like I told you before, you can make a lot money there doing facials."

"Why don't you go?"

"I have my business here."

"Are you making any money?"

"Not yet. Soon I hope."

"If you're not making money here, but you can make a lot of money in the Middle East, I don't see why you don't go to the Middle East. If you can make as much money as you think you can, you can save up, then come back here and invest in a better location."

"Actually, that's probably not a bad idea. We can go as a team. I'll do hair and you do facials. We'll get rich."

"How do we do this?" Min Li asked, genuinely interested, because she genuinely needed to earn money.

"I heard there was an agency that handles things like that down on 14th Wei Road across from the American consulate. It's in Heping District. Isn't that near where you live? We should at least go check it out."

"When do you want to go?"

"Tomorrow morning. I have a dye job at three, so we'll have to be back by then."

"Oh, you're busy," Min Li said using that kind of sarcasm that's safe with friends.

Eighteen

Life for Xiong Yong fell back into the routine when he returned to Panzhihua. Despite his low salary of nine hundred yuan a month, he lived well because he ate in the company dormitory and lived in a small room assigned to him in the worker's dormitory, all provided free to the company's employees. He had few expenses, other than frequent nights out on the town with his coworkers, which typically involved trips to inexpensive karaoke bars and heavy consumption of cheap beer.

Because he worked in the company's offices, most of Xiong Yong's coworkers were office workers of equal or higher status, and Xiong Yong's likable personality allowed him to quickly develop friendships with people of greater authority, some who were members of the Chinese Communist Party. His promotion to scheduling supervisor came as no surprise to anybody, and nobody questioned his admission into the Party, guaranteeing his future success. The promotion came with it three times his normal salary and a bonus, which he used to purchase a small apartment in town.

Chen Ruo Lan noticed Xiong Yong in the company cafeteria, where she often served him meals. She flirted with him whenever possible, gave him extra servings of food, and went out of her way to engage him in conversations. After Xiong Yong's promotion. Chen Ruo Lan redoubled her efforts. Soon thereafter, she managed to ask Xiong Yong how often he went to the movies.

"I've never been to the movies," he answered her.

"That's incredible. I thought everybody goes to the movies at least a few times by the time they're adults."

"I never thought about going. I've seen movies on television, so I figure it's all the same."

"You don't know what you're missing," Chen Ruo Lan offered. "The experience of being in a darkened theater in front of that huge screen with the sound all around you is absolutely spellbinding. You should go."

"It sounds good, but none of my friends would go for it. They're pretty stuck in their routines when they go out. If it interferes with drinking beer, they probably won't do it."

"Then take somebody else."

"Who would I take," Xiong Yong asked naively.

"Well, I'm free this evening. You can take me."

Xiong Yong agreed before he realized how nervous he was about it. He had never been with a woman socially before, and, except for his sisters, the only consortium he ever had with women were coworkers, waitresses, sales clerks, and karaoke bar hostesses, who did not have a good reputation. His having accepted Chen Ruo Lan's proposal to take her to the movies mildly shocked him, and he began walking away without saying another word.

"Don't we need to arrange a time?" Chen Ruo Lan asked.

"Oh yeah. Of course. When would you like me to come by to pick you up?"

"How about seven at the women's number two dorm? I'm on the third floor. Just ask the guard to ring up for me."

Xiong Yong looked at his watch and realized he only had a little over an hour before he was supposed to pick up Chen Ruo Lan. Instead of the city bus, he took a taxi home to save time, took a shower in his new apartment, threw on some clean clothes, and took a taxi to the company dormitory compound just inside the main gate of the company complex. As instructed, he told the guard on the first floor of Chen Ruo Lan's building who picked up an intercom telephone and asked for her by name. After a minute, the guard told Xiong Yong that she was on her way. Within another minute, he and Chen Ruo Lan walked away from the building together toward Xiong Yong's waiting taxi. As he entered the taxi, he noticed at least a dozen women on the third floor of the dormitory watching his every move, pointing, and talking to each other.

Xiong Yong and Chen Ruo Lan regularly saw each other after their first movie date, and she often accompanied him when he went out with his friends. Soon, Xiong Yong's friends began bringing their wives and girlfriends with them to the karaoke bars, changing the texture of Xiong Yong's social life. He was becoming more urbane, and because of the presence of women, conversations shifted from the ribald to the sophisticated, and the group interests changed accordingly. They educated each other on matters ranging from business management and finance to real estate and the arts.

Six months after their first date, Xiong Yong and Chen Ruo Lan married and she officially moved out of the women's dorm into his apartment. It was there, outside the earshot of their friends, that Chen Ruo Lan developed her strategies. As the supervisor of scheduling, Xiong Yong's next promotion made him the director of contracting, toward which he had been working since he first landed in the scheduling office. The opportunity finally arose when his predecessor died of a heart attack during lunch in the company cafeteria. Nobody thought to exam the food that he had eaten.

Life changed dramatically for Xiong Yong after he became the director of contracting. His primary responsibility was to determine the qualifications of contractors and negotiate contracts for the underground mining workforce. The company had an extensive network of mines, mostly underground, and on any given day had eighteen to twenty-two thousand miners employed. These all came from private labor contractors. Considering the number of miners, these contracts could be lucrative.

The contractors clamored after Xiong Yong constantly. In some ways, this was a good thing, because he was often treated to elaborate dinners in plush restaurants and given large cash gifts. But it was also problematic, because the contractors demanded so much of his time, he was unable to complete his work, which also included supervising the entire scheduling office. Chen Ruo Lan came up with the solution. Xiong Yong would only contract with those companies that had been previously vetted by an outside agency, and that agency, for a fee charged to the contractor, would recommend the labor contractor to Xiong Yong's office. But since no such agency then existed in Panzhihua, Chen Ruo Lan would start a company to serve as that agency. Xiong Yong approved and the next day Chen Ruo Lan rented office space downtown.

Thereafter, Xiong Yong's secretary would inform any contractor calling his office that he must first go through Chen Ruo Lan's contract placement agency. Chen Ruo Lan easily hooked the client by guaranteeing that, for a fee, she would obtain a contract with the Panzhihua Minerals Mining Company on behalf of the contractor. Thereafter, the money poured in, as Chen Rou Lan charged a large fee for various steps in the contracting process. There was a fee for an introduction to the director of contracting, there was a fee for assisting the contractor to negotiate a contract, and there was a fee paid at the time of signing the contract. Because the contracts only covered six month, twice a year the contractors had to deal with Chen Ruo Lan.

Gifts continued to flow to Xiong Yong, because the contractors knew that it was still up to him which contractor to use, and there were contractors waiting in the wings in the event an existing contract wasn't renewed. In addition to the agency fees paid to Chen Ruo Lan, contractors also gave her gifts in order to maintain their most favorable contractor status. Within a year of implementing this new agency system, Xiong Yong and Chen Rou Lan owned the top two floors of a high-rise fifteen-story apartment building in a gated executive complex.

For a year and a half, Xiong Yong's busy schedule prevented him from speaking to his sisters. After moving into his lavish new apartment, he called Min Li, telling her simply that he had been promoted and that he is living in a new home with his new wife. With regard to Min Li's life, she simply told him that things did not work out well with the Shenyang Electrical Appliances Company and that she was contemplating a different venture. She did not tell her brother that she was nearly out of money for fear of embarrassment. Her financial dilemma did not diminish her enthusiasm for her brother's success.

"I suppose Mama was right," she told him on the telephone.

"What do you mean?"

'she said that if we find her the perfect place after she died, things would change for our family."

"Are you saying the Zhang family crypt is the perfect place?"

"Absolutely not," she replied. 'mama isn't there."

'she's not there? But I saw Papa set her urn inside the crypt. I closed and locked the door with her in there."

"And then you gave me the key. Remember?"

"You moved her? When did you do that? To where?"

"Early the next morning, while you and Papa slept. Hai Tian and I went up to the crypt and we took her to Pàotǎ Shān. She's now in a small crypt on top of the big boulder."

Xiong Yong remembered the big boulder and how he and Min Li played there as children. "Did Mama know about that place?" he asked out of concern for his mother's wishes.

'she picked it out. She told me to bring her there and not to let Papa know. She used to play there as a child. We went and checked it out before she died. It's truly beautiful there now. She said that if we place here there, she would have good *feng shui* and things would change for the family." Min Li thought about what she had just said. Things did not work out so well for her, but they had for her brother.

"I suppose she was right," Xiong Yong conceded. "Things are going very well for me. You would hardly know that I come from a peasant family. So when will things change for the rest of us? For You?"

"One at a time, I guess. You're the first born," Min Li told her brother as a way of convincing herself.

"Next we'll have to hope that Hai Tian finds a husband."

'she's already married. She married that boy Yang Lin shortly before Mama passed away. You really have been out of touch, haven't you? In fact, she's due to have a baby soon."

"I really need to call more often," Xiong Yong said. "Now I feel guilty for ignoring things at home."

"Don't worry about it," Min Li consoled. 'so when do I get to meet your new wife?"

"We'll be coming home for the New Year holiday."

"I'll see you then."

When the telephone call ended, Min Li thought more about her mother and what she had said about good luck finally coming to her family. Since her mother died, Xiong Yong's career skyrocketed. Hong Qi's fields, which doubled in size with the passing of their mother, were more productive than her neighbors' were. Hai Tian happily lived with her new husband in Xiaguang and would soon have a baby, a son if the sonogram was accurate. Min Li thought about her own life. Her rapid ascent in in the Shenyang Electrical Appliances Company gave her hope for a happy life, but that hope was dashed when the owner ran off to Canada with all the company's money.

Xiong Yong thought about opening up banking accounts in Hong Kong or Macau as a way of hiding it from the inevitable prying eyes of the government.

Nineteen

Min Li and Tong Li Hua arrived by taxi to the barricaded 14th Wei Road right at eight the next morning. The People's Liberation Army Armed Police, tasked with providing external security for the American consulate, as well as the Japanese consulate next door, had placed cement barricades across the opening of the one-block section of 14th Wei Road that housed both consulates on its north side between South 3rd Jing Street and 14th Wei Road Gongxue (Alley). This was intended to prevent vehicular traffic on the street. Various visa assistance agencies and a western style bar lined the south side of 14th Wei Road.

On the street itself, between the American consulate and the visa assistance agencies, stood a large crowd of well over two hundred people, most huddled into small groups of friends and family members. Every few minutes, a Chinese woman appeared at the American consulate and announced a few names, and those people whose names were called hustled to the gate where they were given further instructions while family members and friends yelled good luck after them. And from time to time, people left the consulate compound, some with tears and others jubilant having just been granted a visa. The American consulate in Shenyang typically issued tourist, student, and business visas, and the agencies across the street assembled the application packets and coached the applicants on what to say during their visa interviews. The consulate did not issue residence visas, which had to be obtained more than fourteen hundred miles away in Guangzhou, no matter where a person might live in China.

The agencies, all private companies, helped people obtain visas for other countries, as well, but the most popular was America, and the agencies concentrated their efforts in that area. Tong Li Hua assured Min Li that these agencies could help them as they pushed their way through the crowd and walked up the front steps of the largest of the five agencies lining the street. Once inside, they witnessed a flurry of activity as office workers made photocopies of documents, others made passport photos, and others still gave briefings to clients. Near the back of the large room in which Min Li and Tong Li Hua stood was a door leading to a smaller room marked classroom. There, agency personnel gave classes to their clients on how to answer questions by the consulate officers. One man sat at a drafting table near the classroom and seemed to be busy creating documents. Min Li saw school transcripts, bank statements, and other such official documents, all pasted up and ready for photocopying. Another worker made copies, one at a time, and stamped them in red ink with various rubber stamps.

"It's too late to get in the consulate today," a woman in a grey pantsuit rudely informed Min Li and Tong Li Hua. "The consulate closes the gate at nine, and if they haven't called your name by then, you won't be able to get in."

"Excuse me?" Min Li asked.

"Are you trying to get into the American consulate?" the woman in the gray pantsuit asked.

"I'm afraid not," Min Li answered. "We wanted to learn about visas for various Middle East countries."

The woman in the gray pantsuit looked at both Min Li and Tong Li Hua, tilted her head to the side as if in serious thought, and said, "We can help you. Please, have a seat over here at my desk."

The three women took a seat, and grey pantsuit started talking again. "You'll make more money in Kuwait."

"Why is that?" asked Tong Li Hua.

"There are fewer Chinese women there. Most prefer to go to Dubai, Abu Dhabi, Qatar, or Bahrain. The police don't watch them as much there, and they can have an occasional drink at an international hotel where they serve non-Muslim foreigners. They don't have those in Kuwait, just coffee shops and shopping malls. So demand for Chinese women is higher there. Saudi Arabia is out. They won't even let you in unless you go there with a husband, and that's still in doubt."

'so how do we go to Kuwait?" Tong Li Hua pushed.

"It's a little complicated, but we can arrange everything. First you'll need a sponsor in Kuwait for a work visa. That'll be a Kuwaiti citizen who owns some kind of a business. Sometimes, the business is just a front for doing this or it could be somebody who really wants a Chinese woman to work for him, like maybe the owner of a Chinese restaurant. We send him copies of your passport and whatever else he needs, and he applies for a temporary work permit that allows you to get your visa. He does this for a fee, usually two hundred Kuwaiti Dinar."

"How much is that?" Min LI asked.

"I have a chart here, let me see," the woman said as her finger ran down a list of figures on a piece of paper taped to her desk. "That's seven hundred American dollars, which today is about 5,817 renminbi. Then there's our fee for putting all this together, ten thousand renminbi."

"That's pricey," Tong Li Hua exclaimed.

"Do you have any idea how much the average Chinese woman in Kuwait sends home each month?" asked the other woman. "Of course you don't. But I know one woman from Dalian sending no less than 70,000 yuan each month. I'll give you her contact information in Kuwait. She should be able to show you the ropes."

"We want to work in a beauty parlor," Min Li said. "I'll do facials and my friend here cuts and styles hair. What kind of money will we be able to make?"

"Right. Most of my Kuwait-bound clients are usually sponsored by the owner of a beauty shop. That's how Lan Lan went. That's the lady from Dalian. She started out in a beauty shop doing facials. She's not doing that now, but you have to start somewhere."

"What other expenses are there?" Min Li asked.

"You'll need to fly to Guangzhou and wait there for your visa, which will come in two to three weeks. You'll pay seven thousand yuan for room and board there."

"Why so much?"

"The way station in Guangzhou is part of our network. We have expenses that I can't go into. And of course, you'll stay in a home in Kuwait where you will share cooking duties with other Chinese women. The people there pay for the food and provide you comfortable sleeping arrangements."

"How much is that?"

"Two hundred fifty Kuwaiti Dinars a month."

"That's over seven thousand yuan," Min Li said, after roughly calculating the exchange rate in her head.

"Kuwait is not a cheap place to live. That is why you'll make so much money there. You can stay in Shenyang and pay four hundred a month, but you won't make any money, or you can go to Kuwait, pay seven thousand a month, but send home seventy thousand. Your choice. Oh, and you'll need a passport, so if you're thinking about doing this, go ahead and apply for your passports. We can help you with that too."

The conversation with the lady in the grey pantsuit left both Min Li and Tong Li Hua a little stunned from the sticker shock. They had no idea before what kind of money would be involved in this hair-brained idea of theirs. They thanked the lady for her time and said that they would think about it and get back to her later, then left the building.

Tong Li Hua mentioned she needed to use the restroom, so Min Li waited for her at the top of the steps leading to the agency, about eight feet above street level. From there she could see over the thinning crowd between her and the American consulate, which caused her to once again think about her former American boyfriend and almost fiancé, Peter North. Now she wished she had married him so many years ago. She'd be living in America, maybe with children, and she could have visited her grandparents regularly who lived in Fremont, California, instead of seeing them on their two visits back to China shortly before her Ye Ye passed away from a heart attack. She wondered if Peter was still teaching and if he still looked the same.

She tried to erase these useless, unproductive thoughts from her mind by looking slightly down the street to the Japanese consulate. No crowd milled about in front of the Japanese consulate, just one foreigner walking past on her side of the street carrying a camera. She only saw him from the backside, but his size, shape, and hair color reminded her of Peter. So she watched him some more. He stopped walking as he arrived near the center of the Japanese consulate's compound and walked to the middle of the street, his camera at the ready; then he took a few pictures. Just as he clicked his third photo, two members of the PLA Armed Police came out of the guard booth at the gate and chased after the foreigner with the camera. They yelled at him to stop, but he ran down 14th Wei Road Gongxue, successfully avoiding the confiscation of his camera.

Min Li thought how Peter might have done the same thing, taking photos of things he should not have, thumbing his nose at the Chinese police. She didn't know that it was Peter. He had returned to China for another year of teaching on a leave of absence from his regular teaching job in America. He taught at a university in a nearby city but came to Shenyang once a month with two purposes, to buy western food items to supplement his diet and to find Min Li. He had no idea where to look, but he thought it was worth a shot anyway.

Tong Li Hua interrupted Min Li's daydreaming about Peter by rejoining Min Li outside the door to the agency. They walked down the steps into the crowd on the street below them, finding it easier to wend their way through the crowd that remained, to find a taxi on South 3rd Jing Street. Peter reached the sidewalk as their taxi pulled away. He wasn't certain, but he could have sworn one of the women getting into the taxi was Min Li. Another taxi did not appear for more than two minutes, but by then, Min Li, if that was Min Li, was long gone.

"Do you have that kind of money?" Tong Li Hua asked Min Li in the taxi.

"Hardly, and even if I did it's just too much of a risk. I don't know if I can recoup that kind of money working in Kuwait."

"The lady at the agency said that many Chinese women go there, make good money, and send it back to China. That could just as easily be us," Tong Li Hua argued.

"We don't know if it's true. We only know what the lady said. How do we know she wasn't stretching the truth just to get our money?"

"I suppose we don't," conceded Tong Li Hua. "It'd be nice if we could find out if it's true or not."

"We need to talk to somebody who has actually done it. I really worry about getting someplace like the Middle East and not having the money to come back. Besides, what do we really know about Kuwait?"

'she mentioned somebody from Dalian. Lan Lan, I think she said her name was," offered Tong Li Hua.

"Lan Lan isn't a real name. It's only a nickname, and you know that. What's her family name? How would we contact her? Is that somebody we could trust?"

"Well, let's not put it out of our minds yet. We'll look into it further and see what we can find out," said Tong Li Hua. "Hey, did you see that foreign man running after us before we got into the taxi?"

"What foreign man?"

"He was kind of tall, blond hair, curly and longish. Handsome for a foreigner. He might have been American."

"Why would you think he was an American?"

"Because we were in front of the American consulate."

"That makes since, but why would he be running after us?"

"I don't know. I've never seen him before. Maybe he just wanted to meet Chinese women."

"He ran through a crowd of Chinese people to reach only two women getting into a taxi to meet Chinese women? That's absurd," Min Li chided her friend. "He could have stopped and talked to all sorts of Chinese women standing in that crowd." Min Li wondered if that wasn't Peter she saw earlier after all. "Drive, please take us back to where you picked us up."

The taxi returned to the corner of South 3rd Jing St. and 14th Wei Road, letting Min Li and her friend out on the side opposite the barricade. They walked around, looked in the crowd, and even walked down to the other end of the block past the Japanese consulate. Min Li saw no foreigner described by Tong Li Hua. She saw plenty of foreigners exiting the American consulate, but none of them matched the description. She felt a sudden yearning that she hadn't felt since she and Peter decided to end their relationship on practical grounds. *I'm too Chinese*, Min Li said to herself.

After looking around for twenty minutes with a perplexed Tong Li Hua in tow, Min Li finally gave up. She decided to treat her friend to lunch as a way of apologizing for wasting her time. They caught another taxi and took it to a Sichuan restaurant in her old neighborhood, Min Li explaining to Tong Li Hua that she knew this restaurant had excellent hot pot. However, she actually chose the restaurant because it is where she and Peter went on their first date so many years ago. She secretly hoped that Peter would be there.

Twenty

As soon as she and Tong Li Hua entered the restaurant, Min Li realized her silliness. Expecting Peter to be in this restaurant more than fifteen years later defied logic and common sense. Nevertheless, the restaurant immediate evoked fond memories, which pleased Min Li with her decision to go there. While they waited for a seat, Min Li observed that the decor had changed little since her last visit. Three fake tree trunks, complete with high branches along the ceiling and dusty plastic leaves, separated the dining area into sections. Most of the lunch rush had subsided, and the remaining diners produced a dull cacophony as people slurped the remaining fragments of their hot pots, and clinked near-empty beer bottles against dishes on the tables as their hands grew heavy and their voices slowed to the effects of the afternoon's indulgences.

Three servers, all young women that looked barely to be out of middle school, each dressed in a tight fitting silk chi pao, circulated throughout the restaurant with three-shelved, stainless steel serving carts. They delivered boiling hot water for the hot bots on the tables occupied by customers, various dishes of uncooked prepared meats and vegetables, and more beer. These young girls would not speak unless responding directly to a customer and giggled on cue when a man said something untoward, which the overindulgence of beer would allow him to do. Other young girls, dressed in black slacks and white button-down shirts, cleared dirty dishes from the tables.

"Huānyíng guānglín, Welcome," said a women about Min Li's age, dressed in a long red chi pao. "Two for lunch?"

"If you don't mind, we'd like to sit near the window."

The hostess led Min Li and Tong Li Hua to a table framed by the large plate glass window that fronted the restaurant while handing them some menus. Min Li often sat at this very table with Peter. Businesses vied for foreigners' patronage, and liked to boast in their advertising how foreigners enjoyed their business, sometimes taking photos of unsuspecting foreigners and placing them in newspaper advertisements. When she used to come to this restaurant with Peter, they were always sat in the table in the middle of the window if it was available so that passers-by could see Peter. Inevitably, whenever Peter and Min Li ate there, the restaurant became busier.

The hostess returned to the table and addressed Min Li. "I know you. You used to come here a long time ago."

"Yes, as a matter of fact, I came here many times, but it's been fifteen or sixteen years since."

"You came with some foreigner, an American I think."

"Right again. That was Peter North. We were almost married."

"Why did you marry him?"

Min Li thought this question to be rather rude, but she answered anyway. "We just decided it wouldn't be practical."

"Practical? Are you kidding? If you married him, you'd probably be living in America now getting rich."

"I don't know about being rich, but at least you're half right."

"What do you mean? Everybody is rich in America."

"Not everybody."

'Really? Didn't you see that documentary on CCTV 1?" The hostess was referring to the main news channel of China Central Television.

"Which documentary? There are so many," Tong Li Hua asked, wanting not to be left out of the conversation.

"They were trying to show how poor people in America lived, you know, trying to defeat everybody's claim that America is such a wonderful country. They showed these large apartment buildings in Chicago that they called "projects." They interviewed some of the residents who claimed that the government didn't do anything for them and how they had to live so poorly."

"Yeah, so?" Min Li asked half-interested.

"But the government paid their rent, gave them money for food and utilities, and the all had cars and television sets?"

"What's your point?"

"Our government doesn't even do that, and we're supposed to be a socialist country. You're not poor, yet you can't afford a car."

"But we both have a television," Tong Li Hua chimed in.

'so the poor people in America are better off than the working class in China. You should have gone to America. I bet you wish you had."

Min Li gave that some thought. There are many reasons why she should have married Peter, and none of them had to do with owning a car or a television set. Peter use to say that life should be about quality of experience, not quantity of electronics. She barely understood this before, and simply assumed that Peter was somehow justifying his having taken a teaching job in China that paid less than four hundred dollars a month instead of one in America that paid three thousand dollars a month. He also said that there's time for making money later, but when you start making money, you stop experiencing the world around you. There's too much of the world to see, and once you start making mortgage payments and keeping up with the Joneses, all you can be is a tourist, and tourists see nothing. To this date, she had no idea what a mortgage or a Joneses were, and she made a mental note to look them up.

'shall we order?" Tong Li Hua asked, breaking Min Li's reverie.

They ordered spinach, bok choy, tofu squares, pork strips, cabbage, and shiitake mushrooms in a half and half pot, as well as a pot of green tea. The pot, a round bottomed soup pot, came atop an electric hotplate that brought the already hot water to a soft boil and was divided into two halves with an 's' shaped divider, giving the appearance of a ying and yang symbol. The water on one half was flavored with red chili oil and other spices. The other half was a week chicken broth with a small slice of sea cucumber sitting at the bottom.

The food came on one of the three-shelved carts. While one of the young silk-clad servers set the various dishes containing the raw food on the table, another served them tea, each being poured half a cup, before the server set the teapot on the table. Tong Li Hua began tossing ingredients into the spicy side of the hot pot, while Min Li studied the array of food on the table.

"We forgot to order noodles," Min Li said.

"Do you want noodles?"

"No, but we're supposed to order noodles."

"You don't always have to do what you're supposed to do, you know," her friend said.

"Traditions are made for a reason."

"No they're not. People rely on traditions as an excuse, so they can do things without having to explain why. If you want noodles, order some."

"I don't want noodles."

"I don't either. Tell you what, let's toss caution to the wind and not order noodles."

"Whatever you say," Min Li said, obviously beaten by logic.

"That's why you don't live in America," Tong Li Hua said.

"What do you mean?"

"Noodles."

"I don't get it."

"If you weren't so worried about what you were supposed to do, you would have married Peter North and you would be living in America. You chose your life the same as if you order hot pot. You don't have to have noodles. It's a pity you didn't know that before Peter North left China."

'so I ruined my chance at happiness because of noodles?"

'something like that."

"I suppose it's too late to stop ordering noodles now."

"No it's not. You're what, 34, 35?"

'something like that," Min Li answered, somewhat sarcastically.

"You still have many years ahead of you. It's not too late to stop ordering noodles."

'maybe you're right, but it's so hard to try something new."

"Who are you kidding? Did you forget what brought you to Shenyang? Don't tell me you weren't afraid to try new things."

"I had no choice. It was either start a new life here or marry that rotten Cao Hong Bo and live in misery for the rest of my life in Shangguang."

"But the fact is you came to Shenyang. You didn't marry Cao Hong Bo. You didn't order noodles, then. Do you think life only gives you a one-time shot at changing your destiny?"

'maybe you're right. But making major life changes can be so risky."

"What do you have to risk now?"

"Okay, you win. But I'm not about to traipse off to Kuwait today, and I don't think you are. Let's see if I can't make a go of things again here in Shenyang," Min Li reasoned.

"Fine with me. Maybe we can both make a change without going to Kuwait. Why don't you and I form a partnership?"

"A partnership? You mean with your beauty shop?"

"That's what I mean. I'm really good at cutting hair, styling it, coloring it, and all those things. You're half-good at doing facials, and you can still learn more things. But you are good at managing a business. If we work together, I'm certain you'll be able to help my business grow so that each of our shares would be more than I'm making now. What do you think?"

"I like it. When can we start?"

"Today. I've got an appointment to cut somebody's hair at three. I'll tell her how much more beautiful she would be if you did her facial. We'll take it from there."

"If I'm going to be your partner, we're going to have to move your shop?"

"But it's so cheap where it is. I can't afford higher rent."

"We can if we move. You have hardly any business. We need to be somewhere with a high volume of foot traffic, but not any foot traffic. It has to be where people walk by with money in their pocket in a place where they expect to pay more."

"Where do you suggest?"

"Over on Xiaodong Road near the big Walmart. There's a mall there with many high-end shops. The only people who shop there are people who can afford to. We set up shop there, in or near the mall, and if we have high visibility, we'll do well. You might even need to hire more people to work for you."

"I like it, but I don't have the money for the lease," Tong Li Hua argued.

"We're partners. What money I have left will cover it. I'm certain this will work. Trust me."

Twenty One

The next day found Min Li hunting for shop space in or near the new indoor mall on Xiaodong Road, about a block from one of Shenyang's Walmart stores. She determined the suitability of this area because the large parking structure at Walmart attracted affluent buyers, those with cars, and these people did not bargain shop. People with cars have status, and people with status show it off. That means they will only shop in high-end stores and will not embarrass themselves by negotiating a better price.

The four-story mall hosted a variety of shops and restaurants, all brand names, and despite the fact that most items sold in the shops were made in China, customers paid premium prices, even more than if they purchased the same items in America. A hair cutting shop already occupied space in the basement level, but that didn't deter Min Li. That shop hosted a team of youngish women, barely in their late teens and early twenties, and displayed large posters of modern-coiffed young men and women. They charged a hundred yuan for a simple haircut, five times more than the average shop in other neighborhoods, but its clientele were young upwardly mobiles and children of people with money. Min Li could see that the average, middle-aged Chinese with status did not go near this shop, which was the demographic that Min Li and Tong Li Hua wanted to target.

A recently empty space stood on the third floor, between an Esprit women's clothing store and a Polo store. Min Li knew this location would serve them well, because it could attract both men and women if they marketed it correctly. She looked at many other locations, but decided this one had advantages over the others, mainly because of its location between expensive clothing shops and because it had running water and two restrooms. She signed the one-year lease, paid the deposit and first month's rent, and immediately sat out to buy furnishings for the shop.

  Min Li and Tong Li Hua argued about how the shop should be decorated, Tong Li Hong wanting to create a deep red motif, but Min Li convinced her that they should actually create two motifs, one to appeal to women and the other two men, joined by a common theme. The shop wasn't large, but they could make it look as though it were two shops. The women's shop would have a pink and light grey plan with pictures of expensive homes to appeal to the feminine but well-grounded woman with taste, while the men's side would be painted light blue and light grey with posters of expensive cars. They would install two sinks and two chairs on each side, all black, as well as a hair washing station in the back to be shared by both sides. The sinks would be installed in the center of the room against a wall built to divide the space into two section.

  They also decided to carry an inventory of expensive cosmetics which they would use on their customers and offer for sale at inflated prices, for both men and women, including skin conditioners, anti-aging cream, night creams, and blemish camouflage products. And they definitely need a large stock of hair dye, black and auburn for women and black for men. Men, especially men in positions of importance, found it important to retain a youthful look by keeping their hair black.

  During the nearly four weeks it took to get the shop ready to open, Min Li created signs for the shop windows to announce the grand opening of the most exclusive hair styling shop in Liaoning

Province. She had no idea whether or not similar shops even existed, although she was sure they did. That didn't matter. The window posters also invited future patrons to apply for their V.I.P. membership now while they were available.

This seemed to be the most effective of her marketing gimmicks. People could pay for a V.I.P. membership for the low cost of five hundred yuan, and that would allow them to have priority appointments and preferential treatment while visiting the shop. Such services would include free tea service, free beauty consultations, and advance notice on new products and services. None of this could be worth five hundred yuan, but people were willing to shell out the extra cash in order to be considered special. It gave them more status. By the time they opened the shop, Min Li had already sold more than a hundred V.I.P. memberships, enough to cover the rent for six months. She also set up five appointments for opening day.

Before their grand opening, Min Li and Tong Li Hua hired two more hair cutters, both fairly young but not novices. Tong Li Hua would cut and style hair for the V.I.P. customers, as well as any customer who paid a premium price for the shop's "expert." The other two stylists, Tianshi and Xixi, provided 'standard" services and would primarily work on the men's side of the shop. Min Li would work the front counter and continue to provide facials and cosmetic consultations, although she wasn't quite sure what that meant.

The grand opening of Gaoji Meirong (Premium Beauty) Salon came off without a hitch, and the shop remained busy throughout the day. Women who wanted a premium hairstyle waited for their turn between scheduled appointments, and those who were less finicky allowed Tianshi or Xixi to cut their hair. They did this without much of an investment in advertising, other than the posters that promoted the shop in the days leading up to the grand opening. Min Li sold another thirty or so V.I.P. memberships throughout the day, two to customers that scheduled for the following week.

The shop saw its first male customer after six that evening, then two more before closing at nine. None of them purchased V.I.P. memberships, but two promised they would return for their next haircut.

After a month, the business was well on its way toward reimbursing Min Li for her initial investment, allowing her to breathe easier knowing that the last of her money was finding its way back to her. She hoped to recoup her entire investment within six months or so, but it looked as though her target date would be sooner.

As the capital of Liaoning Province, its proximity to deepwater ports in Dalian and Jinzhou, and its heavy industry, many foreigners make Shenyang their home. This also explains why several nations have consulates in Shenyang, and many foreigners visit Shenyang throughout the year, usually for business purposes. Shenyang's citizens often see foreigners. Many are simply English teachers from English speaking countries. The teachers wouldn't visit Gaoji Meirong Salon simply because of the cost. But other foreigners would, especially those who received salaries in their home countries. Although the services at Gaoji Meirong Salon were cost prohibitive to the average Chinese citizen, those in government, factory owners and managers, foreign diplomats, and most foreigners found the costs to be less than that to which they were accustomed in their own countries, especially considering the level of service. So Gaoji Meirong Salon included many foreigners on its client list.

Having taught English at a local elementary school several years before, Min Li often served as the interpreter for the foreign guests, few of whom could not speak English. Tong Li Hua studied English in middle school, as was required of all Chinese students, but she could never remember more than a few words, certainly not enough to understand foreigners speaking English, let alone have a conversation in English. Tianshi and Xixi also studied English in middle school. Their vocabulary exceeded that of Tong Li Hua only because it had not been so long since they studied it in school. But they couldn't converse either. So Min Li needed to be in the shop whenever foreigners were present, if nothing more than to prevent mistakes resulting from a failure to communicate.

After being opened for business for nearly a year, Gaoji Meirong Salon had its first encounter with Arabic customers. A man in his mid-forties entered the shop with three women in tow. He wore a long white *dishdasha*, a long-sleeved shirt-like garment that nearly reached the floor, and a white scarf, or *gutra*, over his head. Each of the women wore black *abayas*, gowns that covered their other clothes leaving only their head and hands visible, as well as hijabs, black scarves that covered their heads, except for their faces. Each of them, the man and the women, wore expensive Italian shoes. The only accessory on the man was a Rolex watch on his left wrist, but the women wore heavy gold bracelets, some encrusted with emeralds, rubies, and sapphires.

The man stopped at the counter while the women waited quietly behind him. Although he could see Min Li approaching from the back of the shop, he banged on the service bell anyway.

"Huanying guanlin," Min Li greeted the four. 'may I help you?"

"Each of these three ladies require your services, I will come back for them in two hours. I trust they will be finished by then."

"Certainly, sir. Will you need our services today?"

"Don't be silly. Do I look like a woman?"

"Of course not, sir. But perhaps you would like your haircut."

"Not by women, thank you. I will be back in two hours. Good day."

Slightly ruffled by the man's rudeness, Min Li turned to the three women and asked, "Do one of you speak English?"

"I do," responded the youngest of the three who stood behind the other two. She appeared to be around twenty years old. "I am Aliyah."

"And the others?"

"Only Arabic, I'm afraid. This is Huda," Aliyah said pointing to the lady who stood nearest the counter, "and this is Nora." Huda seemed to be nearly as old as the man who brought the women in, and Nora might have been only four or five years older than Aliyah.

'very well, what will the three of you need today?"

"Huda needs to have her hair styled so that it looks a little more modern. But more importantly, she has been fighting some grey hair making her feel old. We think that her mood will improve if you can make her hair all black again. Nora and I only need our hair trimmed and styled, and all three of us would like a facial and make-up. We will be attending a formal dinner at the French consulate this evening."

Min Li assigned Huda to Tong Li Hua, Nora to Xixi, and Aliya to Tianshi. Before sitting in their assigned chairs, each of the women removed their hijabs and abayas, revealing for the first time their expensive Pierre Cardin dresses. Min Li assumed correctly that they did not purchase these dresses at the Wu Ai wholesale market, famous for its designer knock-offs.

Min Li couldn't contain her curiosity, so while Aliyah waited for Huda and Nora to have their hair washed, Min Li started chatting.

"Was that your father who brought you to the shop?"

"No. My father lives in Kuwait. That was my husband."

Min Li wanted to say something about the age difference between Aliyah and her husband, but thought better of it. Such marriages occur frequently in China between rich men who take on young wives. 'so who are Huda and Nora?"

"Those are my sister wives."

'sister wives?"

'my husband's other wives," Aliyah answered matter-of-factly.

'really? I've never seen such a thing. We don't have that in China."

"It was common before 1949," Aliyah responded.

"This is true. Many men had more than one wife, and some may have even had concubines."

"Allah does not allow concubines," Aliyah lectured. "A man may have no more than four wives. I'm Abdul-Aziz's fourth wife. I am his last so long as we all remain alive."

"There are only three here."

"Abdul-Aziz asked his third wife, Mariam, to remain behind to care for the children and the servants."

"How many children does he have?"

"I have not yet given him children, but Huda has given him three daughters. Nora is his favorite wife, because she bore four sons for Abdul-Aziz, as well as a daughter. Mariam has one son and one daughter, but she is again pregnant with another son. I hope to give him many sons."

"This is quite fascinating. I've never spoken to anybody who shared a husband with other wives. How do you feel about that?"

"I don't understand your question. How should I feel?"

"I think most women would be jealous of the other wives. Are you ever jealous of your sister wives?"

"Of course not. I am a lucky woman because Abdul-Aziz chose me to be his last wife. He can have no more after me. She who would be his fifth wife would be jealous of me."

"I suppose it depends on what a person is used to. You said you have servants. China these days has few servants."

"That is because you are a nation of servants."

"I must say I am somewhat offended by that, but I suppose I should gauge your perspective. I'm sure you didn't intend to be rude. What do you mean by saying that we are a nation of servants?"

"Do you own this shop?" Aliyah asked.

"I own half of it. The lady washing Huda's hair owns the other half."

"Then you are the servants of your customers. Although you are the owners, you work the same as your workers doing lowly things. That would never happen in Kuwait. An owner of a business must not stoop to the level of working like a servant. In our beauty parlors, the owner will never touch the dirty hair of another person; he has servants for that. And your farmers, do they farm the land themselves or do they have servants to do that?"

"I come from a farming family. My family had a plot of land that my mother and my sisters farmed while I was in school. They didn't have servants. They had people who helped, especially at harvest time, other farmers, but my family helped them. Nobody in my home village has servants."

'so I am correct."

"Are you saying that people who work in Kuwait are servants?"

"In the sense that they work here. But no Kuwaiti is a servant. Our work is different. We are the administrators, the managers, the supervisors. Some choose work to make a living, but such work is dignified, such as lawyers or doctors."

"What about your teachers."

"A true Kuwaiti would not work in a school unless he or she were a director of that school. We have foreigners to serve our children in that way."

'so even your teachers are servants?"

"Yes, unless they are university professors, then we prefer Kuwaitis for that. It is much more dignified."

"I used to teach here in China. I taught English in an elementary school."

"You could work in a school in Kuwait, but I doubt you could ever teach there."

"Why not?"

"You are Chinese. Chinese women are usually employed as housemaids, or nannies. I have seen some working as nurses in the hospitals or in dental clinics and such."

"What about in beauty shops?"

"You could work there. I have seen Chinese women working in beauty spas. Some do hair, and I know one employed as a masseuse."

"Do the men in that shop ever get the wrong idea about the masseuse?"

"Impossible. Only women can go to that beauty spa. Only women can touch other women, whether it is to give a haircut or a massage. Men have to go to their barbershops where men cut their hair."

"What about massages?"

"They have these places called "health spas" where men like to frequent, but I think they are unseemly."

"What about your husband? Does he ever need a therapeutic massage?"

"He has four wives."

"Do women own businesses in Kuwait?"

"Certainly. A woman may do with her money whatever she wishes. Many invest in businesses and manage them. In fact, Huda has recently talked about buying a beauty spa, one with twenty employees doing many special services, haircutting, pedicures and manicures, massages, facials, waxing, everything."

"What is stopping her from doing it?"

"The place is poorly managed and many of the workers are doing work outside the shop on their own time. Huda thinks they might be providing private services for men, and that could get the owner in trouble. She is looking for a new manager to take over from the start and get things in shape. She is impressed with your operation here, small as it is. I will tell her to hire you."

"Hire me? You must be joking. I have this place to run. I can't give it up to move to another country."

'maybe you can go for six months, then return here. I'm sure your partner can live without you for such a short period of time."

'maybe. But it is a big decision. We're just now running in the black here, and I want to make sure it stays this way."

"Are you afraid to see another part of the world?"

Min Li thought about that. Often she wondered if she didn't marry Peter simply because she was afraid to leave China. If she were to take up this opportunity to work in Kuwait, which would be only for six months, she could learn more about the world. It might even be exciting.

"Do you want me to talk to Huda for you?"

"I don't know. Isn't there a war going on there?"

"Not since 1991 when the Iraqi army was ousted by the Americans."

"Next door in Iraq."

"We don't go to Iraq. You are safe in Kuwait."

"What about the way people dress? Do I have to wear one of those black robes?"

"In Kuwait, women have the option of wearing an *abaya* and a hijab. Many women don't. Those who do wear them are either forced by their husbands, or they wear them as a badge of honor as Kuwaiti women and to distinguish ourselves from those women who are not Kuwaiti. You would not be expected to dress like us, just so long as you dress conservatively, that you do not bare your legs, shoulders, or chest. You will hardly notice the difference."

"Anything else about living there?"

"You will enjoy it. There are Chinese restaurants, coffee shops, and all the other conveniences of western civilization."

"I'll still have to think about it. We don't even know whether Huda will buy the business or not."

'she can make her decision knowing that she has an effective manager who can do what the business needs."

"In that case, you talk to Huda and let her know I'm interested. If nothing else, it could be an exciting change of routine. If things don't work out, I can come back home where I still have a business. I'm sure Tong Li Hua can handle things without me for a few months."

The three Kuwaiti customers chatted amongst themselves while sipping tea and were donning their black abayas and hijabs when Abdul-Aziz returned to reclaim them. Before they left, Huda, through Aliyah, told Min Li that she wanted Min Li to run the beauty spa in Kuwait, and she needed Min Li's assurances that she would do so before she went through with the purchase. Min Li couldn't commit at the moment, but they agreed to exchange email addresses and telephone numbers and would discuss it further by long distance. Although Min Li had an email address, she hadn't used it for anything and couldn't remember it, so she had to look it up on the shop's recently installed computer through the Chinese Yahoo username recovery routine. This took a few minutes, which gave Huda and her husband a chance to inspect the shop's facilities, making mental notes for when they would negotiate the purchase of the beauty spa in Kuwait. Huda, through Aliyah, offered to send more information on the shop, such as photos, diagrams, various accounting documents, over the next few days via email.

When the Kuwaitis left, Min Li sat stunned, wondering how much could happen so fast. She thought about how she could make one decision that might affect the rest of her life. She wondered if this was something she should do, or maybe should not do, or may she was thinking about doing it simply for the sake of the experience. She wondered if her way of life would be changed forever or if she could recover her way of life if things didn't work out to her satisfaction. Tong Li Hua helped her decide.

"Do it and stop thinking about the noodles."

"What about the shop here? I really need to be here helping you," Min Li argued.

"Don't you trust me?"

"Of course I do."

"We'll be here when you get back. It's only for six months. Besides, you can always come home early if things don't work out. Go do something exciting with your life for once."

"Would you do it?"

"In a heartbeat."

Twenty Two

Min Li waited a week after the Kuwaitis left to check her email. To her surprise, she had several emails from Aliyah, most with messages from Huda. Attachments to the emails included a floor plan for the shop in Kuwait that Huda considered buying, as well as photographs of the shop and surrounding businesses, a list of current employees and their responsibilities, and financial ledgers and journals. Much of it confused her because so many of the documents were written in Arabic. But she had become accustomed to dealing with similar financial documents from her time with the Shenyang Electrical Appliances Company.

In short order, Min Li convinced herself that she could improve the net revenue of the beauty spa by applying the same model she had used for the shop in Shenyang. She sent Aliyah an email telling her so and that she was ready to venture to Kuwait to give it a go. Aliyah then informed her of the steps involved in traveling to Kuwait from China.

Min Li needed a passport, which seemed easy enough, after which her sponsor, either Huda or her husband, Abdul-Aziz, would sponsor her for a visa and a work permit, but first she would need to sign a contract. The contract came with the same email in two versions, English and Arabic. According to the English version of the contract, her sponsor intended to hire her as the manager for the beauty spa, pay her a salary of five hundred Kuwaiti dinars a month, provide her with free housing equal to that which she was accustomed in her home country or better, pay for round trip airfare to and from Kuwait from Shenyang, and, after three months, gave her the option of terminating the contract for any reason without penalty. The contract was for a term of five years, which struck Min Li as excessive, but with the cancellation provision after three months, she did not see it as a major problem. After all, they had previously spoken about her doing it for six months. When she asked Aliyah about the five-year term, Aliya said that it was necessary in order to obtain the work permit and residency in Kuwait.

The most attractive part of the contract was the salary. Five hundred Kuwaiti dinars, Min Li calculated, equaled 1,750 American dollars, or 14,525 renminbi. Considering the fact that the average Shenyang resident earned about 500 renminbi each month, the difference was astronomical. Min Li and Tong Li Hua paid themselves more than that, 2,500 renminbi per month. So by going to Kuwait, Min Li's income would multiply by almost six times. The fact that her employer would provide her housing and meals would give Min Li an opportunity to save a great deal of money despite the higher cost of consumer goods in Kuwait.

Min Li agreed to the terms, signed the contract in the spaces provided on both the English and Arabic versions, and went to a computer shop where she could scan the document and email it back. She told Aliyah that she would apply for her passport as soon as possible, but that she didn't know how long that process would take. Min Li took a taxi from the computer shop to the People's Republic of China Ministry of Public Security offices to apply for a passport, where she filled out the necessary forms and handed them to a clerk with her national identification card.

"Do you have your *hukou*?" the clerk asked.

"Why do you need my *hukou*? You have my national I.D. Isn't that enough?"

"Our policy requires that you provide a *hukou*, your family registration."

"Frankly, I don't have a *hukou*. I've lived in Shenyang for eighteen years, and nobody ever asked me for one."

"Where is your *hukou*?"

"I never applied for my own *hukou*. I suppose I'm still listed on my father's *hukou*."

"Then you can bring us his *hukou*."

"But he doesn't live in Shenyang. He lives in Shangguang, about a four-hour train ride from here."

"Oh, so you are not a Shenyang resident."

"I am. I've been here many years like I just said."

"But your *hukou* is somewhere else."

'Shangquan."

"Yes, Shangguang. Where is that?"

"It's near Huludao."

"You're living in Shenyang illegally. I'm surprised you have gotten away with it all these years. You will have to apply for your passport in Huludao. Be sure to have your *hukou* with you when you go."

"You're joking."

"Officers of the Ministry of Public Security do not joke. Please step out of line. I cannot help you in this office."

Min Li never realized that living in Shenyang could be a problem. Now, just to apply for a passport, she had to return to Shangguang, obtain her father's *hukou*, then go to Huludao to apply for a passport. Then she would have to return to Huludao when it was ready. She called Hong Qi to explain the problem to her.

"You're going where?"

"Kuwait."

"Where is that?" Hong Qi asked.

"It's in the Middle East on the Persian Gulf, tucked between Saudi Arabia, Iraq, and Iran."

"How long will you be there?"

'maybe about six months, more or less, depending on how things work out. But I need your help."

"What do you want me to do?"

"When will you see Papa again?"

"I see him almost every day. I go over there to cook his dinner. Sometimes he has a neighbor lady do it for him. Why?"

"I need the *hukou* so I can apply for a passport."

"Why don't you just ask him to send it to you?"

"I don't want the confrontation. Can't you just pick it up today, and I'll stop by your place tomorrow to pick it up from you?"

"That seems like such a nuisance having to come here to Shangguang. I can mail it to you."

"You could, but there's a chance it'll get lost in the mail. Papa can get a new one, but that could take months."

"Why don't I meet you in Huludao? I've wanted to go there and check out some pigs to buy anyway. I can meet you there tomorrow around noon. Will that work out for you?"

"That'll be perfect. I'll buy my train tickets and let you know exactly what time I'll be in Huludao."

Min Li ended the call and took a taxi directly to the train station where she purchased a ticket for Huludao for the next morning at 7:25. The train would arrive in Huludao at 12:15, so she called Hong Qi and told her. Hong Qi agreed to meet her at the train station after she looked at the pigs. Min Li thanked her for that, especially for not involving her with the pigs, making Hong Qi laugh.

Because Min Li arrived during the lunch hour, she assumed that the office for issuing passports would be closed, so she and Hong Qi headed to a restaurant for lunch, which gave Min Li a chance to catch up news at home.

"You're thinking about raising pigs?" Min Li asked.

"We'll make more money if we do and we can have more money throughout the year. You know with corn we get one crop a year, and that money has to last until the next year. If we have a bad year, we don't get to eat."

"How many pigs to you need?"

"I'm looking at buying seven to start with."

"Is that enough?"

"Not really, but if I get the right pigs, we'll have many more in the spring."

"Pigs are more expensive to raise than corn, aren't they?"

"True. With the corn, we only need to buy the seed and fertilizer up front. But pigs have to be fed, and they get sick."

"Where will you get the money to feed them?"

"We're trying to time it with the harvest. We'll feed them our corn and not sell the corn," Hong Qi explained.

"But then you won't have the money from the corn."

"If we can hold out to the spring, then we'll be alright. We can start selling pigs then, one or two at a time."

"It sounds kind of risky to me."

"I think going to Kuwait is more risky."

"How so?"

"You don't know what you're getting into. You'll be in a foreign country with no family or friends. And what about your business in Shenyang? You barely got that going."

"The business will be fine. Tong Li Hua can run things. It's a simple business model. I'm a half-owner, so if things don't work out in Kuwait, I can pick up right where I left off. Besides, I can talk to Tong Li Hua anytime by telephone and email, and I can come back anytime I want."

"What if they won't let you leave?"

"I have a contract that allows me to terminate it anytime and they have to buy me a ticket back to China. Besides, how can they stop me from leaving? Even if they renege on the return airfare, I'll be able to buy that myself and just take a taxi to the airport."

"I hope you're right about that. You hear many stories from other people who go work there."

"Those are stories told by people who work as housemaids or nannies. I'm going there as a manager of a business. That's different."

"You'll still be a Chinese woman in a Middle Eastern country."

'so?"

'really, Min Li, you're smarter than that. Some places don't think highly of Chinese."

"I'm sure our differences are easily overlooked, even in the Middle East, in these modern times. Oh, look at the time. Let's get over to the passport office."

Min Li paid the check for the restaurant, and the two women walked over to the Huludao office of the Ministry of Public Security. Again, Min Li filled out the paperwork for her passport, handed over her national ID, her passport photos, and her father's *hukou*. The clerk then told Min Li to come back in two weeks to pick up her new passport.

"Two weeks? Is it possible to get it sooner?" Min Li asked.

"The law requires that we issue the passport within fifteen days," the clerk responded. "Two weeks is fourteen days. Therefore, we are compliant with the law."

"But I need to send copies out of the country so that my visa can be issued. This will cause a significant delay. Not only that, I live in Shenyang, and coming here isn't very convenient."

"If you like, you may pay an expedite fee and you can have your passport day after tomorrow."

"That's fine. I'll pay the extra fee and stay in Huludao for a couple of days."

Min Li prevailed upon Hong Qi to spend the night with her in Huludao, giving the two sisters time with each other, which had been so rare in the past few years. Hong Qi called her husband, who gave her his blessing and reasoned that it would give her more time to look at the pigs and negotiate prices. Min Li found an internet cafe and sent an email to Aliyah, informing her that she should have her passport within a couple of days. All seemed to be going as planned.

The two sisters spent the next day together, which meant that Min Li went with Hong Qi to look at pigs. She tried to be interested in the pig bartering process, but Min Li lost interest quickly. Standing in the space between stalls, overwhelmed by the smells, Min Li realized how fortunate she was to be living in the city, despite the fact that she did so illegally. China has two kinds of *hukous*, those for the city and those for the countryside. People registered on a countryside *hukou* are destined to remain peasants for their entire life. People fortunate enough to have a city *hukou* have access to jobs, modern healthcare, and opportunity. Min Li, like millions of others, fled the countryside but live in a state of limbo so long as they remain outside their home village. Min Li was luckier than most. She was able to find work and could own two different businesses without ever having to face the issue that she was an undocumented worker in her own country.

Things would have been different if she had children, but she could have resolved any issues while she was still married. If she had children, she would have had her husband register her and the children on his own Shenyang *hukou*; otherwise, her children would not have been allowed to attend school. To register a child in any school in Shenyang, or any other city in China, the parents would have to show that the child legally resided in that city. People who migrate from the countryside to the city, as Min Li had done, often leave their children in the care of the grandparents back in their home village, because that is where the child must attend school.

Finally, Hong Qi and the pig dealer stopped negotiating. Hong Qi managed to buy seven pigs at a favorable price, two of which were already pregnant, a bonus. Using a large, red permanent marker, she wrote the single character for her family name, Zhang, on the side of each pig and arranged for their delivery to her home in Shangguang three days later. She and her husband would need the time to build an enclosure for them. Hong Qi then called her husband to tell him about the purchase, advising him not to wait for her to get home before building a pen to hold the pigs. Thus, Hong Qi had just changed her family's destiny from a life of growing corn to being pig farmers, a definite notch up in the village social hierarchy.

That evening, Hong Qi took the last bus of the day to Shangguang and Min Li returned to her hotel room where she would wait until the next day when her passport would be ready. Like Hong Qi, Min Li was about to change her own destiny by leaving China, like so many Chinese did before her, to make life better for herself.

Twenty Three

Min Li arrived at Shenyang Taoxian International Airport at 6:45 in the morning, more than four hours before her scheduled 11:05 departure. She had never flown before. That, and the prospect of going to a foreign country to live and work, kept her from sleeping well the night before. She worried throughout the evening that she might have forgotten something, that there was something she still needed to tell Tong Li Hua, or that she forgot to pack something. She had packed and repacked her suitcase at least three times, but she could not convince herself that she was not leaving behind anything important. She prepaid her rent on her apartment for a year, had called to shut off the utilities, sealed the windows to keep out dust and covered her furniture with large plastic sheets. Her passport and Kuwait visa sat in her purse. Arrangements were made to be met at the airport in Kuwait. But she still fretted.

Much quieter and cleaner than the train station and located outside of Shenyang, the Shenyang Taoxian International Airport offered a respite from the noises and smells of the city, allowing travelers to relax and reduce their stress before traveling. To Min Li, most of the travelers in the airport were businessmen and women traveling alone. She saw one Chinese family dressed in smart summer clothes, white pants and shorts, sky blue polos, and white baseball caps, dragging designer luggage behind them. Several passengers sat drinking from white paper cups emblazoned with a Starbucks logo. Min Li was always curious about the attraction of drinking coffee from a paper cup that cost five times more than she usually spent for lunch. She told herself that one day she would actually try a cup of Starbucks coffee.

Suddenly, Min Li remembered that she had brought nothing to read. She would be living in an Arabic-speaking, which would likely make finding books written in Chinese difficult. Although she was certain that finding English language reading material would be easy, her English was rusty and reading would be cumbersome and slow. But she would have to wait more than an hour before the airport's bookshop opened. Her flight would take her to Shanghai on China Eastern Airlines, where she would change planes with an Etihad Airways flight to Abu Dhabi. She could purchase a couple of books and magazines in Shanghai, supposing that there would be a larger selection, but she didn't want to take her chances, so she would revisit the bookstore before her flight departed.

After more than two hours of waiting, the check-in counter for her flight to Shanghai opened, and Min Li dragged herself and her belongings over to the line for coach passengers. Four passengers were ahead of her in line for the one airline agent at the counter, and progress was hampered by an argument between the agent and a passenger over the weight of his suitcase. Min Li had only estimated the weight of her own suitcase, guessing that it was about twenty kilograms, two less than the maximum allowed. The argument ended when the man pulled out his wallet and paid an extra fee.

Soon, Min Li found herself at the counter nervously handing her itinerary and passport to the agent.

"You are traveling to Kuwait, I see. How many bags?"

"Just the one," Min Li answered.

"Please place it on the scale to your right," the agent said as she printed out an adhesive-backed baggage claim tag and wrapped it around the handle on Min Li's suitcase.

Min Li watched the digital readout on the scale and saw, to her dismay, that it registered 22.4 kilograms, 400 grams heavier than allowed. "Oh, oh, it's too heavy," she confessed aloud.

"No problem," the agent said. "I won't tell anybody if you don't."

"But that other man, you made him pay extra."

"His bag weighed in at 35 kilograms. That's a little too much to let slide. Do you want to keep the seat shown on your itinerary?"

"I suppose. Why?"

"It's a middle seat. You can have a window seat if you like."

"Oh, I didn't even think about that. I had no idea. Yes, a window seat would be perfect."

The agent punched a few keys on her computer, stared at the monitor for a moment, punched a few more keys, then hit the print key. "I've got you in a window seat all the way from Shanghai, to Abu Dhabi, and then to Kuwait."

By now, Min Li's suitcase was behind the counter on a conveyer belt and passing through an x-ray machine. As Min Li thanked the agent for her help in reassigning her seats, the conveyor belt stopped and the police officer operating the x-ray machine motioned for Min Li to stop. He walked to the counter opposite Min Li and handed her four AAA batteries, two taken from her battery-operated alarm clock and two spares.

"No batteries," the police officer said as he handed the batteries to Min Li.

'sorry. I've never flown before," she responded, taking the batteries and walking away in embarrassment. From there she walked over to the bookstore, hoping to find some worthwhile reading material. She purchased a Chinese travel guide on the Middle East, a collection of modern Chinese short stories, and a mystery novel, shoving them all into her new laptop bag.

Only after she passed through the security gate did Min Li begin to panic. She reasoned with herself that she was doing the right thing, that she would make good money, and that she could return home to China any time she wanted. She thought about the fact that she was leaving her friends behind and her sisters, as well as a business and a lifestyle in Shenyang. But she would make new friends in Kuwait while still keeping the old ones. She and Tong Li Hua promised to communicate frequently, especially if any problem arose with the beauty shop. They both signed up for QQ accounts, a recently popular Chinese social media site. She would frequently call Hong Qi and Hai Tian and give them updates. After a while, Min Li would return to China and resume her normal life in the apartment that she sealed up just before leaving for the airport. The trip to Kuwait will be nothing more than a working vacation. Not only that, she would get her first taste of living in another part of the world, and that idea stimulated her intellectually. She thought how Peter must have felt the same way when he came to China.

Min Li's fear ebbed as the plane leveled after taking off. She looked out the window but could only see a blanket of white below her, stretching for as far she could s see. After an hour or so, breaks appeared in the cloud cover, and Min Li saw patches of blue water, and as the airplane neared Shanghai, the clouds had almost dissipated. By then, the water had turned from blue to a brownish yellow. The passenger seated next to her said that the water looked dirty here because of the sediment from the Yangtze River, renamed the Chang Jiang by Mao Zedong, which emptied into the East China Sea just north of Shanghai.

Min Li was disappointed again as the cloud cover resumed over land, and she was unable to see Shanghai, China's largest and most metropolitan city. She landed at the newer Pudong Airport, far the city. Landing at Pudong Airport gave Min Li her second fright of the day, especially when the airplane's wheels came into contact with the tarmac. It seemed to bounce twice before the wheels grabbed the runway firmly, and only after it made a turn at the end of the runway did Min Li loosen her grip on the armrests. She had to do this twice more before reaching Kuwait.

Much larger than the airport in Shenyang, Pudong airport impressed Min Li with just how busy an airport could be. She saw thousands of people teeming the ticket counters and security gates. Min Li had to wedge her way through a large crowd to get to the security gates for international departures, and came up upon a line more than a hundred meters long. She looked at her watch and saw that she had a little more than an hour to catch her flight to Abu Dhabi and wondered if she would make it. The line moved rather quickly, though, and before long Min Li was handing her passport and visa to a customs and immigration control officer who scrutinized it and checked his computer monitor before returning them to Min Li and waving her through. By the time she reached her departure gate, a line had already formed to board the airplane, although nobody was yet boarding.

Min Li stood in the line, like everybody else, waiting for the door to open leading down the skyway to her airplane. Ten minutes after the airplane should have begun loading, Min Li heard an announcement on the public address system, first in Chinese, then English, and finally in Arabic. The announcement indicated that the departure would be delayed by a half hour or so due to a dust storm approaching Abu Dhabi.

The passengers in line complained, as if Etihad Airways was at fault. Most found a seat in the departure lounge to wait out the delay, although a few remained in line, reminding Min Li of the departure halls in the Shenyang North train station. She found a seat next to an older couple and pulled her travel guide out of her laptop bag, looking in the index for dust storms. She had never experienced one, although she knew China had its share of them west of Beijing.

Middle Eastern dust storms, often called a *haboob* or *shamal*, occur more frequently and, for people experiencing them for the first time, can be quite frightening, turning day into night, reducing visibility to zero, and bringing an entire city to a standstill. Some dust storms can rise to a thousand feet into the air and stretch over a swath of land for more than a hundred kilometers, or sixty miles. *It's no wonder they closed the airport in Abu Dhabi*, thought Min Li.

Before she could finish reading about dust storms, a voice over the public address system announced in Chinese that boarding would begin for the Etihad Airways flight to Abu Dhabi. Before the announcement repeated in English, at least two hundred people reformed the line. Nearly all passengers were in line by the time the announcement was repeated in Arabic. Within minutes, Min Li stood in the starboard side aisle of a Boing 777-300, much larger than the plane she flew on from Shenyang to Shanghai. She found her seat, 22K, next to the window just before the right-side wing, stowed her laptop in the already crowded overhead bin, and sat down ready for the ten-hour flight to Abu Dhabi. Around her sat mostly Middle Eastern men and women who ignored her for the entire flight. She took advantage of this by sleeping most of the rest of the way to Abu Dhabi, which would arrive around breakfast time.

The first two hours of the flight seemed no different than the flight from Shenyang to Shanghai, at least with regard to the view outside Min Li's window. *Cloudy, always cloudy*, Min Li thought.

Maybe if China weren't always so cloudy, people would be happier. But just as she formed these thoughts, the cloud cover broke and snow-capped mountains loomed to her right, the Himalayas. Min Li knew that soon she would be leaving Chinese airspace. She felt strangely anxious and relieved at the same time.

The Abu Dhabi International Airport is certainly that, international. Nearly all flights arrived from or departed from cities in other countries, and Min Li heard more languages spoken at one time than she ever thought imaginable. The airport hosted numerous restaurants, gift shops, bookstores, and duty-free shops, as well as departure lounges and arrival areas, all spread over three terminals connected by concourses. Because Min Li flew in on Etihad Airways and would be continuing on by the same airline, her departure gate was not far from her arrival gate. She had two hours before her next flight departed, so she wondered around the airport, getting a sense of what life was like in the western world.

Already, Min Li could tell that coffee was more popular outside of China, and, like China, there was no shortage of Mc-Donald's restaurants. And she saw Muslim prayer rooms, some for men and some for women. China has Muslims; in fact, ten of the fifty-five nationalities that compose the people of China are Muslim. Officially, China's Bureau of Religious Affairs claims that there are eighteen million Muslims living in China, but Min Li doubted the accuracy of that number. Min Li determined that since she would be living in a Muslim country, she should learn something about the religion.

Time passed quickly for Min Li as she explored the airport, and before she knew it, she heard the public address system announce boarding for her flight to Kuwait. She hustled back to the departure lounge for her flight and found a place at the end of the line as it passed through the ticket gate onto the skyway. In about an hour, she would be in Kuwait.

Twenty Four

Much smaller than Abu Dhabi's, Kuwait's airport did not serve as a hub for any airlines other than one, Kuwait Airways. It was in a true sense only an international airport, because there were no other airports in the country. Most of the people at the airport were Kuwaitis, although there were many Europeans, North Americans, and many Filipinos, Egyptians, Indians, and other South Asians. Min Li immediately sensed that Kuwait was only a place where people lived and worked and was not a tourist destination.

She grabbed her suitcase from the baggage claim area, then proceeded to immigration control where she had to place her suitcase on a conveyor built to be x-rayed. She thought this peculiar getting off an airplane, because she believed this procedure was used elsewhere as a security measure. But it became immediately apparent to Min Li that Kuwait tightly controlled what items entered the country.

After re-claiming her suitcase, she approached one of the immigration enforcement officers and handed him her documents.

"What is your purpose for visiting Kuwait?" the officer asked.

"I'll be working here for a few months."

'really? What do you mean by working?"

"I'll be managing a beauty spa."

"Will there be other Chinese women involved?"

"No, not that I'm aware of."

"Do you have any banned substances in your suitcase?"
"No."
"Any alcohol?"
"No."
"Pork?"
"Pork?" Min Li repeated.
"Yes, pork. You may not bring pork into Kuwait. I know how you Chinese like pork."
"No pork," Min Li answered, remembering seeing something about that in her travel guide.
'sexual products?"
"What?"
"Do you have sexual products with you?"
"I don't even know what those are."
"Please remember that while you are in Kuwait, sexual activities are only allowed between a husband and his wives."
"Thank you for telling me that, but I can assure you that is not an issue with me," Min Li responded indignantly. "Why do you feel a need to ask me this? Do you ask everybody?"
"You are Chinese. You are traveling alone, so I'm assuming you are not married."
'so?"
"I just said, you are Chinese. Enjoy your stay in Kuwait," answered the man as he stamped Min Li's visa in her passport and handed it back to her.

Min Li didn't know whether to be insulted, embarrassed, or angry, maybe all of those. She took her passport with the visa, grabbed her suitcase, and pulled in past the immigration officer into the arrivals lounge. A metal rail marked the farther edge of the lounge, and beyond that stood a large crowd waiting to greet people from arriving airplanes. Min Li scanned the crowd and saw a white poster board sign bearing her name, 'min Li Zhang," with the family name at the end in western style. A young Filipina held it above her head. She wore a grey long-sleeve dress that ended below her knees. The collar and cuffs had a half-inch white trim, and she wore a grey scarf over her hair that matched the dress. Standing next to her was a man dressed in khaki slacks and a white button down, short-sleeve shirt. Min Li later learned that he was from Pakistan. The maid had been sent to meet her at the airport with one of the drivers for her sponsoring family.

"I am Zhang Min Li, I mean Min Li Zhang," she said to the young maid. "Did Aliyah come with you to meet me at the airport?"

"No, ma'am. She sent me instead. It is too hot outside for my lady to come. I am Maria Vanessa, but please call me Vanessa."

Min Li thought how rude it was to not be met at the airport by either Aliyah or Huda, but she accepted it as a cultural difference and thought no more about it. The driver grabbed Min Li's suitcase and offered to take her laptop bag, gut Min Li held firm to it. They walked through the departure area toward the parking garage. Small businesses offering money exchange and mobile telephone services crowded the area. Vanessa suggested that Min Li purchase a local SIM card for her telephone, which Min Li did.

While Min Li waited in line at the Wataniya Telecom counter, she observed several young Chinese women being herded into a group nearby. Most had long braided hair and were dressed very simply. Min Li could hear them talking excitedly, but could not understand their dialect. From time to time, she could hear Mandarin words and phrases. It dawned on Min Li that by the way they dressed and sounded, these were girls from the countryside of Yunnan. She asked Vanessa about them.

"They came here through an agency who will find jobs for them as maids like me."

"What will their life be like here?" Min Li asked.

"Typically, a maid signs a contract for five years. Her sponsor pays for the cost of the maid's transportation to Kuwait, as well as the work visa. She will then work in the sponsor's household, cleaning and doing other household chores."

"Are they paid well?"

"Oh, very well. The average salary is thirty-five Kuwaiti dinars a month, and they have a place to sleep. They also are fed by the host families."

Min Li tried to calculate how much money that was, converting into U.S. dollars first. "That's only a little more than 120 dollars a month, or, let me see, um, about 770 renminbi."

"What's a renminbi?"

"Chinese money."

"That's good, right?"

"I suppose it's okay. It's certainly more than the average Chinese earns, and for those girls, it probably seems like a fortune. They can save a little nest egg and return to their home village where their neighbors will think they are rich."

"Five year contract, huh? It seems like a long time."

"It is standard. After all, the sponsor wants to get his money's worth because he has to pay the agency fee, as well as the cost of transportation at the beginning and end of the contract."

"What if somebody doesn't like the job and they want to leave sooner?"

"They can't."

"What do you mean they can't?"

"If they are guilty of absconding, that means being away from their place of employment without permission of their employer, they can go to jail for six months."

"That seems rather harsh," Min Li said, astounded. "Have you ever thought about leaving?"

"No. I have a good employer. He doesn't beat me, and he tells his wives not to beat me, but Huda doesn't listen too well to that, especially if I don't wash her laundry properly. But that doesn't happen too often. And I get my one day off each week, which is in the contract, and they rarely miss a payday."

"You get one day off a week?"

"Yes. That's required by law. But too many maids in Kuwait don't get their time off. If they leave the house without permission, they get beat or arrested. But I get my time off. Some try to leave for that reason. Some try to leave because they don't get paid. But they still get arrested."

"People beat their servants here?"

"Yes."

"Can't they get in trouble for that?"

"Last month a maid in my neighborhood died from her beatings. The sponsor said she committed suicide, and that's how the police wrote it up. I know, because I read about it in the *Kuwait Times* two days later. But I know they beat her. I heard it going on for more than an hour."

"Do you know why they beat her?"

'she was pregnant. That's illegal here if you're not married."

"How did she have time to have a boyfriend?"

'she didn't have a boyfriend. She never left the house."

"Another servant?"

"Her sponsor."

The unnerving conversation ended abruptly when the customer ahead of Min Li at the counter finished his business. Min Li purchased a SIM card for her cell phone and tucked it into her purse. She glanced over at the small group of Chinese country girls, contemplated their fate for a moment, and then followed the driver through the door into the parking lot. Min Li wondered if Kuwait had office cleaning business like the one she once owned in Shenyang or if the Kuwaitis all had maids to do it.

"Outside the terminal building, Min Li's small party was accosted by several men who wanted to carry the suitcase to the car. The driver, Raja, waved them away, then led Min Li and Vanessa to a late model blue Ford Expedition parked in the metered parking about fifty yards away. By the time they reached the car, Min Li fully appreciated how stifling hot it was outside the air-conditioned airport terminal. According to Raja, the temperature was 46 degrees Celsius (almost 115 degrees Fahrenheit). She expected a drier heat, being in the desert, but Kuwait's proximity to the Persian Gulf caused the humidity to rise, so the relative humidity was close to fifty percent. It wasn't the type of humidity she knew in northeast China, but with the high heat, it seemed worse. If it was twenty degrees cooler with the same moisture in the air, she was certain it would be close to ninety percent. Raja said that it might reach fifty degrees today (122°F), but everything was well air-conditioned. He warned Min Li not to go on long walks in the daytime.

They headed north from the airport on Highway 50, which soon swung east then looped north again where it merged with Highway 51. Desert surrounded them on both sides until they crossed Ring Road 6, and then apartment buildings sprang up on both sides of the road, all painted beige or white, some rising up to ten or eleven stories. On the right, Vanessa pointed out a new mall under construction, the 360 Mall which would have many high-end shops for Kuwaitis and rich expatriates alike.

"Expatriate?" Min Li asked. "I don't know that word."

"Foreigner. They like to use the word "expatriate" for some reason here. Expatriates make up seventy percent of the population here. That neighborhood over there on the left is Abraq Khaitan. Don't go there."

"Why not?"

"It's an expatriate neighborhood. Mostly Pakistanis and Egyptians live there, few women."

"Is that a bad thing?"

"It is if you are a woman, especially an Asian woman. It's dangerous there."

"I'll take your word for it. Where is the beauty spa I'll be managing?"

"That's in Salmiya."

"What kind of a neighborhood is that?"

"It's an expatriate neighborhood, too, but it's much safer than some of the others. Many Kuwaitis go there to shop and to buy services. Most of the expatriates there are either families or Europeans or North Americans. That's where the Marina Mall is, which is right next to the Salmiya Marina. Also, there is a Sultan Center supermarket and a City Center market at Souq Salmiya. You'll enjoy shopping there. Nearby on Salem al Mubarak Street are many small shops, including some 500-Fil stores."

"What's a 500-Fil store?"

"That's half a dinar. Nearly everything inside costs 500 fils. A Kuwaiti dinar has one thousand fils."

"Where are we going now?"

"We're going to the beauty spa where we will meet Huda and Aliyah. Later, we'll take you to your accommodations."

Raja exited Highway 51 and headed east on Ring Road 5, a modern eight-lane freeway, and drove through heavy traffic until they reached an exit that took them into a traffic circle.

"That's Rumaithia, a Kuwaiti neighborhood," Vanessa said, pointing to the right of the car in a southerly direction. That's where Huda and Aliyah live."

The car continued through the traffic circle until it had reached the opposite side of Ring Road 5, and Raja made a sharp right turn onto Al Khansa Street. After passing Souq Salmiya on the right, he turned left onto Qatar Street and drove for another block, turning right on Hamad Al Mubarak Street. By now, Min Li was totally confused as to where she was. They drove a few more blocks, passing Salmiya Park on the left, then turned left onto Al Bahrain Street, a narrow street that took them to Salem Al Mubarak St., a busy road in the middle of a shopping district, then turned right coming to a quick stop on the sidewalk in front of Arabian Beauty Spa.

Aliyah and Huda exited the shop and greeted Min Li at the car. Standing on the sidewalk immediately reminded Min Li how hot it was in Kuwait, so to her relief, the greetings lasted only a moment before she was rushed inside the shop. Much larger than her own Gaoji Meirong Salon, Arabian Beauty Spa had twelve workstations for hairdressers, four pedicure stations with foot baths, and six manicure stations. Each of the hairdressing stations had their own sinks, so customers could have their hair shampooed without having to walk through the shop. Near the rear of the room was a manager's workstation, complete with a desk and computer. In the back was a hallway, on the left side of which were three rooms for added privacy; two had massage tables, and one was set up for body waxing, an uncommon practice in China. On the right side of the hallway were a small sauna and two private showers. At the end of the hallway was a break room with a kitchen. Min Li was immediately impressed.

Most of the shop was in a state of renovation, and Min Li was surprised that the new owners had borrowed the motif from the women's side of her own shop in Shenyang, complete with the pink and light grey paint scheme and photographs of luxury homes, some with snow-capped mountains in the background. One noticeable difference was the lack of windows on the front of the shop. Aliyah explained that it was meant for privacy. Passersby would not be allowed to look through the window to see women who were not completely covered. The floor had been stripped of its original wood laminate and white marble tiles sat stacked in the corner ready to be laid.

"When will the shop be ready?" Min Li asked.

"By the end of the week, Thursday," answered Aliyah.

"Thursday?"

"Yes. The last day of the week in Kuwait is Thursday. Friday and Saturday is the weekend. If we're not finished by Thursday, we can get some workers to finish things up on Saturday. Hopefully, we can open for business Sunday."

"Have you done any advertising?" Min Li asked.

Aliyah grabbed two newspapers, a *Kuwait Times*, an English daily newspaper, and an *Al Watan*, a daily Arabic newspaper, and showed Min Li the quarter page ads in each. "We've run these ads every day for the past two weeks. Many women have already booked appointments."

"Where are the employees during the renovation?"

"We let everybody go. They can apply for their old jobs if they want, but we wanted a fresh break from the old owners and we wanted no confusion with the employees who they worked for. Besides, we didn't want to pay anybody while the shop was closed for renovations."

"Then we better start interviewing. How do we get applicants?"

"We're running some want ads in the *Kuwait Times* tomorrow and the next day. That should give us plenty of applicants."

"Only in the English-speaking newspaper?" Min Li asked.

"Kuwaitis won't apply, and we don't want anybody working for us from other Arabic speaking countries. We hope to hire mostly women from the Philippines or India. We can hire some Chinese too."

"Why?"

Aliyah only looked at Min Li as though she asked an absurd question. "Are you hungry?" she asked.

'very, but I'm also a little tired."

"That's right. You've been traveling for many hours."

"I was able to sleep on the airplane from China to Abu Dhabi, but I wouldn't call it very restful sleep."

"I'm sure. Let's get some shawarma."

"What's shawarma?"

"That's Arabic fast food. It's made with meat cooked on a spit over an open fire, usually lamb or chicken, then shaved onto a piece of pita bread. You add some sauce, spices, and lettuce, cucumbers, tomatoes, or whatever you want. It's very good. You'll need to try it.

'sounds good, but I'm not a big fan of lamb."

"No problem. Eat chicken. It's healthier anyway. We'll go eat, and then we'll take you over to your apartment."

Huda sat in the third seat of the Explorer, while Aliyah and Min Li occupied the center seat behind the driver. Vanessa sat in the front with Raja. Raja made a U-turn in heavy traffic and drove west down Salem Al Mubarak Street. They passed the Sultan Center supermarket on the right, and three small shopping malls on the left. On both sides of the street were several bistro-style coffee shops, including Starbucks and various competitors. The largest of these was Second Cup directly across from Sultan Center, with a large outside sitting area. However, the heat had driven all the patrons inside, and despite the fact that it was a weekday, the place had many patrons.

Arabian Gulf Street ran parallel to Salem Al Mubarak Street, and Min Li caught occasional glimpses of cars speeding by on it. Past Arabian Gulf Street, she saw a marina full of luxury yachts. Soon they were in front of Marina Mall, a large, modern, indoor mall. The facade of the mall faced Salem Al Mubarak Road, but most of the mall was elevated and crossed over Arabian Gulf Street. Near the entrance to the mall stood a Lebanese restaurant, their destination, according to Aliyah. Raja pulled to the side in an area intended for picking up and letting off passengers, letting Huda, Aliyah, and Min Li out, then he and Vanessa drove off, ostensibly to park the car.

Upon entering the restaurant, Huda spoke with the Lebanese host in Arabic, who then led the three to a table with a plush, stuffed sofa on both sides. Min Li sat down, never having sat on a stuffed sofa before, and sank into the leather luxury, surprised at how soft it was. Aliya sat next to her, while Huda sat in the sofa on the other side of the table. Huda did the ordering.

Soon, a Filipina brought a large plate of pickled vegetables, a dish of hummus, and a covered bowl of pita bread. A Filipino brought over a large water pipe with what to Min Li looked like three hoses coming from it, as well as three disposable mouthpieces to fit on the end of the hoses.

"What's this?" Min Li asked, having never seen a water pipe before.

'shisha," Aliyah answered. "Tobacco. The water pipe is called a hookah."

"Oh, I'm afraid I don't smoke."

"You will enjoy this. It's very smooth, not like cigarettes, and the shisha is flavored. Huda usually orders grape."

Min Li looked at the contraption. It stood about two feet tall with a wide bottom that contained water. At the apex of the narrow portion was a bowl, covered in perforated foil, under which was placed the tobacco, or shisha, while a burning ember of charcoal sat on top of the foil. The smoker would suck in on the mouthpiece affixed to the tube, forcing the smoke from the bowl through the water, then out the hose. This had the effect of cooling the smoke, making it much easier to inhale. Min Li, who was not accustomed to tobacco smoke, tried it, but it caused her to cough uncontrollably to the delight of Huda. Huda puffed away as if breathing air, while Aliyah took an occasional puff.

"We smoke shisha as a way of socializing. It's much like how people drink tea in China. We drink tea too, but there is no ceremony attached to it."

"I'm sorry, but I just don't have a knack for it. I hope you are not offended," Min Li apologized.

"Don't worry about it. Everybody has to get used to it. Frankly, although people say it is safe because the water filters the smoke, I don't believe them. In fact, I've heard that it's actually worse than cigarette smoking, but you'll never convince Huda of that."

To Min Li's relief, the Filipina who brought the relish tray returned with three small pots of tea.

'speaking of tea, I could sure use some. But this is red tea. I've never drank that before."

'red tea? Oh, right, it does look red when it's brewed. We just call it tea, but the packages that it comes in say black tea. Sugar?"

'sugar in tea, I've never heard of such a thing. Are you sure?"

'suit yourself. We're used to it very sweet. Maybe you can try it if you like," Aliyah said.

'maybe someday, but for now, I just need the tea. I can barely keep my eyes open. By the way, where are Vanessa and Raja?"

Aliyah looked through the windows toward the courtyard at the entrance to the mall. "There they are. Outside by the staircase."

"Are they not joining us?"

"Of course not. They're servants. Household servants. They can't eat with us. What will people say?"

"I can't imagine what people would say. But they're outside and it's very hot. They need to eat and drink too."

"They'll eat in the kitchen at the house. Please don't worry about them. They are used to it. It is the way things are."

Min Li squirmed uncomfortably on the plush sofa thinking about this. She had never treated anybody the way Aliyah and Huda treated Vanessa and Raja. To Min Li, they were people employed to do a job and the Kuwaiti women were their employers. They were all people, and people should be treated with dignity and respect. She knew that wasn't always the case, not in China anyway, but there it was not so blatant. Sometimes government officials would treat people like this, but that was rare. People knew their place in society, yet everybody was provided human dignity. Leaving Vanessa and Raja outside was, to Min Li, like treating them the same as livestock. Min Li couldn't stop thinking about this throughout lunch.

When the three women finished eating and Huda had exhausted the package of shisha, Aliyah paid for the lunch. Raja saw this from outside the restaurant and took this as a clue to fetch the car. He ran off for that purpose, leaving Vanessa waiting alone outside for the three women to exit the restaurant. After a few minutes, Aliya motioned to Huda that Raja was there with the car. When Huda rose, Aliya and Min Li also arose, and they headed for the door.

"We'll take you to your new home now so you can get some sleep," Aliyah said. "Tomorrow we'll take you shopping for things you might need that aren't already in the apartment, but you should have the essentials already."

They drove away from Marina Mall and over to Al Mughira Bin Shu'ba Street. Not far from Hamad Al Mubarak Street, they pulled into a concrete parking area in front of a plain looking, eight-story apartment building. The two Kuwaiti women and Min Li entered the ground floor of the building, leaving Vanessa and Raja in the car. Huda pressed the call button for the elevator, and Aliyah told Min Li that her apartment was on the fourth story.

"Fourth floor?" Min Li asked for confirmation.

"Actually, it's the fifth floor. Here, the first floor is the ground floor. The first story is the next one up, the second floor. You'll get used to it."

When the elevator opened on the fourth story, or fifth floor, Min Li was overwhelmed with the smell of curry. Aliyah saw the face Min Li made and explained that some Indian families lived in the building. They walked down the hallway toward the front of the building, and Huda pulled out a key. Inside, Min Li was taken by the fact that the living room had four bunk beds. There was no television, no sofa, nothing that would make it look like a living room.

The apartment had three bedrooms, two bathrooms, and a kitchen. Each of the bedrooms was likewise furnished with four bunk beds.

"Why are there so many beds here?" Min Li asked.

"Your staff will be living here when we hire them."

"I have to share an apartment with fifteen other women?" Min Li asked incredulously.

"We won't hire that many, I'm sure," Aliyah said. "Likely only ten or so to start with. So you'll need to be careful whom you hire. They will be your roommates."

Flabbergasted, Min Li said nothing because she was too tired. As the first person in the apartment, she was able to choose where she would sleep. She chose the first bedroom past the living room, threw her suitcase on one of the bottom bunks, and plopped down on the other bottom bunk. Aliyah went into the hallway, grabbed some bed linens, and brought them into the room Min Li had selected.

"We'll come by and pick you up tomorrow around eight," Aliyah said. "There's no food in the kitchen, so we'll go to breakfast first thing, then out to Avenues Mall."

"Okay, I'll see you then. Are there any towels here? I want to take a shower."

"In the linen closet by the first bathroom. I think there is a bar of soap in the shower. Pleasant dreams," Aliyah said as she handed a door key to Min Li.

Min Li took her shower, thinking all the while about how to deal with her new living arrangements. She would come up with a plan to maximize her privacy. After all, although it certainly didn't feel like it now, she was the boss. She would have to figure out what to do with the six extra bunk beds and to do it before her hosts found other uses for them.

Twenty Five

Min Li knew about the six daily calls to prayer in Kuwait from reading her travel guide, but she didn't know about the loud speakers on top of mosques in every neighborhood. The first call to prayer, called *fajr*, around four in the morning, frightened her out of bed. One of the huge loudspeakers on a mosque a block behind her must have been pointed directly at her apartment building. She looked at the time on her watch and managed to go back to bed, knowing that she had to wake up in three hours, her portable alarm clock having been set for seven. But less than two hours later, the sunrise call to prayer woke her again.

She couldn't sleep after that, and decided to get dressed and explore the apartment. She still had a little more than two hours before Aliya and Huda would pick her up to go shopping. First she went into the kitchen, which she immediately noticed to be much larger than the average Chinese kitchen. One wall contained cupboards above a counter and cabinets below. In the middle of the wall-length counter, she saw a double stainless steel sink with both hot and cold running water. A microwave oven sat at one end of the counter. On the opposite wall in the corner to the left of the doorway stood a full refrigerator, taller than Min Li's 5 feet 2 inches. Between the refrigerator and the cupboards stood a four-burner electric stove with an oven. On the wall to the right of the doorway was a table with six chairs. People would have to eat in shifts, thought Min Li.

Min Li had seen none of this before. She ran the water in the skink, waiting until it ran from cold to hot, then turned on all four burners on the stove's range top, watching as they turned red hot. She went through the cupboards and cabinets, locating dishes, pots and pans, flatware, everything except chopsticks and a teakettle. Min Li grew more excited about the prospects that lay ahead of her. She could learn to use a fork, or maybe purchase some chopsticks if they could be found in Kuwait.

Beyond the kitchen, she found a utility room of sorts where she saw a washing machine and a clothes dryer. She soon figured out what the washing machine did, but she had never contemplated before a machine that dried clothes. She thought that odd considering the heat in Kuwait. The utility room had no air conditioning as did the other rooms, and she thought that clothes would dry quickly in there if hung on a rack. It was only a few minutes after six in the morning, and already the temperature in the utility room was more than 35 degrees Celsius (95ºF).

Min Li explored the bedrooms next. All three each had four bunk beds, all stacked in pairs, and there were two four-drawer chests of drawers in each bedroom. Min Li calculated that two people would each share one chest of drawers, giving them two drawers each. A large wooden wardrobe was also placed in each bedroom, which Min Li could see would cause some concern as the future occupants would be fighting over available space. Min Li would have to establish rules. One of the things that she decided early on was that if she hired a staff of only ten, not including herself, there would be no need for any beds in the living room. She wanted to move the beds out and move in some sofas with a television. People needed to relax when they were home, and it wouldn't be possible without a living room.

With the time she had before Huda and Aliyah picked her up, Min Li disassembled the bunk beds in the living room, leaned their parts against the far wall, and cleaned the floor where they once stood. Before she finished, she developed a thirst but had nothing in the apartment to drink. Normally, she would have opened a bottle of water or boiled water in a teakettle. Instead, she found a four-quart saucepan, filled it with water from the sink, and brought it to a boil on the electric stove. After it had boiled a few minutes, she found some coffee cups in the cupboard, poured herself a cup of water, and sipped it, remarking to herself how the water tasted good. She later learned that the water found in Kuwaiti homes is actually distilled seawater. Kuwait had no population-wide water distribution system, so trucks brought it into the neighborhoods and filled up large cisterns situated at each building. Boiling the water wasn't necessary, but Min Li would continue to do so, mostly out of habit. She had learned after moving to Shenyang never to drink the water from the faucet.

Aliyah and Huda arrived about twenty minutes late and found Min Li sitting in the kitchen sipping her boiled water. Min Li found it a little unnerving that they let themselves in without knocking but assumed that was the result of another cultural difference.

"What happened to the beds?" Aliyah asked.

"I took them apart, just the ones in the living room. We won't need them, and I'd like to turn that room back into a sitting room for our staff."

"I suppose that makes sense," Aliya said. "We didn't think much about it. This apartment came with the business when we bought it, so we haven't done anything with it."

"People need to feel like they are in a real home," Min Li reasoned. "That will help them be more productive at work. Do you have a way of getting some sofas and a television for the living room?"

"We can stop by the Friday Market and pick some things out."

"Friday Market?"

"It's a big outdoor market west of here out on Ring Road 4. You can buy almost anything there cheaply."

"But it's not Friday."

"That's not a problem. It started out as a flea market on Fridays for expatriates, but it's grown and it's open every day now. We'll go there right after breakfast."

"Breakfast sounds good. I've been up since before six when those loudspeakers woke me up."

"Oh, the call to prayer. You'll get used to that and sleep through it as we do. Let's go eat."

The three women left the apartment and climbed into the Expedition again. Raja then drove them down Arabian Gulf Street to Souq Sharq, an upscale shopping center on the shore of the Persian Gulf, called the Arabian Gulf by Kuwaitis, near Kuwait City. Huda ordered Chai Haleeb, black tea infused with milk and flavored with cinnamon and cardamom. They ate Irani bread, a type of flat bread, and eggs cooked with tomatoes. Min Li thought about asking if people in Kuwait ate porridge, but thought better about it. She would not need to get used to eating like the Kuwaitis so long as she had a kitchen and access to the right foods to cook. Raja remained outside while the three ate.

They finished eating around ten, and by then the temperature had already exceeded 43ºC (109ºF). Min Li wondered how Huda and Aliyah could handle the heat the way they dressed. Like when she first met them in Shenyang, they each still wore a black abaya over their regular clothes and a hijab over their head to hide their hair. They almost looked like some Catholic nuns she once saw in a photograph she had seen in the old church in Shangguang.

They drove south on Al Riyadh Road to Ring Road 4 until they reached Airport Road, turned right, then left again on Airport Road, pulling off onto a roughly paved service road that took them into a large dirt parking area, at least a kilometer deep. The parking area was about a third full with cars and pickup trucks parked haphazardly, barely forming rows. Raja drove past the parked cars up to a large permanent awning at least 20 meters high and 150 meters wide, under which sat the Friday Market.

The women alit from the car and wondered through the aisles marking the clothing section. They crossed over a wide aisle, which seemed to separate sections and found themselves in the furniture section. There, they looked at several sofas, bargained with the men who operated various stalls, and finally settled on two matching sofas covered with a brown corduroy fabric that almost matched. In another stall, they found a matching set of two end tables and a coffee table. Aliyah called Raja on her cell phone and told him where to find them. He appeared within minutes. Huda gave him instructions in Arabic, and he left again. Next, the three walked over to the rug section, and Huda picked out a rug of approximately twelve square meters. The rug was new and looked expensive with a red and gold Persian design, but Aliyah said that it was most certainly a fake, especially at that price.

Their last stop was at a stall that sold used televisions, and Huda again negotiated a price for a 35-inch flat panel late model television. She made sure it worked before paying for it. By then, Raja had reappeared with three workers pushing a large three-wheeled trolley. He would have them gather Huda's purchases and load them onto a truck. They gave one of the three of these men the address of the apartment on Al Mughira Bin Shu'ba Street. Raja would meet them with a key after dropping the women off at Souq Salmiya, which Min Li later learned was walking distance from her new home.

According to Aliyah, Souq Salmiya had everything she would need, clothing, food items, shoes, household goods, and other items. They browsed around the mall for a while, going up and down the various aisles with many small shops selling cheap clothing, shoes, luggage, almost all bearing fake designer labels, and everything being made in China.

Souq Salmiya boasted at least three coffee shops on the ground floor, and several fast food restaurants on the second floor, some American, such as McDonalds, and others of Middle Eastern origins, many of which sold shawarmas, lamb stews, and roasted chicken. The largest feature of the Souq was the two-story City Centre Supermarket. There, Min Li loaded up a shopping cart with a 20 kg bag of long grain rice, noodles, corn grain, jars of spices, various dry goods, cartons of fresh milk, and vegetables. She skipped those vegetables she had never seen before and was disappointed that she could not find any daikon radishes. When she came to the fruits, Min Li was quite pleased with the selection of Fuji apples, a favorite of people from Liaoning Province.

Their last stop in the supermarket was the meat counter. Min Li chose some nice selections of chicken, but there was no pork, not a single piece. She was about to say something when she remembered her being peppered with questions at the airport the day before. Min Li would have to learn to live without pork, which is banned in Kuwait. *That's going to be hard*, Min Li thought to herself. *Pork is practically the national meat of China.* She decided to take some more beef to make up for the lack of pork, the chose a small grouper fish to add to the basket. She couldn't think of anything else she needed, so she pushed the teeming shopping cart to the front checkout stands with Huda and Aliyah following close behind.

Huda paid for Min Li's purchases, and they pushed the cart through the doors of City Centre leading out to the rest of the mall. Aliya found them a free table at one of the coffee shops and purchased three cafe lattes, the first "designer" coffee Min Li ever tasted. According to Aliya, it's the same as one would buy at a Starbucks. Min Li had to add three packets of sugar before she could handle the strong coffee taste.

As they sipped their coffee, Huda and Aliyah talked to each other in Arabic, allowing Min Li a chance to watch the people around her. Two tables away, Min Li saw two Kuwaiti women sipping coffee while three children sat with them drinking hot chocolate. Standing next to them holding a baby was a Filipina woman, dressed much like Vanessa, but wearing pink instead of grey. She stood the whole time and tended to the baby, never once sitting down. Nor was she drinking anything. After a moment, one of the Kuwaiti women took the baby from the Filipina's arms, bounced the baby a little, kissed it on the face, and handed it back to the Filipina who remained standing the whole time.

She observed several Kuwaiti men wearing traditional white dishdashas walking together holding hands. From time to time, she saw men greet each other and then kiss each other on both cheeks. *This never happened in China*, she thought, but again, she chalked it up as a cultural difference, because, as she had read in her travel guide, homosexual conduct is illegal in Kuwait. She saw a Kuwaiti family walking through the mall, a man dressed in a dishdasha, followed by two wives and five children. She even saw one man with four wives.

Aliyah's cell phone rang, and Raja told her that he was just outside the north entrance. The three women gathered up their things and Min Li pushed the shopping basket after Huda, who led the trio to the north entrance. Min Li couldn't lead, because she had completely lost her bearings and couldn't identify north from south.

"Vanessa will meet us at your apartment to help put things away," Aliyah said. We haven't much time. After we drop off your purchases, we have to hurry to the spa to interview job applicants. The ad in today's paper said to apply in person after three o'clock today."

"What about the furniture?"

"Already there. The four beds you took apart have been taken to the storage shed behind our house in Rumaithiya. Vanessa will remain and clean the apartment and help you sort things out when you get home tonight."

"Well, I came here to work," Min Li acknowledged. "Now is as good a time as ever."

Min Li spent only about fifteen minutes at the apartment unloading her purchases from the car while Raja helped. Huda and Aliyah remained in the air-conditioned car and waited for Min Li to finish her two trips upstairs. Min Li was grateful for the elevator. Most apartment buildings in China didn't have elevators unless they were more than seven stories high, but most apartment buildings were seven stories or less.

The car pulled up to the front of the shop about a quarter to three. Already, a line had formed outside in the hot sun, and no fewer than a hundred applicants had responded to the ad. The ad had specifically stated that the shop was looking for women from the Philippines, Southeast Asia, or China, yet many of those in line were southern Asian, such as Indians, Sri Lankans, Bangladeshis, and Pakistanis. Min Li didn't care where the applicants were from, but she could tell that Huda was upset by her rapid-fire Arabic. Aliyah had told Min Li why.

"Customers will believe that eastern Asian women are better at this sort of work."

"Indians can't cut hair?" Min Li asked.

"I'm sure they can, perhaps some better than most, but that's not the point."

"What difference does it make?"

"If we hire Indians or other people from their part of the continent, we will lose business."

"That doesn't seem fair. What do they think of Chinese?"

"Chinese make good massage therapists."

Min Li thought about that for a moment. She had gone to a massage shop a few times in Shenyang, but never remembered receiving an excellent massage. Blind people staff most legitimate massage shops in China. The government, which still likes to select careers for its people, seems always to send blind people to massage school. Most people think that it's because people are shy and a blind person cannot see the person upon whom they are working. That rationale never worked for Min Li, though, because in China people leave their clothes on for legitimate massages. But the Kuwaitis believed that Chinese make good massage therapists, so they were included in the help wanted ad.

The car drove around to the alley in the back and let the women out there so that they could go in through the backdoor to avoid the large crowd out front. Min Li set herself at the manager's station, while Raja handed out application forms to the women in line outside.

"Open the door so they can come in and get cool," Min Li demanded. "They can stand in here in the air conditioning. I'll interview in the break room."

Raja opened the door and screened the applicants for country of origin pursuant to Huda's instructions, turning away all women from India, Pakistan, Bangladesh, and Sri Lanka. Two women were Egyptian, three Lebanese, and two who claimed they were Kuwaiti. When Min Li asked why the Kuwaitis were rejected, Aliyah told her that they were not really Kuwaiti; otherwise, they would have Kuwaiti ID. They were Bedouin who were born in the desert who claim that their proof of birth was destroyed during the invasion by Iraq in 1990. These women were, in fact, stateless, and could claim to be citizens of no country.

'so how does that keep us from hiring them?" Min Li asked, still puzzled.

"If we hire them, they can use that to legitimize their claim for Kuwaiti citizenship. We can't have that."

Min Li was still confused, and she reviewed the list of other requirements given to her in English by Aliyah. There were only a few. The applicants must have proof that they are in Kuwait legally and that they are not otherwise in an employment contract. They must speak English, and it would be nice if they could also speak Arabic. They must be qualified to do the job for the position for which they are applying. They must be single. They must be honest. They must not be Muslim.

"Why can they not be Muslim?" Min Li asked, confused. "This is a Muslim country."

'Muslims in the servant class from other countries are lazy," Aliyah said without hesitation.

"What?"

"They will stop working every time there is a call to prayer. The shop will be open for four of them."

"Isn't that part of their religion?"

"Not everybody heeds the call to prayer. We stopped employing Muslims in our household because they would stop working, using the call to prayer as an excuse. That takes five minutes away from their work."

Min Li considered the rationale and how Aliyah disapproved of her household servants taking a five-minute break four, maybe five times a day. *How hard do they work their servants?* Min Li asked herself.

By the time Raja had weeded out the obvious "rejects" from the line of applicant, no more applicants stood outside in the hot sun. The big room of the shop was large enough to accommodate the remainder, although it was still tight and standing room only. Min Li rose from the table in the break room and went into the big room to make an announcement. "Those of you who are finished completing the application please form one line beginning here." Three women immediately stood next to Min Li. She pointed to the first one and led her back into the break room.

"I'm Min Li Zhang, and you?"
"Ma Linda Estrella."
"Ma Linda?" Min Li clarified.
"Actually Maria Linda. Most people call me Ma Linda."
"Where are you from, Ma Linda?"
"I'm from the Philippines, from Cebu."
"What brought you to Kuwait?"
"I came as a maid twelve years ago."
"What did you do before you were a maid, when you were in the Philippines?"
"Nothing. Just a housewife."
"Are you married?"
"Yes."
"Where is your husband?"
"In Cebu."
"Why did you come to Kuwait?"

"To be a maid. My family needed money."

"How long were you a maid?"

"Five years, like everybody else."

"Were you able to send money home as a maid?"

"Oh, yes. I earned thirty-five Kuwaiti dinars at first, and I sent twenty-five home every month. Later, I was earning fifty a month, so I sent home forty. I did quite well."

"You didn't go back to Cebu after your five-year contract?"

"No. I could make more money in Kuwait if I wasn't a maid. My family needed the money."

"What did you do when your maid contract was finished?"

"First I worked in a KFC for about two years. I was earning 150 a month there, but I had to use some of that to live on, so I could only send 50 a month home. After that, I got a job here."

"Here?"

"I worked in this salon before it was purchased by the new owners."

"What did you do here?"

"Pedicures and manicures. I was quite good at it. Would you like to see some photos of my work?"

"You have photos?"

"Yes." Ma Linda took out a small portfolio with at least 200 photos of fingernail designs and flipped through the pages for Min Li to see.

"Did you like working here?"

"It was nice. I was earning 300 a month, more than the other girl, because I had so many repeat customers. They liked my work."

"How were you paid?"

"I had a base salary of 150, and the owner gave me half the tips I earned."

"Half? That doesn't sound so good."

"It's real good. Some places, the owners don't share the tips."

"What about your living arrangements? Did you live in the apartment on Al Mughira Bin Shu'ba Street?"

"That wasn't so good. It was two crowded. There were sixteen beds and twenty-one people living there. Some people slept on the floor. Then it was hard to enforce the chore schedule. Sometimes people whose turn it was to cook wouldn't come home, and nobody wanted to clean their mess. The kitchen was horrible, and the bathrooms were worse."

"Would you mind living there again if only eleven people lived there and we had a strict chore schedule?"

"That might be better."

"Where are you staying now?"

"With some Filipino friends that I met over the years."

"Do you ever plan to return to Cebu?"

"I don't know. It's been too long. My children don't live with my husband anymore."

"Where do they live?"

"Two are already grown, and my youngest lives with my mother."

'so your husband is alone. Does he miss you?"

"No and no."

"I see. Have you thought about divorcing him? I'm not trying to encourage you, but it just seems that after all these years, you two don't really have a marriage anymore."

"I can't."

"Why not?"

"I can't divorce him here for two reasons, I'm not Kuwaiti and I'm not a man. I can't divorce him in the Philippines because there is no such thing as divorce there."

"That doesn't sound very good."

"I'm fine. I live in Kuwait where I can make money. If I went back to the Philippines, I wouldn't make money and I'd be stuck at home with nothing to do. This is better."

"Can you start work Wednesday? That's the day after tomorrow."

"Yes, but the sign out front said the grand opening is Friday."

"We want to do some training and get everybody's station ready. We'll have new rules to teach everybody."

"I can be here. When can I move into the apartment?"

"This evening at eight. I'll be there to let you in."

Min Li had just hired the first employee for Arabian Beauty Spa. She had nine more to go. Min Li told Ma Linda she was looking forward to working with her and asked her to send the next person in line. A few seconds later, a Chinese woman walked in who looked to be in her mid-thirties.

"*Ni hao. Ni shi zhongguoren ma?*" (Hello, are you Chinese?), Min Li asked.

'Shi" (I am).

"Can you speak English?" Min Li asked, which was a requirement for the job.

"*Yi dian, ne ge*, I mean a little."

"I'm Zhang Min Li, which I suppose is Min Li Zhang here. And you are?"

"Hui Jing Jing. People say Jing Jing."

"Where are you from, Jing Jing?"

"China."

"I mean, what part of China, which city?"

"Liaoning. Jinzhou."

"I know Jinzhou. I'm from Shenyang. Well, actually I'm from nearby Hululdao, but I moved to Shenyang almost twenty years ago."

'many girls from Liaoning here."

'really? I only arrived yesterday. You're the first Chinese I met. What do you do?"

"*An ma, ne ge*, massage. I very good."

"Where did you learn English, Jing Jing."

"In middle school in China, but that no good. Most I learn in Kuwait."

"How long have you been in Kuwait?"

"Two years."

"What brought you here?"

"I came to work in doctor's office."

"Doing what?"

"They tell me I be nurse, but I have to do massage."

"Is that where you learned to do massage?"

"Yes, both kinds."

"What do you mean both kinds?"

"Good kind and bad kind. More money for bad kind, but I don't like."

"Why didn't you just quit?"

"I quit after three months but they put me in jail for six months. Can't quit in Kuwait."

"You're here now. Do you still work for the doctor's office?"

"Contract finished two weeks ago. If I don't find new job *kuai le* must leave Kuwait."

"Here you can only do good massages with women customers."

"Good."

"You can't do private massages."

"Good."

"If you do, you'll be terminated and your work permit will be revoked. You'll have to leave Kuwait."

"Good."

"Please tell me about your massages."

"I give three massage. First is Swedish. That easy massage use oil. Very relax. And I give deep massage. Hurt more but good if body bad. Not too many customers like. And I can do Thai massage. Many stretch muscles."

"Do you have a following?"

'*Shenme*?'

"Will your regular customers follow you here from where you worked before?"

"No want following. Only want new customers. But all customers come back again. No problem. I good massage."

"How much were you paid at the doctor's office?"

"I get five K.D. for good massage, ten for bad."

"Here, you will earn three hundred Kuwaiti dinars a month, and you can keep the tips."

"*Zhende ma*? I want job. When to start?"

"Day after tomorrow, *hou tian*."

"Where are you living now?"

"No place. Job ended. Last night I stay at friend's. Night before I stay in park. I worry bad people and police see me."

"Bring your things to this address on Al Mughira Bin Shu"ba Street at eight tonight. You can sleep in my room. Maybe I can help your English."

"*Xie xie, a yi*. I come tonight. Happy day."

By seven o'clock, Min Li had finally finished interviewing all the applicants. She hired ten women: one massage therapist, two manicurists, six hair stylists, and an aesthetician, somebody to do make-up and waxings. Four of them would meet her at the apartment at eight, and the others will come the next day. With the exception of the room in which Min Li slept, the bunks would go on a first come, first serve basis. Jing Jing would sleep in the same room as Min Li, being the only other Chinese employee. Min Li would cook a late dinner for five people that evening, and establish house rules with a duty roster by the next day.

Everybody agreed to start work two days later to set up their stations and to go over procedures. They would also do each other's hair and nails, and Min Li would make sure they all knew how to apply make-up for themselves. Everybody working in a beauty shop must be beautiful. It wouldn't make sense otherwise. By Wednesday, uniforms would be delivered, pink work dresses and black shoes. Min Li hoped that nobody lied about their sizes, because there would be no time to exchange them before opening day Thursday. Shoes were another matter, and Min Li encouraged Huda and Aliya to bring extra pairs to ensure that everybody had well-fitting, comfortable shoes, because they would be on their feet all day. The shop would open on-time Thursday promptly at ten in the morning and remain open until nine that night.

As exhausted as Min Li was, still suffering from jet lag, she felt energized and ready to work some more. She would sleep well her second night in Kuwait.

Twenty Six

When Peter North finished his recent year of teaching in China, he headed to Nevada instead of the school district from which he had obtained a year's leave of absence. Peter believed that teaching in China provided him a unique insight in the science, or maybe art, of teaching. He hoped to apply these unique skills in what he thought would be a typical American school district outside the influence of Silicon Valley, so he chose to teach in Reno, only a few hours from the civilization to which he was accustomed.

His first time in China, Peter taught conversational English at a university in Shenyang. It was a typical English as a Second Language (ESL) job, and it gave him his first taste of China. There, he met and fell in love with a Chinese elementary school English teacher, Zhang Min Li. She taught him various aspects of Chinese culture that he could never have known otherwise, and he fell in love with the Chinese people. He remained at odds with the Chinese system of government, which never set well with his American sense of democracy and his commitment to human rights issues. The things about the Chinese people that he liked the most was their industry, their willingness to get on with their lives, no matter what obstacles they faced, and their hope in the face of oppression.

He would have married Min Li. Unfortunately, they had both settled into what Peter called life's "practical mode," and they reasoned that their marriage would not be well considered. He was American with loyalties in America where he planned to keep his roots, and she was Chinese with loyalties in China where she planned to keep her roots. They never talked about compromise, and neither knew whether the other was capable of it. They just assumed that it would be unfair to expect the other to make a compromise, so they thought that the "practical" thing to do was to go on with their lives separately. For Peter, this was a mistake.

He couldn't keep his mind off China. More accurately, he couldn't keep his mind off Min Li. To advance his career in education, Peter earned a master's degree, choosing as his thesis topic *Integrating the Beneficial Aspects of Chinese Education in American Schools*. As he researched and wrote his thesis, one Chinese face haunted him, that of Min Li. He often wondered if maybe the only reason he had an interest in China was because of her. By then, he had married a nice American woman, and the marriage worked well for more than fifteen years. But Peter felt compelled to return to China, at least for a year, to learn more about the Chinese and about teaching to Chinese.

He landed a job with a Canadian program in Changchun in Jilin province, only two hours by train from Shenyang. There, he would teach the Nova Scotia curriculum in a special program for Chinese students who wanted to attend university in Canada. All classes were taught in English, and the students graduated with both a Chinese and a Canadian high school diploma. Peter was thrilled, because he would be teaching regular English literature, not ESL, although his students' English skills varied greatly. Rather than teaching them how to make greetings and invite friends to a party, he could teach them *King Lear* and the principles of rhetoric.

His wife would have nothing to do with that. They had grown apart over the past couple of years anyway, and she never could understand Peter's fascination with the Chinese. Their divorce was amicable, and she promised to keep Peter's half of their household furnishings until he returned from China, which was a simple thing to do, since his things would remain in the house in which the two of them resided together. Peter applied for and obtained a one-year leave of absence from his school district and was again China-bound.

Always in the back of his mind, Peter thought about Min Li. He had no contact information for her in Shenyang, so he thought that his chances of finding her were nonexistent, but he often thought how wonderful it would be if he ran into her in Shenyang. Of course, that might have presented some problems, particularly if she were married. And there was the problem that she might have lost interest in him. He wouldn't set his heart on re-uniting with Min Li. He was going back to China to teach, and he would focus on that. But still, if they did see each other, that could only be a good thing.

After arriving in Changchun, Peter learned something about his Chinese students that he couldn't know when teaching only ESL. They do their homework. As an English teacher in an American school, Peter knew that when he gave an essay assignment, on the due date he could grade all the turned in essays and still have time for a leisurely dinner and a movie. He would be lucky if even half the students turned in the assignments on time. However, when he assigned a due date for an essay in China, all 161 students turned their assignments in on time. Had he not promised his students to grade all assignments and have them posted by the next day, he could have enjoyed that dinner and movie. Instead, Peter would work until one in the morning grading essays, no easy task considering his students were not native-English speakers.

Peter worked his students hard, because he taught twelfth graders and had to make sure they could pass the Nova Scotia Provincial Exam, which was designed for native-English speakers.

But Chinese students are used to working hard. They typically start school at 7:30 and get an hour and a half break for lunch. Then they're back in school until 6:00 that evening when they get another break for dinner. They study again until 9:00 p.m. when those who live nearby go home for the evening. The students who reside in dormitories remain in the classroom until 10:00. All but one of his students managed to pass the Nova Scotia Provincial Exam in English Language Arts.

Once a month, Peter took the train into Shenyang. He knew Shenyang well, having taught there fifteen years earlier, and he needed to replenish his supplies of western food products, which were much more abundantly available in Shenyang due to the large number of foreigners. Every time Peter went to Shenyang, he kept his eyes open for Min Li. He knew it was silly to expect to see her in such a large city with a population of more than five million in the urban area.

He actually thought he saw her once outside the American consulate. He was in the neighborhood and tried to take photos of both the American and Japanese consulates before he was chased off by Chinese guards. He barely caught a glimpse of her face, if it actually was her, before she turned and walked away. She was with another woman talking, so she would have been too distracted to notice him. He ran to catch up to her, but just before he broke through a crowd milling in front of the American consulate, the woman that looked like Min Li caught a taxi. She was gone before she could even hear him shout. He felt foolish and stopped looking for her after that.

Then he went to Reno. Reno seemed like a great place, open spaces, blue skies, four seasons. His school even had wild horses that sometimes grazed on the front lawn. But he wasn't used to teaching American students, especially ninth-graders. Not only did they not do their work, either in class or at home, but there was hardly any incentive for them to do so. Peter learned that in Reno, students are passed from one grade to the next regardless of whether they pass their classes or not, even in middle school. Many of Peter's ninth graders hadn't passed any of their core subjects in any of their three years of middle school. Yet they were still promoted to high school, and those who failed three years of middle school English did not feel obliged to do their work in high school.

This created classroom discipline problems that Peter never experienced, not even in the school where he taught in California. Because there was no reason to do their work, at least in the minds of a good number of his students, they didn't do their work. And because they were not working, class became boring. When class becomes boring, kids act up. Peter sent a few kids to the dean's office, but it was the dean's first year on the job. Her only real teaching experience was as a special education aide, then a little time as a special education teacher after getting her teaching license. Before turning to education, the dean majored in psychology, so instead of being a dean and disciplining the misbehaving students, she wanted to psychoanalyze them, which did nothing for student discipline.

The school where Peter taught in Reno became a nightmare. Students quickly learned that they could get special treatment by writing out false statements against teachers, that they could get away with not doing their work by blaming the teacher, and that, when their four years of high school was nearly finished, they could be placed in a special classroom to make up all their missing credits during the last semester and still graduate with their peers. Peter enjoyed teaching too much to remain at a school where the culture had evolved to this. Teaching should be fun, which makes learning fun, Peter always believed. But when an administration facilitates empowerment of underachieving students while constantly telling them that they are successful no matter what, working at such a school is no different from working in a factory. Teachers learned to get along, to keep their mouths closed, and to not be noticed.

The by-word at his school was to keep peace in the classroom. Don't do anything that would cause a parent complaint, no matter what the intention was and how well the students learned from it. Keep students out of the office by 're-teaching expectations." In other words, maintain the status quo. This particularly distressed Peter who had learned some very interesting teaching techniques while earning his master's degree, but each time he tried to implement any of them, he was chastised for "not following best practices," practices that his administrators might have learned years before and may or may not have used themselves in a classroom. The fact that his students performed better on standardized testing, and the fact that fewer of his students failed than in other classes, made little difference. Peter did not fit in, and it became clear that he would never fit in unless he lowered his principles.

Peter loved teaching, and he wanted to be in a school that supported his belief that hard work, nurtured by a caring teacher, will develop a desire for lifelong learning in a student. That wasn't going to happen at his school in Reno. He thought about teaching again in China, but he thought he was narrowing his focus too much. He wanted to know if students other than in China could care as much about their education. Then he received an email inviting him to serve as a mentor teacher in the United Arab Emirates.

The email came from a private contractor providing services to the UAE Ministry of Education. After reviewing his application and interviewing him three times, they told Peter that they wanted him, as soon as the Ministry signed the contract. Peter became interested in teaching in the Middle East, having researched various aspects of it. He was attracted to it because the Middle Easterners, particularly in the Gulf States, placed so much emphasis on education. He decided that it would give him good experience, and he would be able to broaden his cultural horizons, making him a better teacher back home.

The UAE job never came through, but by then, Peter had been researching teaching positions in Qatar, Bahrain, Saudi Arabia, and Kuwait. He settled for a school in Kuwait that taught the New York curriculum. He applied, was interviewed via Skype, and was on his way to Kuwait within two weeks. The first day of school would occur two days after arriving, so he would spend nearly the entire time writing lesson plans, course syllabi, and numerous other documents and preparing worksheets for his students.

Peter found himself teaching four classes of 12th grade British literature and one speech class in a walled off school in the middle of Abraq Khaitan, a neighborhood dominated by rough Egyptian day laborers. The school had three gates, heavily guarded by armed retired Nepalese army veterans. It was divided into three campuses, the elementary school, the girls' upper school, and the boys' upper school. Peter taught one 12th grade girls' class, and had to walk across campus, through the walled divider, to teach the girls.

The school provided the expatriate teachers with suitable housing. It rented a block of apartments in a building in Hawally, abutting Ring Road 4, as well as a block of apartments in a building off Amman Street near Ring Road 5 in Salmiya, about ten miles from campus. After the first week, the teachers were responsible for their own transportation. Most took taxis or car-pooled with other teachers, but Peter opted to lease a car, which would give him more freedom of movement and the ability to explore Kuwait.

Although he didn't earn quite what he did in America, Peter couldn't complain. The difference was more than made up by the housing. The school provided each teacher with his or her own one-bedroom apartment. Peter's had a spacious living room with an eighth-floor balcony overlooking a portion of Salmiya. He had two sofas and an easy chair, a television with satellite reception and numerous English channels, which certainly beat the one English language channel in China, which broadcast Chinese propaganda all day every day. His bedroom included a king size bed with a memory foam mattress, a large wardrobe, and a full dresser. The kitchen was "western," in that it had regular cupboards, a countertop, a full refrigerator, a small four-burner stove with oven, as well as a stacking washer-dryer unit. He would have had none of this in China. Even more special was a regular western-style bathroom with a shower and bathtub. The one feature that even his apartment in America didn't have was a bidet faucet near the toilet, which took some time for Peter to learn to use.

Peter enjoyed cooking for himself, and quickly made friends with the Iranians who operated the produce market next to his apartment building. Every day, they'd see Peter pull into his apartment's parking lot in his rented Mazda 6, and they'd bring him some bananas. Peter purchased all of his fresh produce there, regardless of whether he planned to shop elsewhere for his other groceries.

Nearly every day after dinner and after grading papers, Peter enjoyed driving down to Salem Al Mubarak Street, where he would read each of Kuwait's three English-language newspapers at the Second Cup Coffee shop across from the Sultan Center, a large, busy supermarket. Often, he would take his friend, Habib, the Lebanese math teacher, with him to the coffee shop. Peter read the newspapers while Habib played chess with a group of Lebanese physicians. When Habib wasn't playing chess, he and Peter would talk about the difference between western and Islamic culture, between Kuwait and Lebanon, and about women.

Because Kuwait has no bars, not even for foreigners like some of the other Gulf States, Kuwait had an abundance of coffee shops.

The evenings often saw the coffee shops crowded, and one was certain to run into foreigners there. Indians would sit at a table discussing Indian politics, in English because their Indian dialects were too diverse for them to understand each other. Another table would find a group of Lebanese. Several tables would be taken up by Kuwaitis. The Filipinos worked behind the counter and cleaned the tables. And always there was a soccer game or other sport contest on the wide screen television. Were it not for other negative aspects of Kuwait, Peter would have enjoyed his time in Kuwait. It was a time of leisure, reflection, and intellectual stimulation.

Too often Peter saw how the local citizens treated the servant class. One day shopping in Sultan Center, Peter saw a Filipino stock clerk carrying three heavy flats of vegetables toward the produce section, when a man wearing a dishdasha asked him a question. The Filipino had already passed the other man and didn't know he was being addressed. Frustrated that the Filipino didn't stop what he was doing, the man wearing the dishdasha slapped the Filipino, nearly causing him to drop the heavy flats of vegetables. The Filipino dared not complain. Too often, he observed Kuwaiti families out for an evening in a nice restaurant while their Filipina nanny stood nearby, often holding a baby, never being allowed to sit and never being given food or drink.

Peter learned of a secret group of Filipinos that help domestic workers escape their employers by smuggling them out of the country. He first met members of this group at his church, one of only four in the country, and the only church with a Chinese congregation, which met on an upper floor while English services were conducted below. He started carrying with him business cards from that group, which he would secretly hand to domestic workers that he saw being abused. Of course, Peter saw very little compared to what actually happened in the privacy of the sponsors' homes. Those often resulted in atrocities that he could read about in the newspapers.

Peter lived rather comfortably in Kuwait, despite the things he saw that gave him discomfort. He still was an expatriate, but he was an American, and that gave him a certain status that other expatriates did not enjoy. He was almost as good as Kuwaiti. More importantly, Peter's students respected him, they responded to him, and they did well under his instruction. And he had made many friends, mostly non-Kuwaitis, which made living in Kuwait good enough.

Living in a new environment, learning a different culture, and adapting his lifestyle gave Peter the chance he needed to take his mind off Min Li. He still loved her, and probably always would, but at least he could take his mind and spirit to another place where the pain in his heart could no longer be felt.

Twenty Seven

Min Li never worked so hard, at least not that she could remember. Not only was she managing a busy day spa, but she also managed a household with eleven women. She thought it would be easier than it turned out to be. She created a duty schedule that she strictly enforced in the apartment, but dealing with the diverse cultures of the residents required a certain finesse. Naturally, she and Jing Jing preferred Chinese food, but the six Filipinas demanded Filipino food, which Jing Jing complained about incessantly. Fortunately, nobody complained about dinner when it was Vietnamese night or when either of the two Thais cooked, except that the Thai food was sometimes too spicy.

At least half the household couldn't remember to keep the shower curtains closed, and nearly everybody used too much hot water, so half the time some of the women had to take cold showers. Min Li resolved this by encouraging some of the women to take showers at work, either first thing in the morning or before they went home for the evening.

Working in the beauty spa presented fewer problems. Everybody was typically busy with the services that each provided and there were few customer complaints that couldn't be resolved. From the day the shop opened, Arabian Beauty Spa had a steady flow of customers, due in large part to the ubiquitous print advertising, as well as a large network the owner's friends and associates. The shop made more money than Min Li expected during its first month in operation, and all of its employees looked forward to fat paychecks at the end of the month.

Min Li expected nothing more than her salary of 500 Kuwaiti dinars. The others worked for much smaller salaries, but were promised that they would be allowed to keep their tips. All of the tips were collected by the shop, banked until payday, and then paid back out to the employees. Aliya explained that this was Kuwaiti law. From time to time, the employees were allowed to take an advance on their salaries in order to purchase personal necessities, but these advances were minimal at best. Min Li kept accurate records of both advances and tips collected, so each of the women always knew where they stood.

Then it was payday, and Min Li learned just how hard her job would be. Huda had deducted from each woman's salary 200 Kuwaiti dinars for rent and 100 Kuwaiti dinars for food, as well as any advances each employee may have taken over the past month. Some women were able to put no more than thirty dinars in her pocket. Min Li received nothing. Deducted from Min Li's 500-dinar salary was not only the rent and groceries, but also the cost of her airfare from China, the 35-dinar visa fee, and a 200-dinar fee for processing the visa. Not only that, her visa was only valid for one month, and she would have to pay another 235 dinars for a one-month extension. If she wanted, she could pay 2,000 dinars for a one-year work permit, but that was up to her.

It only took a second for Min Li to realize that if she were to stay in Kuwait under these conditions, she couldn't net even 100 dinars a month, and that is without factoring in the cost of her airfare. She called Aliya to ask about these surprises.

"The contract said that you would provide airfare, visa, and housing, in addition to a salary of 500 dinars a month," she said trying not to show her temper.

"There must have been an error in the English version of the contract," Aliya responded.

"The business is making more than enough money to pay what you promised me."

"But we have to pay what the contract requires. That is the law."

"But that's what the contract says," Min Li thought she was repeating herself.

"That is a mistake in the English version."

"That is what I signed."

"But the Arabic version is what is enforced. That is the law. You should have read the Arabic version. The English version was provided only as a courtesy."

"Where does it say that in the contract?" Min Li almost shouted.

"In the Arabic version."

"But I don't speak Arabic. I certainly don't read it."

"You should have had somebody read it for you. A lawyer perhaps."

"In Shenyang? You hired me in China. The contract should have been in Chinese."

"I'm sorry. We are in Kuwait. We must follow Kuwait's laws. Please don't forget that you are a guest in this country."

"Well, I certainly don't feel like a guest."

"I'm sorry. That is the law."

"I'm sorry, too," Min Li said, this time almost shouting. "I'm going back to my business in Shenyang. I feel that I have been cheated."

"You cannot do that," Aliya explained. "You have a contract. You must stay until the end of your contract."

"Do you really expect me to work for almost free for five years?"

"We expect you to comply with the terms of your contract."

"Then I'm exercising my right to cancel the contract at any time I choose. And you must provide me with return airfare."

"That's not in the contract."

"It most certainly is." As soon as Min Li said this, she assumed that it was not in the Arabic version. She closed her phone without saying good-bye, went into the break room, closed the door, sat down, and cried.

By now, the other workers were no longer angry with Min Li. They had surmised what had happened from listening to Min Li's side of the telephone conversation. They left her alone, not knowing what they could say to console her. They could only hear Min Li's sobbing.

When Min Li had finally spent her tears, she remained sitting in the break room, thankful that nobody had come it to see her in such an undignified state. This felt worse than it did when the owner of the Shenyang Electrical Appliances Company skipped town. At least she received some regular salary then. But under these conditions, Min Li would be working for practically nothing, and she would have nothing to show for her time in Kuwait except more experience, experience that she did not need. And she wasn't getting any younger. She was nearly forty years old, and she realized that the prime of her life had already passed her.

Closing time came at seven, and before Min Li could lock the front door, the other women had to do their closing chores, sweeping their area, emptying trash, cleaning the sinks, and washing, drying, and folding towels. Everybody did what she was supposed to do without Min Li having to remind them. While they worked, Min Li stared at the cash box that held the day's receipts, and for the first time in her life thought about doing something dishonest. But she couldn't even keep the thought in her head. Some things are more important than money, namely her reputation, and she would not allow that to be destroyed.

Min Li took the cash box and locked it in the floor safe behind the manager's station. Now the safe held more than three thousand Kuwaiti dollars because Huda had not picked up the money to make a deposit. Min Li thought it strange that Huda would not even be concerned about getting the money to the bank, especially in light of her having cheated Min Li out of her salary. Huda obviously wasn't hurting for money. If so, Min Li might understand what had happened. She supposed that it was just the nature of some people.

At seven, Min Li locked up the front and the eleven women slipped out the back door into a short alley that emptied into a parking lot. As was their daily custom, they walked the eight blocks as a group back to the apartment. They learned shortly after opening the shop a month ago always to remain in a large group. That's when Ma Linda and another Filipina made a detour to buy some toothpaste, shampoo, and mangoes at Sultan Center. The rest of the group went on without them.

After making their purchases, the two had only walked two blocks before a car stopped near them and the driver offered them a ride. They both knew better and refused. The driver told them that he was an undercover police officer, and he was placing them both under arrest for prostitution, his evidence being that they were two single Asian women out alone at night. This had happened to Ma Linda before, but instead of being taken to the police station, the driver took her to a rented apartment in Fahaiheel. He dragged her from the car but she broke free and ran. She later learned that the police had arrested a gang operating out of the same building who was buying women, mostly Filipinas, to force them into prostitution. She wasn't going to allow that to happen, so she grabbed her friend and they ran into the Al Fanar Complex, a small upscale mall on Salem al Mubarak Street. Thereafter, all eleven women stayed together after hours. If one needed to go shopping, they all went with her.

When the group reached the apartment, Min Li headed to the kitchen. It was her turn to cook. Ma Linda and Jing Jing both offered to take her turn cooking. When Min Li assented, they argued amongst themselves, because Ma Linda did not want to each Chinese food and Jing Jing had no tolerance for Filipino food that night. The argument was settled when May, one of the two Thai women, offered to cook. Nobody ever refused her food. May would cook, and Ma Linda and Jing Jing agreed to clean up the kitchen. Min Li went into her room to think.

Min Li thought about her mother. It seemed like decades since her mother died, although it really had only been about three years. She remembered her mother making her promise to leave her on Pàotǎ Shān, that good things will happen to her family if she did so. And so they did for her brother, Xiong Yong. He advanced rapidly and now made enough money to own two houses. He was making so much money, he was hiding it in banks in other cities. The last time she talked to him, he was planning a trip to Hong Kong where he wanted to open a bank account.

Her sisters were doing well, considering. Hai Tian finally was married, and Hong Qi was on her way to being a pig farmer, which would be much more lucrative than merely farming corn. But Min Li's life had taken a turn for the worse. Sure, she had a successful business again in Shenyang, but she wasn't in Shenyang. She was stuck in Kuwait with the prospect of working a seven-day-a-week job for next to nothing. *This isn't better*, Min Li said to herself. In fact, she couldn't think of how to make it better. She found herself in a dark place from which there was no escape, and her mother's *feng shui* couldn't help her.

Min Li knew she needed a plan, and moping in her bedroom wasn't going to get anything done. But it was too late in the day to do much, but she needed to get her hands on her money. She had not yet had time to open a bank account in Kuwait, so there was no way to transfer money from her bank account in China.

Min Li called Tong Li Hua, forgetting that it was after midnight. After Tong Li Hua was fully awake, Min Li gave her instructions to wire money to Western Union, which fortunately operated in both counties. Min Li needed to buy an airplane ticket back to Shenyang, and she would probably need at least two thousand American dollars. She specifically told Tong Li Hua not to wire renminbi, Chinese money, because she would lose too much when she converted it. Dollars were safer and more easily converted back into renminbi later. Tong Li Hua agreed to do it before she opened the shop the next day, which would be available in Kuwait as soon as a Western Union outlet opened there.

It was only a part of a plan, but it was enough of a plan to give Min Li some peace of mind. She ate May's dinner, took a shower, and slept well, knowing that she could buy a plane ticket the next day to go home. But the happiness brought by this plan was dampened knowing that she would miss her new friends in Kuwait. To make things worse, she couldn't even say good-bye, because she didn't want Aliya or Huda to know she was leaving.

Twenty Eight

Min Li woke up the next morning at 5:30 and packed her suitcase, being careful not to let the other women know. She returned her packed suitcase under her bunk where she normally kept it, slipped her passport into her purse, and then prepared breakfast for her housemates. Knowing that everybody would wake up in a bad mood after yesterday's payday debacle, Min Li fixed a large breakfast that everybody would enjoy, including scrambled eggs with tomatoes, toasted bread, hard boiled eggs, cornmeal mush, steamed buns, and two kinds of tea. At least nobody would complain that morning about breakfast.

When the women had cleaned up the breakfast dishes, washed their faces or showered, and finished dressing, she headed them out the door for their eight-block walk to the shop. It was hot already, at 7:30, but by now Min Li was getting used to the heat. They would be well within the air-conditioned shop before the outside temperatures became unbearable.

After unlocking the shop, Min Li made sure everybody's station was ready for business, made a mental inventory of supplies, and did a hair and face check of each of the workers. Some could cut hair but not apply make-up, and she wanted to make sure that everybody who worked in the beauty spa was beautiful. Then she waited. She needed to go to the Western Union outlet five blocks down Salem Al Mubarak Street, but it did not open until nine. Min

Li avoided temptation by staying away from the floor safe behind the manager's station.

At 8:45, Min Li grabbed her purse and announced that she had to run an errand and would be back in an hour or two. She left the keys to the shop in a drawer at the manager's station, grabbed her purse, and walked out the front door, walking briskly to the east, toward the Western Union outlet situated in a Federal Express office. It was already 44ºC (111ºF), and she regretted that she did not at least take enough money from the shop to pay for a taxi.

Min Li reached the Federal Express office a couple of minutes past nine, and the clerk was still getting things ready for the day's business, so she had to wait a few nervous minutes. Finally, he asked if he could help her.

"I'm expecting some money from Western Union."

"I'll need your I.D."

Min Li handed the clerk her passport and waited while he scrutinized it. Finally, he turned on the computer and waited for it to boot up, three minutes that seemed like thirty, logged in, and found Min Li's name and identifying information.

"You want dollars?" the clerk asked.

"Isn't that what the wire is for?"

"Yes, but I wanted to make sure. I can change it to Kuwaiti dinars for you."

"I'll take fifty dinars, but give me the rest in dollars, please."

"No problem."

No Min Li had to wait for the clerk to open the time-delay safe, another three minutes.

"Oh, oh."

"What?" Min Li asked with anticipation.

'somebody forgot to restock dollars. I've only got about three hundred. You sure you don't want dinars?"

"I really need dollars."

"Okay, but it'll be a few minutes. I'll call the boss and he can pick some up at the bank on his way it."

Min Li had no choice but to wait, but the few minutes turned into forty-five minutes, and despite the frigid air conditioning at the Federal Express office, Min Li sweated profusely. Then when the manager finally arrived, she again had to prove who she was. The manager counted out twenty one-hundred dollar bills, handed her eighteen of them, then handed her fifty Kuwaiti dinars as she requested and another American twenty, keeping five dollars as a fee for exchanging the money. Min Li didn't argue but grabbed the money and headed out to the street without even thinking about the illegal fee. She had no time for that.

Min Li then took a taxi to the apartment, now that the outside temperature had risen even more, and asked the driver to wait for her while she retrieved her suitcase. She returned to the taxi in four minutes and instructed the driver to take her to the airport. The driver wanted to chat.

"Where are you going? Vacation?"

Min Li didn't want to chat, "Wo bu ming bai le." That was enough to keep the driver from talking, as he assumed she could speak no English. Less than twenty minutes later, Min Li exited the taxi at the departure's area at Kuwait's only airport. Now, all she had to do was to buy a plane ticket to China, anywhere in China. Once in China, she could buy another ticket to Shenyang, or take the train if it was near enough.

Pulling her one suitcase behind her, Min Li approached the first airline counter she knew that had flights to China, Etihad Airways, the same airline she had taken to come to Kuwait.

"Have you any flights to China? This morning?" she asked the ticket agent.

"We have a flight to Shanghai leaving in about an hour. Would you care to book that?"

"That'll do? How much?"

"When will you be returning?"

"One way please."

"You won't be coming back to Kuwait?"

"No. My business here is finished. I had a lovely time, but I really must get home."

'very well then. May I see your passport and entry visa, please?"

Min Li handed over her passport, turning it open to the page with the Kuwait visa.

"You are Zhang Min Li?"

"Yes. Min Li Zhang or Zhang Min Li. Zhang is the family name."

"I'm sorry, ma'am, but the computer says that you have a travel ban. This is your name and passport number."

"A travel ban?"

"I'm afraid so. I'm not allowed to sell you a ticket. It seems you have unfinished business in Kuwait."

"What authority issued the travel ban?"

"It's really a simple matter, ma'am. Anybody who has a civil claim against you can file a form with the Ministry of the Interior. After that form is filed, the Ministry enters your name in the travel ban database. Once that happens, you may not leave Kuwait until the person filing the form files another form releasing the ban. This usually happens if somebody thinks you owe them money. Once that is resolved, we can help you with a flight to China."

This news dumfounded Min Li. She had an argument with Aliya at the end of the day the day before, certainly after the Ministry's offices closed. And there could not have been enough time to issue the ban so early the next day. "When was this ban placed?" Min Li asked.

"Let me see here," the woman said in a fake cheerful voice. "It looks like it was place almost a month ago, twenty-eight days to be exact."

"That was two days after I entered the country. I couldn't have had a dispute with anybody so soon. How do I contest this travel ban?"

"You would have to go to court and have a judge order it lifted. That is if the person filing the application for the ban doesn't refuse to lift it. But you're going to have another problem starting tomorrow."

"What problem is that?"

"You visa expires today. You will be fined for each day you overstay your visa. After a while, you might have to stay in jail for a little while. You will need to have your sponsor renew your visa."

'my sponsor filed the travel ban and they want another two hundred dinars to extend my visa for another month. Not only that, they aren't paying me."

"I'm sorry to hear that. You might want to file a complaint with the Ministry of Labor, unless you are a domestic worker, in which case you have no right to file a complaint. Why don't you call your sponsor and simply ask him to lift the travel ban?"

"I'll do that. Thank you." Min Li knew that calling Huda, by way of Aliya, would resolve nothing. She wouldn't lift the travel ban if she went through so much trouble to get Min Li to Kuwait to work for free, especially if Huda filed the travel ban only two days after arriving in Kuwait. No, Huda knew what she was doing, and this couldn't be resolved with a phone call and saying please."

Min Li had no idea what she was going to do. She did not want to return to the shop or the apartment, especially now that she'd been gone for nearly two hours. She had to extricate herself from this horrible situation in which she found herself. She needed a different plan. Unfortunately, Min Li knew nobody in Kuwait, other than Huda, Aliyah, and the eleven women who worked at the shop, and she couldn't tell any of them. But how was she going to know other people, people that had the connections she needed to get out of Kuwait? She needed to think.

Min Li took a taxi back to the apartment. She couldn't stay at the airport, and she couldn't wonder about Kuwait towing a suitcase with her. When she arrived at the apartment, she called the shop and talked to Ma Linda, telling her that she felt terribly ill and that she was going to remain home in bed for a few hours. She also told Ma Linda where to find the shop keys at the manager's station, just in case she didn't return to work before closing time. Then she called Tong Li Hua.

'min Li, are you coming home?"

"No. I tried to buy a ticket at the airport, but there is some kind of a travel ban. I can't leave Kuwait."

"What do you mean you can't leave Kuwait? Just leave."

"It's not that simple. I have to go to court, and that could take months."

"Go the Chinese embassy. Maybe they can help you. I've got to go now. I'm in the middle of a dye job and it's time to rinse. Call me back."

The embassy, why didn't I think of that? Min Li asked herself. She immediately left the apartment and caught a taxi to the Embassy of the People's Republic of China in Yarmouk, just off Ring Road 4. There she was able to talk to a deputy consul who explained the travel ban procedures in Kuwait. The embassy could not help her, except maybe to assist her in applying for an extension to her visa allowing her to remain legally in Kuwait long enough to resolve the travel ban in court so that she could legally leave Kuwait. The mere fact that she could be in Kuwait illegally while being legally prevented from leaving Kuwait infuriated Min Li and offended her sense of logic. Min Li thanked the deputy consul for his time and said that she would likely return soon for their help in extending her visa. She didn't want help extending her visa, because she didn't want to stay in Kuwait. Somehow or another she would leave. At the moment, she didn't know how.

Min Li caught another taxi and took it back to Salmiya. She didn't want to go to the shop or the apartment, so she had him drop her off at Marina Mall. No sooner had she paid the driver a Kuwaiti man walked up to her and offered her his telephone number on a scrap of paper. Min Li thanked him and placed the number in her purse. She later learned that the man had committed the crime of "Eve baiting" by giving her his number. He assumed that she was a prostitute.

She then walked west down Salem Al Mubarak Street, occasionally ducking into department stores and shopping centers to momentarily escape the oppressive heat. Eventually, she reached the Sultan Center supermarket and stood in front of it for a while, facing the road when another Kuwaiti man offered her his telephone number on a scrap of paper. She thanked him, too, and placed it in her purse next to the other number.

Looking across the street, she studied the facade of the coffee shop known as Second Cup. Larger than most of the coffee shops, it occupied about half of the first floor of a small indoor shopping center on the side nearest Salem Al Mubarak Street. Through the large plate glass windows, Min Li could see several men, mostly foreigners, drinking coffee, reading newspapers, and chatting with friends. She could also see some women, two by themselves, and a group of three. The two solitary women were not Kuwaiti. Second

Cup Coffee Shop looked like a safe place to sit and think, and because there were unescorted single women there, she could likewise sit there and not be noticed. She crossed the street, entered the coffee shop through the large glass door, and approached the counter.

"May I help you ma'am," asked the petite Filipina behind the counter.

"I'd like a coffee, but I don't know what to order. What do you recommend?"

The barista patiently explained each of the coffee drinks on the menu, all of which confused Min Li.

"Why don't you recommend something for me?" Min Li said out of frustration.

"We have tea."

"Tea? Oh, I'd prefer tea. Do you have any oolong?"

"Naturally. One cup of oolong tea coming up. It's from Sri Lanka, you know."

"Not from China? Sounds exciting. I never tried tea from anywhere else before."

Min Li paid for the tea and sat down at a small booth away from the window where she tried to relax. The place was relatively quiet, as it was still the afternoon, and she could watch shoppers occasionally walk by inside the shopping center, which the backside of the coffee shop opened into. A minute later, a Chinese woman plopped herself down in Min Li's booth across the table from her.

"Are you Chinese?" the woman asked in broken English.

"Yes."

"I'm Lan Lan. Why haven't I seen you before?" the woman asked, switching to Mandarin.

"I can't answer that question," Min Li answered, not knowing where Lan Lan was going with her question.

"I know all the Chinese girls in Salmiya. Most of them work for me. Who do you work for and why are you in Salmiya?"

"I work down the street at Arabian Beauty Spa. I'm the manager there. What do you mean most of them work for you?"

"You can't be that naive," Lan Lan chided.

"Naive about what? I really don't know what you are talking about. Do you have a business?"

"You can call it that. I guess you really aren't working for somebody."

"I just told you I was."

"That's not what I meant."

"What kind of work are you talking about?"

"The only kind that allows Chinese women a chance to make good money."

"I earn a salary of five hundred dinars a month," Min Li said proudly, ignoring the fact that her employer refused to pay her.

"That's nothing. You should be sending that much home every week."

"Doing what?"

"Taking care of the needs of men?"

"Oh. I see. No, that's not me."

"It's really quite easy you know. People call me, tell me where they are, and I call one of my girls to go there. They usually charge thirty dinar for a visit and give me ten. Or I have them standing around at the Marina Mall or across the street at Sultan Center. Men come up, give them a phone number, I call the men and check them out, then set up a date."

"Two men gave me their phone numbers this afternoon. Is that what they think I am?"

"If you don't need them, let me have those numbers."

Min Li dug into her purse and handed over the two pieces of paper with the phone numbers. She was glad to be rid of them.

"Anyways," Lan Lan continued, "it's a good set up. If you need a place to stay, I can put you up in an apartment with other Chinese women where you can sleep, keep your things, and eat. From time to time you'll have to cook. You know how to cook, don't you?"

"I can cook. But I . . ."

"You pay a hundred dinar a month to stay there. Then I have somebody take care of your visa. That'll cost you two hundred for a one-month visa. It's a working visa, and we make it look like you're working at a beauty parlor to get the visa. Most girls pay for a one-year work visa. That's two thousand dinars, but you can do that later."

This all sounded too familiar to Min Li, and listening to Lan Lan only made her more angry, not at Lan Lan but at her own sponsor.

"What I want is to go back to China," Min Li said.

"Why? You can't make any money in China. Chinese men are too cheap, and at your age you'd be lucky to make a hundred yuan a night."

"I want to go back to Shenyang. I have other work there."

'so what's stopping you?"

"Travel ban. They wouldn't sell me a ticket at the airport," Min Li explained.

"Then get a different passport?"

"How do I do that?"

"I can arrange it."

"How much?"

"Five thousand."

'renminbi?"

"No, of course not. Kuwaiti dinars."

"I don't have that kind of money. That simply won't work."

"If you work for me, you'll have it in two months."

'sorry. I'll work something else out."

Peter's coffee had grown cold as he immersed himself in the crime section of the Kuwait Times. He folded the newspaper, grabbed his almost empty cup, and started toward the counter to buy another cup. His eye caught two women talking in Mandarin, and he could clearly see Lan Lan's seriously animated face as she explained something to the other Chinese woman.

Interesting, Peter thought. *Chinese women in Kuwait. I wonder if I can remember how to say a few things.* He was bored anyway, and it had been so long since he talked to a woman who wasn't a teacher, he thought he'd have some fun by meeting the two Chinese women in the coffee shop and telling them that he twice lived in China.

As Peter approached their table, Lan Lan saw him and said to Min Li, "I think I've got to go work soon."

Min Li looked at Lan Lan, confused, when she heard a man standing behind her speaking horrible Mandarin.

"Ni hao. Ni shi zhongguoren ma?"

Min Li almost laughed, the accent was so horrible. She turned and looked at the fool speaking it, and she screamed, "Peter North!"

Lan Lan looked surprised.

Peter looked ever more surprised.

Min Li jumped from her seat and threw her arms around Peter's neck, almost sobbing from joy, and said, 'my mother is in a perfect place."

Now Peter was even more confused. He stepped back, looked her in the face, and said, 'min Li? Is that you?"

"Ai tian! Peter, you're here in Kuwait."

"You're in Kuwait. How? Why? I looked for you—in Shenyang, but you're here. I can't believe it. I even prayed to God to let me find you. But you're in Kuwait."

"I guess you two know each other," Lan Lan said, disappointed that she had no customer yet amused at the spectacle she was seeing. "You two better get your hands off each other before the police see you. You're in Kuwait, you know."

"Yes, I know," Min Li answered without taking her eyes off Peter, "and my mother is in a perfect place."

Twenty Nine

Peter sat in awe as Min Li unfolded for him the events of her life since they last saw each other. He had tales of his own, but they paled in comparison to those of Min Li. He heard about her office cleaning business and her marriage to a man who almost had her killed because of his dealing with the *heishehui*. She talked about her mother succumbing to cancer, and how her remains were secreted to Pàotǎ Shān, as well as her brother's meteoric rise in status in Panzhihua. Min Li impressed Peter with her description of the beauty shop in Shenyang. He would never have seen it, because he never shopped in that mall, but he did often visit the Walmart nearby, and he was surprised that he never saw her on the street.

And they both had a story about when they each thought they saw the other in front of the American consulate in Shenyang, both of them regretting not trying harder to verify their suspicions. After several minutes of competing "only ifs," the subject turned to Min Li's current dilemma. How was she going to get out of Kuwait? On the other hand, she and Peter were together, and they realized that they had always wanted to be together. They ended their relationship nearly twenty years ago because they wanted to be practical. They had reasoned themselves into twenty years of unhappiness. But they were together now, at least for the moment, making Min Li's situation bearable.

Peter assured her that they could make a plan, a plan to extract Min Li from Kuwait despite the travel ban. All they had to do was to wait for solutions to present themselves, and now that Peter was on the scene, Min Li could at least relax knowing she didn't have to go back to the shop or the apartment. It would be easier to avoid being noticed, to stay off the grid as they say. So the first part of their plan, the only part they had so far, would be to grab Min Li's things from the apartment on Al Mughira Bin Shu"ba Street and secretly move in temporarily with Peter.

It had to be secret for two reasons, mainly because it was illegal in Kuwait for an unmarried man and an unmarried woman to live together no matter what the circumstances, and because Peter's employment contract prevented him from moving anybody into his apartment with him. They thought about getting married, but that solution was immediately out of the question. Peter still did not have residency in Kuwait, working on a three-month visitor's visa that he renewed by leaving the country and returning, and because Min Li was, or soon would be, wanted by the law. Discussing marriage came too easy, Min Li thought, as did Peter. They both naturally assumed that it was their destiny to be married. After all, they almost married once before; although, it was nearly twenty years earlier.

By the time they had settled on part one of the plan, Min Li realized that it was nearly nine o'clock. All the women from the shop would be back at the apartment and Min Li wouldn't be there. She had told them that she was sick, so they would have expected her to be there when they returned. Min Li panicked and told Peter she needed to get her suitcase and laptop from the apartment. Peter offered Lan Lan a ride to wherever she needed to go. Lan Lan, who had taken several "work" calls, opted to remain in the coffee shop and said that she was sure she'd see them later.

Peter led Min Li to the parking lot behind the shopping center and to his car. Min Li never visualized Peter with a car, because they had only known each other in China, where few foreigners even attempt to drive a car, and a foreigner obtaining a driver's license there was next to impossible. Peter could use his international driver's license in Kuwait.

Min Li then directed Peter to her apartment on Al Mughira Bin Shu"ba Street. When he parked, Min Li asked him to remain in the car while she fetched her things. After more than a half hour, Peter began to worry, because he only expected Min Li to be gone five minutes or so. They hadn't yet exchanged cell phone numbers, and Min Li did not say what floor she lived on. Peter had no choice but to continue waiting, but the more he waited, the more he worried. Finally, just before Peter talked himself into banging on every door in the apartment building, Min Li reappeared from the ground floor entry. Peter hopped out and opened the trunk for her suitcase and laptop.

"Hurry," Min Li said as they sat back in the car.

Peter sped off going north on Al Mughira Bin Shu"ba Street and was two blocks away when he asked her why the hurry.

'some of the girls didn't want me to leave. They tried to talk me into staying."

"Why?"

"They didn't trust the owners and they didn't know what would happen to them. They like me, I guess."

"But that doesn't explain the hurry."

"One of them told me that Huda was on her way to the apartment building to look for me. It seems she heard I wasn't at work today, and she found out I wasn't home when the rest of the girls got off work. I didn't want to be there when she showed up."

"That might have been bad," Peter acknowledged.

Peter drove east on Ring Road 5 to the second exit at Amman Street. He then drove north on Amman Street four blocks, and turned left. A half a block further, just past High Market, he pulled into his building's parking lot and helped Min Li out of the car. He looked around to make sure nobody was around to see Min Li enter the building with him, and, thinking the coast was clear, escorted Min Li to the elevator at the base of the building. Just as they entered the elevator, Peter glanced over at the produce market next to his building, and one of the Iranian's gave him the thumbs up. *Lecherous fool*, Peter thought.

Peter pushed the button for the seventh story, really the eighth floor, and they rode the elevator up. When the elevator door opened, Peter poked his head out to make sure nobody was standing in the hall, then escorted Min Li from across the hall to his apartment only fifteen feet away. He fumbled with his keys for a moment out nervousness, dropped them to the floor, picked them up, and finally managed to get his door opened.

Min Li was immediately impressed by the spacious and well-appointed apartment, smaller than the one on Al Mughira Bin Shu"ba Street only because it had one bedroom. She immediately walked across the living room to the sliding glass door leading to the balcony and threw open the curtains so that she could see the skyline of west Salmiya. She sat on the sofa then the loveseat, then the easy chair, each time feeling the softness of the cushions. She walked into the bathroom and the kitchen.

"You have a nice apartment," she said, 'much better than the one on Al Mughira Bin Shu"ba Street. How do you keep it so clean?

"It's only me here," Peter answered, "and once a week I have somebody come in to clean it for ten dinars, but it only takes her about twenty or thirty minutes."

"You won't have to have her come anymore, now that I'm here," Min Li said.

"I wish that were true, but you can't stay here long. Don't forget, we have to get you out of the country. I really wish you could stay longer, though."

'me too. What's going to happen, Peter?"

"I don't know, but we'll think of something. I have a few friends that can help maybe. I met them at church. But tonight, we'll relax and we'll tackle the problem tomorrow, after I get home from work, of course."

That evening, Peter made a late dinner, Min Li's first ever spaghetti. He also made a salad from fresh iceberg lettuce, tomatoes, cucumbers, apple wedges, and toasted sunflower seeds with a peanut oil and apple vinegar dressing. Min Li had never eaten iceberg lettuce before. In fact, this was her first ever green salad, and was surprised how well vegetables could taste without cooking them. She'd never even eaten iceberg lettuce until then, and she was surprised how much she liked it.

The next morning, Peter said good-bye to Min Li and headed down stairs to go to work where he would meet Habib, his co-worker, who carpooled with him. As Peter got off the elevator, Habib asked him whom he was with the night before.

"Nobody," Peter answered. "Why do you ask?"

"I saw you get out of your car with an Asian woman. Who is she?"

"An old friend."

'she went into the building with you, and I think she's still in your apartment."

"What if she is?"

"The apartment belongs to the school. If the school finds out, you're out of a job."

"I'll get another job." Peter thought about that for a moment. He could easily get another teaching job, but that time of year, there were few openings. He'd have to wait a few months before he worked again, unless he took a less than favorable teaching post or was lucky enough to find an unexpected vacancy. Then he thought about his students. Sometimes students joyously accept news of a new teacher, but most of the time the students suffer while the new teacher adjusts to the students and the curriculum. He had a good rapport with his students, which didn't come easy, and he didn't want to let them down. "The school won't find out," he told Habib.

"I don't care one way or another. You're my friend and I congratulate you on finding a new diversion."

"It's not like that."

"Whatever. But you know if I saw you, other people can see you, including Mona," referring to the school's assistant principal for the boy's upper school.

Mona didn't like anybody, and she took particular delight in reporting anybody's transgressions, not matter the source or the reason. She often wondered the halls in the school building and placed her ear to the wall outside of a classroom surreptitiously to listen in. Once, Peter was reviewing characters in a story one of his twelfth grade boys' class had just read, which had an evil female character named Mona. The real Mona overheard him talking about what an evil person the Mona character was, and she reported Peter to the school's director. Peter had to defend himself by showing the director the story in the textbook.

Mona's jealousy of Peter's popularity with the students produced some peculiar backlash. For example, a group of boys in the quad saw Peter walking in their direction and started singing a song, incorporating his name in the song. Mona heard it and disciplined the boys by not allowing them to use the school's cafeteria for a week. And Mona could never get a handle on her unabashed use of sarcasm whenever she spoke with Peter. Sometimes she called him in the middle of class, and then chew him out for answering the telephone.

The situation became so bad that Peter had to ask the director to intervene, resulting in Mona being prohibited form communicating with him. First she was simply told not to talk to Peter, but then she simply sent him absurdly demanding emails. After being banned from sending him emails, she sent messages to him by way of students. After that, to the relief of Peter's students, the director banned Mona from speaking with Peter's students, making life a little more pleasant for Peter. But she lived in the same building as Peter, and if Mona saw Min Li, there would be trouble.

"You're right," Peter acknowledged. "I should be very careful, but I hope she won't be here long, as much as I'd like her to be."

Peter explained as much as he could about Min Li during the twenty-minute drive to school, the longest part of which was the last three blocks, because he had to wade through a crowd of Egyptian day laborers that filled the street waiting to be hired for the day. When the retired Nepalese army first sergeant pulled the gate open at the school so that Peter could drive into the parking lot, he told Habib that he would finish the story on the way home.

During his English classes, Peter wanted his students to do a writing assignment about some aspect of Kuwait that they knew to be different from countries outside the region. He stimulated a discussion about guest workers, visa, travel bans, and such, and the boys easily entered into a lively conversation, taking both sides of various controversial issues. The fathers of several students worked in government, and one actually worked in the Ministry of Interior Affairs, the agency responsible for issuing visa, work permits, residency permits, and travel bans. That student boasted that he had more knowledge on those topics than the other students had and pretended to be an expert. From this conversation, and the essays that followed, Peter surmised that getting Min Li out of the country would be no easy task.

While the students were busy writing, during his prep period, and during lunch, all Peter did was think about Min Li's dilemma. The two Iranians that ran the produce shop next to his apartment often talked about the things they smuggled in and out of Kuwait, but their adventures always involved travel between Iran and Kuwait. The last thing Peter wanted to do was to send Min Li into Iran.

Then there was the possibility of getting her out by taking her through Saudi Arabia to Qatar, which did not routinely honor travel bans from the other Gulf States. The problem with that would be getting her into Saudi Arabia. As a Chinese citizen, she would need a visa before traveling to Saudi Arabia, whereas Peter could obtain an entry permit at the border because of his American citizenship. But before they even arrived in the Saudi border checkpoint, they would have to pass through Kuwait exit controls at the border. Qatar would give Min Li an entry permit, but she would have to go through the Kuwaiti exit control, Saudi entry control, then Saudi exit control before reaching Qatar. Min Li would have to ride in the trunk of Peter's car for some portion of the trip, twice, and the trunk had no air conditioning. With temperatures in the high 40's, this was not a valid option. And if they were caught, everybody would go to jail, either in Kuwait or Saudi Arabia, resulting in a life altering, or life ending, nightmare.

He would talk to the Filipinos he met at church, the ones that assisted Filipina maids and nannies escape their employment when conditions proved too brutal. But church services weren't until Friday, three days away. On the way home from school, Peter discussed these options with Habib. He hoped that Habib, who was a native to this part of the world, would have some insight.

"If we were in Lebanon, we would have no problem. This is not Lebanon. This is Kuwait, so everything is dangerous if you are not Kuwaiti," Habib responded. 'she needs a new passport with a fake visa showing her entry into Kuwait."

"Yeah, for three thousand dinars, which I don't have," Peter said in desperation.

"I'm sure you will find a way, God willing."

"Let me know if you can think of anything. You speak Arabic, so you can ask around for me."

"I will ask some people I know, but I won't ask any Kuwaitis. It's too risky. If she were Lebanese, I could get her out. All I'd have to do is have her trade passports with another Lebanese lady who looked similar and mail the passport back when we were finished with it."

"That's an idea," Peter said. 'some Lebanese cover themselves, don't they?"

"Not many, but a few conservative ones do."

"Do they wear veils?"

'some."

"When a Muslim woman goes through passport control at the airport, are they required to remove their veils?"

"Never. That would be an insult to the woman."

"Then why can't Min Li be a Lebanese woman for a day? I can fly her to Qatar, and then she can change back into a Chinese woman and use her Chinese passport to fly home to China."

"That might work, but I'd have to find a Lebanese woman the same height as your friend who would be willing to risk using her passport that way. It could be trouble at both ends."

"That won't work," Peter said dejectedly. "They would want to see her Qatar entry visa at the airport before she got on the airplane."

'sometimes."

'sometimes?"

"They don't always check. It depends how busy they are. They would check at the ticket counter if you purchased the ticket at the airport."

"Then I'll buy the ticket online. No checking there."

"It might work. I'll make some discrete inquiries."

'meanwhile, I'll check my Filipino connections," Peter said, now with a hint of hope in his voice.

Peter explained the possible plan to Min Li, that she could impersonate a veiled Lebanese woman, fly to Qatar, then on to China. She didn't like the plan because of the risks involved, but she knew any plan would have risks. It certainly sounded better than crossing into Saudi Arabia in the trunk of a car. In any event, whether they went with that plan or another, it would at least be a few days before Min Li could leave Kuwait, and Peter wanted to enjoy his time with her. They watched television together, and Peter found the English version of China Central Television on his satellite service, but it was a boring propaganda piece on China's pig farmers. All that did was make her a little homesick. So Peter offered to take her down to Marina Mall for some shopping, to which Min Li readily assented.

The drove down to Salem Al Mubarak Street and parked the car in the large parking garage situated under the mall. While strolling the mall, Peter and Min Li both had to fight the urge to hold hands. That might have caused them both to be arrested, and Min Li's visa had just expired, so they had to be extra vigilant. Soon, they realized they were risking unwarranted exposure at the mall. Min Li was just a Chinese woman walking with an American man, and it seems that nobody assumed they were together, despite their close physical proximity. Three times a Kuwaiti man approached Min Li to give her a slip of paper with his telephone number on it. Three times Peter had to say, 'she's with me." Three times he was asked why he was with a Chinese woman. Three times he had to fight the urge to deck somebody for saying something rude about a Chinese woman with a white man. After the third time, Peter suggested they go elsewhere, so they drove down Salem Al Mubarak and ordered coffee at Second Cup where they ran into Lan Lan.

When they told Lan Lan that they had just come from Marina Mall, Lan Lan asked if Min Li had any new phone numbers. Peter answered for her. He let Min Li and Lan Lan talk awhile, mostly about China and Liaoning Province. Lan Lan was from Dalian, the port city due south of Shenyang in Liaoning, and Min Li had visited there before. They spoke in Mandarin, but Peter thought he heard them talking about Dalian as a good place to spend a honeymoon. His Mandarin wasn't good enough to be certain.

Lan Lan took a call and said she had work to do and that she would see Min Li and Peter again if they were still there in a couple of hours. This gave Peter and Min Li a chance to enjoy each other's company. Tired of sitting in one place, they decided to stroll down Salem Al Mubarak Street, going in and out of clothing shops and shoe stores, and stopping for an avocado and strawberry smoothie, another new taste sensation for Min Li. Near the end of the evening, they walked back to Peter's car and drove home.

As Peter pulled into the parking lot at his apartment building, he saw two people exit a white Jeep Cherokee with U.N. license plates, a man and a woman, Mona. They entered the apartment building while Peter and Min Li watched from the car, remaining there until Peter was certain Mona was well inside her own apartment, only then leaving the car and approaching the elevator. The next morning, the Jeep Cherokee was still there.

This knowledge came in handy the next morning. Because she wanted to buy some produce next door, Min Li descended in the elevator with Peter when he left for work. The elevator stopped on the fourth floor and Mona hopped on.

"Who is your friend?" she asked Peter.

"This is my fiancée Min Li."

"Why is she here at 7:20 in the morning? You know you can't have somebody living with you."

'she is merely visiting me," Peter responded, trying to remain friendly.

"I think there's more to it than that. I will have to let the director know."

"Go ahead. When she calls me into her office, I will show her pictures of you and your friend with the Jeep Cherokee." Peter lied, because he had no photos.

"That's a different matter."

"You're in Kuwait," Peter reminded her. "And you are a single woman. Your consequences will be worse than mine. I suggest you mind your own business, and I will reciprocate." Peter felt a tinge of guilt when he said this. He was not the type to blackmail anybody, but for Mona he could set those feelings aside. He had to get the upper hand on her and keep her mouth closed, at least until he could get Min Li out of Kuwait.

When Friday morning came, he fixed a quick breakfast for both Min Li and himself, and drove them both to Mishref. There, the local Anglican Church met in a large private residence without any external markings showing it as a place of worship. Muslim calls to prayers echoed off the walls of surrounding houses while church members congregated on the front steps and in the small front yard.

Peter wasn't an Anglican, which would be an Episcopalian in America, but he enjoyed this church for two reasons. The congregation was small and friendly, and it co-existed with the only Chinese Christian congregation in Kuwait. Although Kuwait had a large Catholic church in Kuwait City, it was a much further drive and, despite the building being very large, was always crowded. Since

Catholics are allowed to receive sacraments in Anglican churches under some circumstances, Peter assumed there would be no moral problem associated with him attending the smaller church in Mishref. And there, Min Li would meet Chinese Christians, another first for her.

Min Li enjoyed her time with the Chinese members, and didn't mind it so much when the group split into two allowing the Chinese to attend a Mandarin service in a large room on the ground floor, and an English service in the larger basement. When the two separate services were complete, Peter rushed outside to find the Filipino men who he knew were associated with the secret rescue organization, Miguel and Renaldo.

They told him that the Kuwaiti government was chartering a Kuwaiti Airways flight to Manila in about a week for the purpose of repatriating Filipino children. These were actually children born of Filipinas who became pregnant while working as maids and nannies for their Kuwaiti sponsors. Nearly all the children were half Kuwaiti, but the Kuwaiti government did not grant them citizenship. Since they were residing illegally in Kuwait as citizens of the Philippines, they were being deported to their "home" country, a country they had never seen, where they would be placed in the care of relatives of the affected maids and nannies.

Because this happened with some regularity, and because it required coordination with Philippine authorizes, the Philippine embassy was able to demand that the Kuwaiti government allow a certain number of Filipina maids and nannies, who had taken asylum in the embassy, to be returned to the Philippines, no questions asked. The Philippines Ambassador was able to convince the Kuwaiti officials that such an arrangement would ensure minimal embarrassment for Kuwait. It was possible that the embassy could assist Min Li in leaving the country, disguised as a Filipina maid. She would, of course, be issued a fake Philippines passport and given a fake name. But this plan could not be assured, and it certainly could not be made known to the ambassador.

Peter explained to Min Li the possibility of the Filipino plan. Certainly better than anything else so far, this plan had the smallest risk. It would be much easier for Min Li to pass herself off as a Filipina than as a Lebanese. She asked Peter about the travel documents she would need.

"You'd be given a fake Philippe passport," he explained. "Not a fake one, but a real one made with fake information. It would even have a work visa and an entry stamp. That part might be faked. The plane is scheduled to leave Kuwait next Saturday, so we'd have get ready. You'll need a passport photo by tomorrow, and some more information for Miguel and Renaldo. They'll take care of most everything, and all I have to do is drop you off at the airport or the Philippine embassy. They'll let me know which later."

"How much are we going to have to pay them?"

"Nothing."

"They do this for free?"

"They do this to help. They're not making a living doing it. Everybody involved is a volunteer."

"I've never heard of such a thing. Too many people just want to get rich."

"That's because you come from a country where government controls charity. You'll find that people in the West have different attitudes about that. They did ask us to give some money to help cover their expenses, but that's only if we can afford it," Peter continued. "They're expenses aren't much. Cost of materials, gasoline for the bus, that sort of thing. Most of the people they help don't own a single fil."

"I have some money in my suitcase," Min Li offered. "We can give them some."

Both Min Li and Peter moods had lifted considerably, knowing that they had a plan. Being Friday, most businesses were closed in Muslim countries, Kuwait being no exception, except for supermarkets and some of the consumer goods stores. They would wait until the next day to buy some passport photos for Min Li. For the rest of the drive home, they talked about whether she could be made to look like a Filipina, but Peter assured her that the Philippines had a large Chinese population, so that would not be a problem. Min Li acknowledged that her skin was darker than the average Chinese woman's, because she was from the countryside, and maybe she could pull off being a Filipina.

Peter called Renaldo on his cell phone, told him that Min Li wanted to leave with the "baby flight," and Renaldo said he would work on it and reminded Peter to get the passport photos. Rinaldo or Miguel would be in touch the next evening.

Thirty

Saturday morning, Peter woke Min Li up to the smell of pancakes and fried eggs cooking in the kitchen. They wanted to get an early start to the day, and Peter didn't want Min Li fussing over him. Besides, Min Li had never eaten pancakes, and this was a good opportunity to introduce her to them. If all went well, Min Li and Peter only had a few days together, and he wanted to do as much with her as possible.

Peter cleaned up the kitchen while Min Li did her make-up and watched television, and they were out the door by 8:30 to get her passport pictures made, Min Li taking a plastic shopping bag with extra shirts. They didn't need to go far, because the photo shop was just around the corner on Amman Street, so they walked. It took a little longer than Peter had planned, because Min Li had several photos taken, changing tops and restyling her hair. She wanted to look as Filipina as possible, but Peter thought any difference would be too subtle for the typical airport official to notice. He reminded her that many Filipinas were offspring of Chinese immigrants, so it really didn't make much difference, but Min Li didn't want to chance it, because there may be no more opportunities to take more photos.

They finally left the photo shop almost two hours later, and they walked over to the dry cleaners a block behind Peter's apartment building where Peter dropped off four shirts and two pairs of pants. He would pick them up the following Thursday. Next, they walked back to Peter's apartment and caught the elevator just as Mona and her male friend were getting off. Peter said good morning to Mona's friend and smiled at Mona, who returned his greeting with a sneer. Peter felt as though he won a small victory.

After dropping off Min Li's bag of extra shirts and the dry cleaning claim ticket, they headed back down to the car. They needed to meet Miguel and Renaldo to deliver the passport photos. They drove north on Amman Street to the Starbucks attached to the Al Rashid Hospital, parking on a side street. Miguel and Renaldo sat inside waiting for them in a corner away from the windows. They chose this particular Starbucks because it was not unusual to see Filipinos there as customers rather than as just employees. Peter handed the photos to Miguel.

"Why so many photos? We only needed six copies of the same photo. There must be more than fifty photos here?"

'sixty," Peter said, 'min Li wanted to make sure you had good ones. She's worried that she doesn't look like a Filipina."

"Any of these are fine," Miguel answered.

"We have a seat for her on the plane," Renaldo offered. "It'll leave Thursday night at 11:40 and fly directly to Manila. Min Li will need to meet us at the Philippines embassy at 9:30 where an officer of the Ministry of the Interior will verify the identities of the passengers and confirm them against a list provided by the embassy. She will go by the name of Esmeralda Maria Chang."

"That's an interesting name, Spanish and Chinese," Peter remarked.

"There are many Chinese families that have assimilated into the Philippine culture," Miguel explained. "Chang is a common Chinese family name there. This will alleviate any suspicion the Kuwaiti authorities might have if Min Li doesn't look Filipina enough."

"What about her accent?" Peter asked. "'min Li speaks English well, but it's obvious that she's Chinese. People from the Philippines speak with a different accent."

"That won't be a problem. When we've done this before, the officer from the Ministry of the Interior doesn't bother asking questions. They always seem in too much of a hurry to get off the bus. If somebody says anything, we'll just say that she's from Mindanao."

"Do they have a differ accent in Mindanao?"

"Not really, but no Kuwaiti will know that. She can bring one suitcase and nothing else. Everything has to fit in that one suitcase, including a laptop, if she has one."

"Why can't she take her laptop separate?"

"Because they won't be going through the normal security check at the airport to avoid publicity. Kuwait is ridding itself of a constant embarrassment, and there will likely be reporters at the airport. The bus will drive onto the tarmac and the passengers will offload there. Baggage handlers will take the suitcases off the bus and load them onto the plane, and the passengers will go through a metal detector. There won't be any secondary check of carry-on items, so they can't have them. She'll need to keep her passport and other papers in her pocket. No coins, cell phone, or metal objects."

"Will we hear from you between now and then?" Peter asked.

"Only if there is a change of plans, which isn't likely," Renaldo said. "We'll have her passport waiting for her at the bus at 9:30. The Ministry of the Interior official will show up around 9:45, and she needs to be seated on the bus tending to children at that time."

"This sounds exciting," Min Li said, speaking for the first time. "Do you want any money from us?"

"We do this for free, but we gladly accept donations whenever we can get them." Miguel answered.

"I have about eighteen hundred dollars back home."

"You'll need that to buy a ticket to China. We can't help you with that."

Peter reached into his pocket, took out a hundred Kuwaiti dinars, and handed it to Miguel. "That's all I have on me."

"This is most gracious of you," Miguel said. What we get from the church donations is never enough."

Peter shook the hands of both Miguel and Renaldo, and then departed with Min Li. They were both excited.

"You're leaving in only five days," Peter said.

"I know. I'll be so glad to leave."

"But it took me two decades to find you."

"Do you expect this to be our last good-bye?" Min Li asked.

"No, of course not. We have some planning to do."

They drove toward Kuwait City on Arabian Gulf Street to do some sightseeing. While they drove, they talked about their future. Peter still had a few months left on his contract with the school in Abraq Khaitan, and they agreed that he should complete his contract, which would make getting another teaching post easier. Meanwhile, he would put his feelers out for teaching jobs in China. Min Li would return to Shenyang where she had an ongoing business in partnership with Tong Li Hua and where she had an apartment with paid up rent. They could talk everyday using Peter's Skype on his laptop. He was very glad that he already had it on his computer before he came to Kuwait, because the program's download web site is blocked in Kuwait. But as long as he already had it, he could use it.

Peter realized that he had a week off in April for spring break, and the two of them would meet up then. Unfortunately, because Peter did not have residency in Kuwait, the Chinese embassy there would not give him a visa, so he would either have to go back to America to obtain a Chinese visa from China's consulate in San Francisco or Los Angeles, or they could meet in a third country, likely Malaysia. Peter thought that was a better idea. Chinese can obtain a visa at the airport in Malaysia, and being an American, Peter would simply need his passport. Neither had ever been to Malaysia, and it would be an interesting experience they both thought.

When Peter's contract finished, he would travel back to the United States, obtain a Chinese tourist visa, and then travel to Shenyang where he and Min Li would marry. He'd wait with Min Li in Shenyang for his new teaching contract in China to start, wherever that would be; then they would move together to whatever city in which he would be teaching and start the process for obtaining a visa for Min Li to travel to America. But for the time being, they would enjoy each other's company as much as possible. Spring was still a ways off.

By the time Thursday came, Min Li had packed and repacked her suitcase at least twelve times. She had everything in there that would fit, including her laptop and purse. She left out her paper money, which she would keep in her pocket, and nothing else. She would also keep her new Philippine passport in her pocket when she received it that night. It was a little after three, and Peter would not be home from work until around four, but she had too much nervous energy to just sit around and wait. She saw the dry cleaners claim check on the table and decided to go pick up Peter's dry cleaning, which he had paid for in advance.

Min Li took the elevator to the ground floor and exited the building on the backside, before crossing the dirt road behind Peter's apartment building, she saw Hamed, the Iranian manager of the produce market breaking down cardboard boxes in the back. She waved to him, and he waved back. When she passed the dumpster on the other side of the dirt road, a car came speeding toward her and skidded to a stop, kicking up gravel and dust and attracting Hamed's glance. Hamed knew the driver, not well but by name, Siamak, and was about to wave to him, when a passenger in the car jumped out and dragged Min Li into the backseat, holding her head down while the car sped away, throwing up more gravel.

Hamed was not only shocked by what he saw, but he was in a quandary. He knew about Min Li's legal status in Kuwait, that she was living illegally with Peter on an expired visa and that she had a travel ban placed on her. If he called the police, they would arrest Min Li. On the other hand, that might be a better option, because Siamak was a fellow Iranian who worked out of an underground brothel down the coast in Fintas. Siamak had once bragged to Hamed that he had kidnapped Filipinas and forced them to work as prostitutes. Maybe he could help Peter rescue her, but he couldn't think of how to do that. Siamak was a scary person.

Hamed waited in the front of his produce shop for Peter, keeping the parking space in front of Peter's apartment building that was closest to the produce shop open by shooing away other drivers. Peter returned home a little earlier that day, having raced home in the afternoon traffic to spend more time with Min Li. Hamed waved him over to the open parking spot that he had saved for Peter and approached Peter's car.

"They take your Chinese friend," Hamed announced.

"What are you talking about?"

'some men, Iranians. I know one. Your friend was on street back of building, and they stopped car and made her get in. I saw it happen almost hour ago."

"They took her? Took her where? Does she know these people?"

"Bad people. I help find them. Man's name is Siamak. Very bad man."

"Why?" Peter was getting desperate.

'make her whore. All I know is Fintas. I make call."

Hamed went into the produce shop, thumbed through some scraps of paper, and found a phone number. He spoke a few minutes in Farsi, wrote down another telephone number, and spoke to Peter.

"They probably take her to Fintas to secret whore place. I have phone number."

"Let me have it," Peter demanded.

'maybe no English. They Iranian. I call."

"Tell them you have an American friend that likes Chinese women. Ask if they have any Chinese women and make an appointment or whatever it is they call it."

Hamed made the call and spoke for a few minutes. To Peter, it sounded like Hamed was arguing with the other person. After a few minutes, Hamed wrote down an address in Fintas, then closed his phone and turned to Peter. "We go now. Must hurry, though. They say Chinese girl popular and have other clients later."

"You're going with me?"

"You need my help. Maybe they steal your money and beat you up if you go alone. If I go, you okay. I speak Farsi. I can help you. Do you have forty dinars?"

"Forty dinars?"

"They wanted sixty, but I said twenty, so they say forty."

Peter checked his wallet. He had forgotten it was empty because he had given his cash to Miguel and Renaldo. "We'll have to stop by my bank on the way."

"No time. I have money in store. I lend you." Hamed ran into the produce shop and grabbed four bills, ten dinars each, and was in Peter's car a few seconds later. "Go now. Take Highway 40, is quicker."

Nearly twenty minutes later, they were driving through a derelict neighborhood of apartment buildings that reminded Peter of East Cleveland, except that the buildings were all beige or white. The residents in this neighborhood were all foreigners, mostly from Egypt, India, Pakistan, and Iran. They were all poor, and it looked to Peter as though several people lived in each apartment. Finally, they pulled up to the address given to Hamed, and Peter parked in the street. Peter saw three men standing about, lookouts. Before they exited the car, Peter opened his glove compartment and pulled out a three-cell flashlight with a hardened aluminum body. When he stood up, he placed the flashlight in the back of his waistband under his shirt, being careful not to be noticed by the lookouts.

Peter suggested they walk up to the fourth floor where the secret brothel was located instead of using the elevator. He wanted to check out the stairs for obstructions because it was unlikely he'd be exiting the building by elevator. The stairs were clear except for a bicycle chained to the handrail near the second floor landing. They entered the hallway on the fourth floor and Peter, the smell of curry and dirty laundry momentarily overwhelming Peter, making his eyes water. He regained his bearings quickly and allowed Hamed to knock on the door of apartment twenty-four. Inside the smell was worse. The place lacked any ambiance whatsoever, not like what Peter imagined a brothel would be like, and immediately he was confronted by a large Iranian. Hamed stepped up and said that his American friend had an appointment with a Chinese woman.

Peter paid the forty dinars to the doorkeeper and was led down the hallway to a bedroom where the doorkeeper motioned for him to wait. A full-size bed with dirty sheets occupied the room in the corner, nothing else. Two minutes later, the Iranian reentered the room pulling a Chinese woman by the wrist, thrusting her in the direction of Peter. In broken English, the man said, "Thirty minutes or pay more." He then left the room, closing the door behind him. Peter thought he could hear his heart pounding.

It wasn't Min Li. This woman was at least three inches taller and ten pounds lighter than Min Li. Peter stuck his head out the door and yelled down the hallway toward Hamed.

"Hamed, tell him she's too tall. I like short Chinese woman."

Hamed spoke to the other Iranian for a moment, then yelled down toward Peter. "He says shorter one cost fifty dinars."

Peter had forty dinars of Hamed's money. He couldn't go to the bank now, and he wasn't leaving without Min Li. He had to bluff. "Tell him to let me have the shorter Chinese woman or I'll go somewhere else.

A minute later, the doorkeeper came back to the room, grabbed the poor Chinese woman by the wrist and dragged her out, slamming the door as he left. Peter waited while his heart pounded. And he waited some more. He heard yelling coming from the room next door, then screaming, and the sound of a man's large hand slapping the face of a woman and then a shriek. He knew that was Min Li. He ran out of the room, yelled at Hamed to hold the door to the apartment opened and rushed into the other room. The big Iranian was about to hit Min Li again when Peter entered the room, and Peter reached for the flashlight from his waistband. The Iranian heard Peter's footsteps rushing toward him and reached into his back pocket for a switchblade knife, but Peter was quicker.

Peter's flashlight smashed into the left temple of the Iranian with all the force Peter could muster. It broke apart, and the batteries flew against the wall as the heavy aluminum tube of the flashlight collapsed against the Iranian's head, dazing him and causing him to fall backward onto the bed where three other women were sitting, making them scream.

Peter grabbed Min Li hand and pulled her from the room while he looked over his shoulder at the dazed Iranian. "Run for the door!" he yelled at Min Li, and she rushed past Hamed holding the door for her. Peter ran after her, pushing Hamed through the door with him, and veered Min Li toward the staircase. He could hear the big Iranian yelling out the window at the three sentries at the base of the building. Before they exited the stairwell, Peter grabbed a metal bucket that he'd seen earlier and rushed out the ground floor stairway exit ahead of Min Li and Hamed. He tossed his car keys to Hamed and told him to get Min Li in the car just as the first sentry appeared at the bottom of the stairwell.

Before the sentry could react, Peter had already knocked him off his feet with the heavy bucket, allowing Hamed and Min Li to make a dash for the car, Peter right behind them as the other two sentries caught up to Peter, pulling him hard to the ground. Hamed opened the car door for Min Li, closed and locked it, and fumbled with the keys to get the trunk open. Peter now had one of the two remaining sentries on top of him, pounding Peter with his fists, while the other stood kicking at Peter's head and ribs.

Hamed found what he was looking for, the tire iron, and walked quickly up to the man kicking Peter and brained him with the tire iron. The man went down instantly and lay there, bleeding and unconscious, as Hamed swung at the man on top of Peter, dispatching him as quickly as the other. Hamed placed his hands on his hips and surveyed the carnage he had just created.

"I was sergeant in army," he told Peter who was trying to pull himself up after his beating. Peter's face was nearly black from beating, his lip swollen and bleeding, and one eye was swollen shut. He thought some ribs were broken. He looked over at the car and was relieved to see Min Li sitting in the back seat, crying at the sight of Peter. Hamed offered his had to Peter, helping him to stand.

"You drive, my friend," Peter said to Hamed, as he crawled into the front passenger seat. "It's a good thing it's Thursday."

"Why is that?" Hamed asked.

"I don't have to work tomorrow."

Hamed turned the key in the ignition, looked around for any trouble, then drove off, leaving tire marks in the pavement. After he had driven four blocks, Peter told him to stop the car and handed Hamed his cell phone.

"Who you want me call?" Hamed asked.

"Call the police to get those other women out of there. Give them the address and tell them to come now before those guys regain their strength."

When they arrived at Peter's apartment building, Peter had recovered somewhat from the beatings, but he still suffered a great deal of pain. He could at least help himself out of the car, slowly though. He met Hamed at the front of the car and hugged him.

"You are a good friend, Hamed. I will never forget this."

"Any time, Peter. You best American I know."

Min Li thanked Hamed for helping rescue her and helped Peter to the elevator. Once inside the apartment, Min Li spent the better part of two hours helping Peter clean up and bandage his wounds. They had soup for dinner, because Peter couldn't chew without causing more pain. While Min Li was cleaning Peter's face, Hamed stopped by with a bottle of aspirin and a bunch of bananas.

At 8:45, Peter and Min Li rode the elevator down together for the last time, and Peter, who still didn't feel much better from his pummeling, drove Min Li to the Philippine embassy. Night had come sooner, and there was little traffic. Despite the fact that they were in Kuwait, Min Li and Peter hugged and kissed good-bye, softly only because of Peter's busted lip, while the passengers already on the bus cheered.

"Have a safe trip, Esmeralda Maria Chang," Peter said.

"I'll see you in Malaysia, my hero."

"You will most certainly. And with any luck, I'll be well enough to give you a proper hug and kiss."

Miguel came up to them and grabbed Min Li's suitcase and tossed it in the luggage compartment under the bus. 'she should get on now."

Min Li kissed Peter again, turned, and hopped on the bus, sitting at a window so she could look out at Peter.

"What happened to you?" Miguel asked Peter.

"We had a little trouble getting here."

Thirty One

Min Li finally sent Peter a text message the next morning at ten. She had arrived in Manila safely, and was waiting for clearance to leave the Philippines using her Chinese passport, the matter being complicated by the fact that there was no record of Zhang Min Li having entered the country. The immigration control police at the Nino Aquino International Airport in Manila cleared up the matter by telephoning the duty officer at the Philippine Department of Foreign Affairs, who in turn contacted the Philippine embassy in Kuwait. This matter took only about a half hour to clear up.

Within an hour, Min Li purchased a ticket on Philippine Airlines from Manila to Guangzhou Baiyun Airport that would leave that evening at 10:40, 5:40 p.m. Peter's time. From there she would take a direct flight on China Southern Airlines to Shenyang, arriving late Saturday evening. Min Li found an electrical socket into which to plug her laptop to charge her batteries and she made a video Skype call to Peter. It took him a few minutes to get to his computer.

"How are you feeling today," Min Li asked. "You look horrible."

Peter's face had turned a nasty hue of purple, his lower lip had swollen even more, and one eye remained swollen shut. Scabs had formed on the left side of his face, and he hadn't combed his hair due to the pain. "I'm doing great. Couldn't feel better," Peter lied.

"I'm really proud of you rescuing me like that."

"I had no choice."

"Of course you did."

"I didn't wait so long to be with you to lose you again after such a short time together. Of course, had I thought things through better, I might not have ended up like this."

"And I might still be in Kuwait. You should go to the doctor."

"I'm okay. I ate a banana. It made me feel better. Later I'll go to the pharmacy and buy some stuff. The doctor would do the same thing and tell me to take it easy."

"You might have a broken rib."

"Or two. I'll keep an eye on it, but there's not much one can do about broken ribs except to lay still."

"You're not going to church today?"

"No. People will ask questions. I don't mind answering them, but it hurts to talk."

"I'm sorry. I guess talking to me is hurting you." Min Li was being sincere and not sarcastic.

"It's worth it. Call me from Guangzhou. Use Skype to call my cell phone. Remember the Skype to Go number I set up for you?"

"Why your cell phone?"

"I'm going to Second Cup with Habib. He wants to play chess tonight and I want to read the newspapers."

"Why don't you just stay home tonight and rest?"

"Because you're not here. This place is sad without you. Besides, I think Habib has been a little jealous of my time with you the past several days."

"Well, he's got you now."

"And I need to go to the bank and get some cash. I owe Hamed forty dinars."

"We owe him more than that."

After the call, Peter took a slow shower and dressed. He spent the rest of the afternoon researching hotels and attractions in and around Kuala Lumpur, Malaysia. In a few short months, he and Min Li would be able to spend a week with each other, and he wanted to make their time count. He found an Outback Steakhouse online and looked over its menu, including its cocktail selections. The sold mojitos, which for some reason sounded good to Peter at the moment, but for the time being, he'd have to handle his pain with aspirins.

The next day, Peter and Min Li began their daily Skype video calls, and Peter thanked God for modern technology. He wondered what might have happened if Skype was around when he left China so many years ago. He and Min Li might have stayed together, married, and, well, it didn't really matter. What now mattered was that Min Li was safe in Shenyang, she and Peter were reunited, and they had the remainder of their lives planned. At the moment, they were not together physically, yet they were still together. They knew their hearts were in the perfect place.

Acknowledgments

The inspiration for *Min Li's Perfect Place* came from Zhang Min Li, the main character in my first book, *The Crystal Monkey*. That book ended with Min Li having broken free from the shackles of domestic servitude and having illegally migrated from the countryside to the city in in the early years of China's opening. Too many of my readers begged to know what happened next, and frankly, so did I. Fifteen years after Min Li liberated herself, we find her enmeshed in China's new commercialism and having to work through the complexities of unrequited love, a failed marriage, organized crime, corrupt officials and business owners, and human trafficking.

This book was made possible by my listening to the stories of my wife, many of which were relived in *Min Li's Perfect Place* with a few embellishments, as well as the memories of other Chinese who remembered why they left China.

Then there were those who graciously read the book for me, giving me much needed criticism, such as Debby Hellen, an English teacher where I also teach English and an author in her own right (*Chasing Evil's Shadow*) and Joseph Bell, who has a moral obligation to be truthful with me as a Deacon in the Catholic Church. I also had the good fortune of receiving criticism from Larry Hyslop, who has a degree in history and taught with me in China before retiring to Canada.

I cannot forget to thank my mother, who frequently asked me if I finished the new book yet, as well as my high school students who are more impressed with the fact that their English teacher wrote a book than they would be if they actually read the book. But I wrote the book for them, because one can only really learn history when it comes to life in the form of stories of the people who lived that history.

I did not write *The Perfect Place* to glorify China's rulers or the Chinese government. I wrote it despite them. My aim was to show the spirit of the Chinese people, nearly all of whom desire more than anything else to be successful in their endeavors and to elevate their families to a more glorious life. They are the true inspiration for this book, and to whom I am eternally grateful.

Finally, I need to thank my agent, Erik L. Miller, who worked tirelessly to find a publisher who was not afraid of publishing a book critical of the Chinese Communist Party.

Glossary of Chinese Words and Names
Used in the novel *Min Li's Perfect Place*
by Patrick Nohrden

All Chinese words in this book are spelled using the modern pinyin system instead of the older Wades-Giles system. Therefore, instead of Peking, I write Beijing (the pronunciation was always supposed to be the same, but westerners found it difficult to pronounce a "b" when a "p" was written, and likewise pronouncing a "j" when a "k" was written.

Also, in China, family names are always used first followed by the given name. Children take the family name of their father, and after 1949, women retained their family name after marrying, which explains why the main character Zhang Min Li, has a different family name than her mother Zhou Lian Min.

Below are the important words and names that the reader will encounter in *The Crystal Monkey* with some attempt very unsophisticated way to show pronunciations when needed.

Bai Jiu (bye j-yo)—strong alcoholic beverage usually exceeding 100 proof made from sorghum.
Bohai (bō high)—a large gulf branching off the yellow sea formed by the Dalian Peninsula to the east and Qingdao to the south.
Cao Hong Bo (chow hōng buh)—Min Li's nemesis, the boy who tried to rape her twice and the son of Cao Hong Li, a local Communist party official.
Chen Ruo Lan (chŭn rō lan)—wife of Min Li's brother Xiong Yong.
Chi pao (chee pow)—traditional Chinese dress typically made of silk with fabric buttons and floral print.
Da Yi (da yee)—the older sister of a person's mother.

Deng Xiaoping (dung show ping)—After being twice purged from leadership within the Chinese Communist Party for his "rightist" thinking, Deng Xiaoping took over leadership of China after the death of Mao Zedong. His forward thinking allowed China to become more open and encouraged the production of wealth and both private and public ownership of industry. Although he had no official title at the time, it was Deng Xiaoping who ordered the Army into Beijing in June 1989 that led to the Tiananmen Square Massacre.

Fen—one-hundredth of a yuan.

Gao Kao (gow cow)—China's national college examination, a grueling three-day test.

Great Leap Forward—a period between 1957 and 1963 that resulted in the deaths of 30-40 million Chinese, mostly from starvation, resulting on failed agricultural and industrial policies.

Hai Tian/Zhang Hai Tian (jāng high tea-ann)—the youngest sister of the book's main character, Min Li.

Heishehui (hay-shǔ-whee)—organized crime, literally, the underworld.

Hong bao (hōng bow)—a small red envelope used for giving money as gifts.

Hong Qi/Zhang Hong Qi (jāng hōng chee)—The next oldest sister after Min Li.

Hukou (who-kō)—family register used to record all members of the household and is the only method of registering births.

Huludao (hoo-loo-dow)—a major city in Northeast China on the coast of the Bohai Sea just east of where the Great Wall of China meets the sea.

Jiang Qing (jee-ang ching)—otherwise known as Madame Mao, she was the last wife of Mao Zedong and was placed in charge of cultural affairs, causing the Cultural Revolution in 1966 which lasted until Mao Zedong's death and her imprisonment in 1976.

Jie Jie (jee-ah jee-ah)—big sister, often used as a term of respect and in lieu of a name.

Jin (gin)—the standard unit of measure in China, which has been redefined in modern times to equal exactly 500 grams or roughly 1.1 pounds.

Jinzhou (gin-joe)—a city larger than Huludao about sixty miles east on the way to Shenyang. Jinzhou is the major agricultural and financial center for eastern Liaoning Province.

Kang—a raised wooden platform that served as a bed for her family in rural China.

Lao Gong (like "loud" without the "d" and gong)—an affection form of the word husband.

Lao Po (like "loud" without the "d" and puh)—an affection form of the word wife.

Lian Min/Zhou Lian Min (joe lee-ann mean)—the mother of the book's main character.

Little Red Book—a collection of sayings by Mao Zedong, which was virtually the only reading allowed to school children during most of the Cultural Revolution (1966-1976). All citizens were required to have a copy with them and most were required to memorize parts of it.

Liu Yuncun (lee-oo yoon chun)—the husband of Hong Qi.

Mah Jong (sometimes mah jongg)—A popular Chinese table game played with unique dominoes. Typically, players gamble on the outcome of the games.

Mao Zedong—also known as Mao Tse-Tung, the founder of the People's Republic of China and head of the Chinese Communist Party until his death in 1976.

Mei guan xi (may gu-wang see)—frequent Chinese expression meaning "no problem" or "it doesn't matter."

Min Li/Zhang Min Li (jāng mean lee)—the main character.

Mei Mei (may may)—little sister.

Nai Nai (nigh nigh)—paternal grandmother.

Nian Dou Bao (nee-ann dough bough)—literally, sticky filled pouch. Sticky rice, often with a red bean paste center, wrapped in bamboo leaves in the shape of a triangle.

Panzhihua (pan-ji-wha)—city in southwestern Sichuan Province which is the steel-producing center for China.

Pàotǎ Shān—literally, Turret Hill.

Red Guards—most simply, members of a militant youth group made up beginning in 1966 who were loosely organized and allowed to inflict terror on the Chinese populace in the guise of advancing the ideas of Mao Zedong and to root out rightists, counterrevolutionaries, capitalist roaders, intellectuals, persons who associate with foreigners, reactionaries, and other class enemies. Their methods were often brutal.

Renminbi (ren-min-bee)—the official name of Chinese money, literally People's Currency. During the time in which this book is set, one U.S. dollar equaled roughly 8.2 yuan, Currently, one U.S. dollar is worth about six yuan).

Shangguang (shong guong)—a small village in southwest Liaoning province, the eastern most province of the three northeast provinces that make up Manchuria.

Shenyang—the capital city of Liaoning Province and former capital of Manchuria before it became a part of China during the Qing Dynasty (1644-1911), the last dynasty of China.

Sun Dongyu—Min Li's husband.

Tang Dynasty—a period of Chinese history from a.d. 618-906 known for its militaristic rulers and beautiful poetry.

Tieguanyin—an expensive tea from Fujian Province.

Tong Li Hua (tǒng lee hwa)—friend of Min Li.

Xiaguang (she-aw gu-wang)—a village nearby Shangguang.

Xiao (show)—small.

Xiong Yong/Zhang Xiong Yong (jāng sshee-ong yōng)—the brother of the book's main character.

Ye Ye (yeah yeah)—paternal grandfather.

Young Pioneers—the entry-level organization of the Chinese Communist Party. Typically, all elementary age children are members and wear red scarves showing their membership. Children of "black" families, those who have been accused of being rightist, counterrevolutionary, capitalist roaders, etc., are not allowed membership and cannot wear the red scarves. Membership becomes even more selective in middle school, high school, and college, where members may be invited to join the Communist Youth League based upon their academic standing and correctness of thinking. A select few of these will later join the Chinese Communist Party.

Yuan (you-ann, but quickly so that it sounds more like "yen")—the unofficial name for the standard unit of currency (officially called the renminbi—see above).

Zhang Zhi Hao (jāng ji how)—Min Li's father.